# FADING SHADOWS

## SHADOWS LANDING #8

## KATHLEEN BROOKS

*Forever Concealed*

*Forever Devoted*

*Forever Hunted*

*Forever Guarded*

*Forever Notorious*

*Forever Ventured*

*Forever Freed*

*Forever Saved*

*Forever Bold*

*Forever Thrown*

*Forever Lies*

*Forever Protected (coming Aug/Sep 2022)*

## *Shadows Landing Series*

*Saving Shadows*

*Sunken Shadows*

*Lasting Shadows*

*Fierce Shadows*

*Broken Shadows*

*Framed Shadows*

*Endless Shadows*

*Fading Shadows*

*Damaged Shadows (coming Oct 2022)*

## Women of Power Series

*Chosen for Power*

*Built for Power*

*Fashioned for Power*

*Destined for Power*

# PROLOGUE

*Arlington National Cemetery, Arlington, Virginia . . .*

Three years, six visits, and it never got easier.

Edie took a deep breath as she walked among the headstones belonging to brave soldiers, including her husband. It had been three years since a traitor killed her husband during a mission. She'd prepared herself for losing him in action, but to be murdered by one of his own teammates had made it harder to accept and even harder to move on.

However, that's what she was determined to do—move on in her own way. Edie's brother, Walker Greene, had been the sole survivor of that mission and he'd made sure the traitor got what he deserved. While that brought closure, it couldn't bring her husband back. Nothing would, but there had to be balance. She'd been living in the shadows of life for three years now and it was time to step out of them and start participating among the living again.

SHANE JOHN WECKER
SOC
US NAVY SEAL

There he was. Her husband. Edie read his name and forced her eyes past the date of death down to the bottom of the marker.

OPERATION NIGERIAN WATERS
PURPLE HEART
BELOVED HUSBAND

"Hello, Shane. I've missed you," Edie said, taking a seat in front of the marker. It was April and Washington, D.C., was in full bloom. Cherry trees with their fluffy blossoms, tulips and daffodils in full bloom, green grass, new leaves pushing toward the sunlight, birds chirping all around her and her husband's white headstone.

Edie placed her hand on Shane's headstone and used her fingers to trace his name as the tears fell. They always fell. She visited him twice a year to talk to him, to promise she'd never forget him, and to tell him she still loved him. Even as time went by, her feelings for him never faded.

"I've been managing a treasure museum belonging to my friends, Wade and Darcy Faulkner. Do you remember me telling you about the sunken treasure hunt I helped with? Well, I took over managing the museum. It's nice to walk to work every day, talk to the tourists, and to be honest, keep all the personal questions at bay. It appears to everyone that I'm okay, but I can still feel isolated even when I'm in the middle of town."

Edie took a deep breath as she scooted closer as if Shane were still there holding her. Instead of his warm body, she leaned against the cold, hard headstone. She scrolled through her phone to a picture of her and Shane at Virginia Beach. His arm was around her, her face was buried in his chest, and they were both laughing.

"Walker and Layne had the cutest baby girl last year. She's not quite one now. Carolina Miles Walker Greene. Miles after Layne's father and Walker after my brother. Layne said it was to give Carolina the strength of the two most important men in her life who will always look out for her and protect her. Speaking of Walker and Layne, you'll be proud of me. I'm taking a big step forward. They invited me to go to Europe with them and I'm going. I'm actually here on a layover on our way to Paris. Walker wanted to come with me to visit, but I asked him to come see you on the way home. I wanted to talk to you alone first."

Edie felt the tears start again as her hand shook where it lay against Shane's name. Her other hand gripped his wedding band that she wore on a long necklace. "I'm so scared, Shane. I'm scared to start living again. I know you'd be mad at me for acting like this, but I just couldn't seem to make myself want to live. I love my brother, I love my friends, and I love my family, but you're not here and I felt like an empty shell just hiding in the shadows instead of living. I finally decided I was tired. Tired of pretending to be okay. Tired of pretending I'm actually living instead of just making it through the days. I joined a support group for veteran spouses and it's helped me see I'm not the only one who feels like this and that I'm not alone. It's as if the sun is beginning to shine through the fog I've been in since you died. I'm thirty-three, Shane. We'd wanted a family of two children by now. I grieve for the kids we didn't get to have even though they never existed. I'm so lonely and I feel the loss of all we dreamed about. But I'm determined to be brave, Shane. I've decided to do all the things we talked about. We talked about taking a romantic trip to Europe. We talked about getting matching tattoos and living life to the fullest. All the things we wanted to do and see. I'm going to do them all and more. I'll just do them with you in my heart instead of by my side."

Edie let the tears roll down her cheeks as she took a shaky breath.

"I don't have much time. The flight leaves soon, but I had to talk to you. I had to, I don't know, I guess ask your blessing to begin moving on. To laugh again. To live again. It doesn't feel right to do it without you, Shane, but I also know you'd want me to live, have a real life again. It's going to be hard. Please give me a sign that you want me to do this. We believed in signs. We believed in gut feelings we couldn't explain. You said they kept you alive. Well, now I need them to live again. I need your strength and I need your courage."

Edie closed her eyes as she held on to Shane's wedding ring and remembered his face, the way he'd touch her, the way he'd kiss her, and the way he laughed with his whole body.

The screech of a hawk brought her up straight with a start. Her breath caught in her throat as a red-tailed hawk suddenly dove from the sky. The hawk raced toward the ground only to pull up and float by her with its wings outstretched. Fresh tears flowed from Edie's eyes as she turned back to the phone leaning against the grave. "Thank you, Shane," she choked out between sobs as she looked at the tattoo on Shane's chest, a beautifully detailed red-tailed hawk.

Edie lay there with her head resting against his headstone until her tears slowed. She tucked the ring back under her shirt, placed her phone back in her purse, and turned back to Shane's name. Edie leaned forward and kissed the headstone. "I'll be back with Walker and we'll tell you all about our trip. I love you forever."

Edie stood on wobbly legs and made the long walk back to the area where taxis waited, bringing tourists and families to and from the cemetery. She felt wrung-out and weary, her heart heavy with memories, as she took a taxi to the airport, but she also felt lighter. It was time to have an adventure. It was time to live again.

# 1

_Millevia, Europe . . ._

Tristan Durand was a damn good government asset, and as such he knew when to keep his mouth shut. This was one of those times.

Tristan stood at attention with his hands behind his back as the "president" of Millevia gave him a new assignment. Annette Pastor hadn't been elected. Instead, she'd filled the power vacuum when the beloved president, Christian Gastaud, had been killed in a horseback riding accident one year earlier. Annette Pastor had been President Gastaud's Head of Armed Services. She'd served her adult life in Millevia's military before Gastaud appointed her as the head of the military many years ago. When Gastaud died, Pastor had immediately stepped forward declaring herself president and prevented legitimate elections. She leveraged the power of the military to take the presidency before firing all other cabinet leaders and putting in all her own people in key government jobs.

To avoid the term *military coup*, Pastor had held a national election, but it was an election in name only. There'd been rampant voter intimidation and opposition candidates mysteriously decided to pull out of the election, wound up dead, or simply disappeared. Those candidates brave enough to fight through until the end found ballots missing and ballot numbers that didn't match up anywhere close to exit polls that showed an embarrassingly large percentage of the people had voted against Pastor. Yet, she somehow still "won" with seventy-three percent of the votes.

Millevia, a small country on the Mediterranean Sea, sat between France and Italy, and just east of Monaco. It was not an international powerhouse, and under Gastaud it didn't pretend to be. Instead, Millevia had focused on banking, luxury tourism, and a very large port for business. However, Pastor was trying to rile up the citizens by saying Millevia should be more of an international player. She played the victim and claimed other countries were disrespecting and cheating Millevia. As such, she'd called in Tristan every couple of weeks to carry out some kind of clandestine operation for her.

Tristan has been a highly trusted asset under Gastaud's presidency. That was a fancy way of saying government assassin. However, President Gastaud conferred with Tristan and his team before any assignment. They'd go over all the evidence and all the intelligence before deciding on the goals of the mission. Only then, when everyone agreed the target was a danger, did Gastaud order Tristan to capture or to take them out. Most of the time, Gastaud's orders were to capture and only kill as the last resort.

Annette Pastor was a different story. She didn't consult with anyone. As far as Tristan could tell, she'd have someone taken out because she didn't like the color of their shirt.

"I'm tired of them disrespecting Millevia and you should be too," Pastor was ranting. "They were supposed to enter into a major shipping contract with us, but since Gastaud died, they are now refusing to go through with it. It makes us look weak on the international stage right when I'm poised to take Millevia global. I won't have it. I want this woman taken so you can turn her to get them to fall into line. Everything you need to know is in the file. Instructions, backgrounds, pertinent people. Got it?"

Tristan looked in the opened file and tried not to frown. His target was some American woman from a small town, an innocent. She had nothing to do with that shipping contract. However, he knew better than to say anything. Pastor was more vindictive than a snake whose tail had been stepped on, and Tristan preferred to stay alive.

"This is your most important mission, Durand. Capture her, torture her, and send pieces of her to the address there to scare them into getting this contract back up and running or you'd better run, because I'll send your own team after you. Failure is not an option, got it?" Pastor snapped.

"Understood, ma'am." Tristan kept his hands clasped behind him until Pastor shoved the file across her desk indicating he should take it.

"Make this happen and there's a place on my cabinet for you." Sure, she tried to encourage him by dangling a reward immediately after implying she'd kill him if he failed. That was Pastor for you.

"Yes, ma'am."

Tristan reached for the file and tucked it under his arm. He saluted Pastor and waited for her to formally dismiss him. She loved her power and kept him waiting almost a full minute.

"Dismissed."

Tristan turned on his heel and stepped from the office. He didn't dare say anything until he was back at the military base that housed his elite team of assets.

"Hey, Tris. What's the assignment?" David Parodi asked as soon as Tristan sat down in his bare-bones office. There was a heavy wooden desk, a relatively new computer, filing cabinet, and bookshelf. There was one chair opposite the desk that was thick, dark-gray plastic and incredibly uncomfortable.

Tristan put his finger to his lips and David nodded in understanding. There was a very strong likelihood his office was bugged and everything reported back to Pastor. "This is a solo operation. Thanks, David. You, Jean, and the rest of the boys have this week off."

Tris slid the file across the desk to his best friend. David talked about what he was going to do this weekend as he glanced over the file. David shook his head when he handed it back, and with a nod to the football field outside, they wrapped up their conversation about Millevia's pro football team and he left.

David closed the door and Tristan took his time to review the file. It didn't make sense. Why was this woman from a small town in America so important to a shipping contract? He turned to the best place to find information on a subject—Google. There wasn't much about to learn about her. Very little social media presence. No big job announcement, no news interviews. Nothing that should make her a target. But then he saw the picture and the pieces started to fall together.

Tristan waited thirty minutes before leaving the office to

meet David on the football pitch. In the center of the field, David stood kicking the white and black ball around and bouncing it from knee to knee. They didn't speak until Tristan arrived there and David kicked the ball to him. "What the hell, Tris? She's not a political figure. She's not a danger to Millevia. You can't do this."

"Pastor told me if I failed, she'd send you, Jean, and the team to kill me." Tris kicked the ball back to David so if anyone looked at them it would look like they were just taking a break and playing around.

David was quiet for a moment. "You know I'd never do it. However, I think she's already turned Jean. He's been acting differently these past months," he said of their third teammate. "Plus, there are those missions he decided to overrule you on and killed the target, claiming it was the only option when it clearly wasn't."

"I think she's turned him too." Tris frowned. "It makes sense. He was the outsider. You and I grew up in the orphanage together and attended military school together. It would be hard to separate us. However, Jean has only been on the team for two years. He has no loyalties to us."

"What do we do?" David asked.

"We watch each other's back, just as we always have." Tris gave David a small smile. Tristan's parents had been murdered when he was six and he was placed in the state-run orphanage where David had been his assigned bunkmate. They'd become like brothers. They shared their food, protected each other from bullies, and studied hard so when the time came, they could make a good life away from the orphanage. That had come when they'd turned thirteen. The military offered free food, housing, and a lifetime career if they met certain academic and physical requirements. Once they turned eighteen, they'd have a free university education, a salary, a retirement plan, and be independent.

David and Tris studied nonstop and together aced both the test and physical assessment. They spent the rest of the years having each other's backs through military school where they were thrown in as the charity cases. Sure, there were others who were not well off, but there were also the sons and daughters of the richest people in Millevia. They were in officer training for the cushiony jobs while Tristan and David had been trained as soldiers.

Tris and David worked hard to master every class, task, and technique and their talents had been undeniable. They finished at the top of their class and both had been recruited into the elite Special Forces of Millevia's military. Now thirty-six, they'd spent thirty years as brothers in arms, in life, and of the heart if not blood.

"What about the target?" David asked and Tristan knew he meant the woman he was supposed to capture.

"She's set to arrive tomorrow and will be here for three days. I'll observe and then try to come up with some way to protect her and not get myself killed."

David was quiet once again as they kicked the ball back and forth. "I bought a boat under a fake name," he said in a whisper. "In case I have to leave in a hurry. It's at Millevia Med Marina. Her name is *Sea Symphony*. If you need her, she's there for you."

Tristan took a deep breath. "Thank you, brother. I hope we'll never need it."

"There has to be a way to overthrow Pastor," David said so quietly that Tris could hardly hear him.

Tris tightened his jaw. He'd been thinking the same thing. "I've been working on it. We need proof Pastor killed Gastaud. It's the only way I can think to get the international community to come to our aid and to get the citizens riled up enough to forget their fear of reprisals and stand up against her."

"Do you have any evidence?" David asked.

"No. She's smart, but she's also led by emotion and that can cause someone to slip up. Gastaud's daughter, Emily, swears her father would never take that jump, but that's only enough to cast doubt on the accident. It has nothing to do with Pastor. Emily did say Pastor was a frequent visitor and went riding with her father every day when she stayed at the castle."

David nodded. "So, Pastor knew the trails Gastaud would take on his morning ride. The question is how she, or whoever, got him off his normal path and over that jump where he supposedly fell."

"It's smart," Tristan reluctantly said. "No bullet. No strangulation. No signs of foul play."

"There has to be something." David let out a long breath before reaching for the ball and picking it up. "Jean's coming. Let me know if you need anything."

"If I ever take *Sea Symphony*, I'll leave her in that marina in Monaco with a note hidden in our spot," Tristan said quickly before Jean got within earshot.

"Be safe, brother," David said quietly before turning a smile to Jean. "Jean! Perfect timing. Tris is being boring and doesn't want to play anymore. Come on, see if you can score a goal on me!"

Tris laughed as David ran toward the goal and pretended to be a ninja blocking imaginary goal shots. Jean didn't give Tristan a second glance after Tris wished Jean luck and headed back to his office. He had less than twenty-four hours to figure out how to save an innocent woman, along with his own life.

## 2

Edie bounced Carolina on her hip as she waited for the gelato. Carolina giggled as she wrapped her drool-covered fist into Edie's hair and yanked.

Edie smiled and handed over the money to the waitress at the sidewalk cart before pulling her hair free and taking the cup of gelato. "Here now, Caro," Edie cooed to her niece as she set her in the stroller and walked over to a bistro table along the edge of the blooming gardens in the capital of Millevia. The ancient oceanfront country was stunning. They were staying at a lovely old resort on the top of a cliff overlooking the sea. There was even a little tram that would take guests down to the beach directly below the resort.

This was day two of three in Millevia, and Walker and Layne had wanted to have a romantic lunch while their friends Dylan and Abby, who were joining them as part of a babymoon, planned to spend the afternoon on the beach. Edie volunteered to take Carolina for the day so the couples could do their own thing while Edie did hers, Carolina in tow.

Abby and Dylan lived in the small town of Keeneston,

Kentucky where her brother and his wife lived. They were great and she was so happy for them, expecting their first child, but it was becoming a problem. They weren't personally the problem, just like the insanely happy-in-love Walker and Layne weren't the problem. It was that Edie very much felt like a fifth wheel during talks with Walker and Layne of marriage and babies Abby and Dylan would have. They were all very kind to Edie and kept the talk to a minimum, which actually made her feel worse.

Most of the days in Paris, Edie had taken Carolina to have their own adventures. It felt good to be needed again and she found herself smiling and laughing right along with her young niece. Plus, Walker and Layne appreciated their romantic time together so it was a win-win. However, Millevia had seemed to just speak to Edie the second they got off the train. She'd have Carolina this afternoon but for the rest of her time here she was on her own and she had plans. Something about this small country made her feel safe, adventurous, and ready to step out on her own. Paris had been overwhelming, in a big-city way, but Millevia was different.

"Here, try this. Don't tell Mommy or Daddy. This is why aunties are the best. We get to sugar you up and then hand you back to your parents."

Edie held the spoon while Carolina slowly stuck out her tongue. The second she tasted the gelato, her little chubby hand grabbed the spoon and shoved it into her mouth.

"Caro!" How was an eight month old baby this strong?

Edie and Carolina entered a battle over the spoon. Edie tried to gently dislodge the spoon from the baby's mouth and Caro, using some super baby strength, yanked it back to keep it in her mouth.

"Let go for Auntie Edie," Edie cooed, but Caro just

drooled strawberry gelato. "You're going to make me play dirty, aren't you? You've been warned. I can play dirty," Edie teased as she bent and blew a little raspberry on Caro's knee.

Caro squealed with delight as the spoon covered in drool and half-melted gelato went flying out of her hand.

"Victory is mine!" Edie cheered as she turned in her chair to pick up the spoon only to find it stuck to the bottom of a man's white T-shirt instead of the cobblestones as she had imagined. "Oh my gosh! I'm so sorry!"

Edie looked up from where the melting gelato stuck to the hem of his shirt to find a flat stomach, a wide chest, muscular arms, broad shoulders, and a smooth-shaven face with a small scar on his square chin. She then looked up higher to find short-cut dark blond hair and deep brown eyes filled with a mix of disbelief and amusement. "I'm so sorry! I will buy you a new shirt," Edie said with a cringe as the man reached down and plucked off the slobbery gelato-covered spoon.

"I believe this belongs to you," the man said in English with just a slight French accent mixed with a smidge of Italian. His voice was deep and Edie felt as if it rumbled through her as he held out the dripping spoon. "Or should I say, to your daughter? I think she was winning the battle before you cheated."

Edie laughed as she took the spoon. "This is my niece and she was winning. It's like some kind of baby superpower. Again, I'm so sorry for your shirt. I hope it'll wash out. Or seriously, let me give you some money for a new one." Edie reached for her purse, but the man's hand reached out and stopped her. At the touch, her heart sped up and her cheeks heated. Edie hoped she wasn't blushing too badly.

"That's not necessary. Enjoy the rest of your day."

Edie watched as the man turned to continue walking. "Wait," Edie blurted as she gave Carolina her favorite binky to snuggle before standing up and taking a step toward him. "Are you from here?"

The man smiled as he looked down at her. Goodness, he was even taller than Walker, which meant he had to be around six foot three or so.

"I am. I take it you are not?"

Edie shook her head. "I'm from South Carolina. It's in America. Can I ask for some recommendations?"

"Sure. There're several things for tourists to do."

Edie shook her head again and nibbled on her lower lip before speaking. "I'm looking for a place to get a really nice tattoo, but I'll need several drinks beforehand."

The man's lips turned up into a smile. "You want to get drunk and get a tattoo while on vacation? What will your husband say?"

Edie saw his eyes flash down to her hand. Only he didn't notice her ring was now on her right hand instead of the left. "I'm a widow."

His smile immediately fell. "I'm very sorry, madame. I wouldn't be a gentleman if I let you go to a bar, get drunk, and then get a tattoo alone. Who knows what tattoo you'd end up with? I had a friend get drunk and have his girlfriend's face tattooed on his arm only for her to break up with him the next day."

Edie smiled and gave a little laugh. Was this sexy man flirting with her? Even after saying she was a widow? That word usually sent most people running in the other direction. Either way, it felt nice to just talk to him. "Why did she do that?"

"Because under her picture he tattooed *I love Gina* in French," the man told her.

"I don't get it? Why was she mad?" Edie asked.

The man's smile widened. "Because her name was Aria."

Edie burst out laughing. It felt so good. To talk, to laugh, to flirt.

"Where are you staying?" the man asked.

Edie told him the name of the resort and he nodded as he glanced off in the direction of the resort. "How about I meet you here tonight at ten. There's a great bar nearby and a block away from it is a very reputable tattoo parlor. I'll make sure they even spell your tattoo right."

"You don't have to do that. I'm sure you have better things to do on a Friday night than play tour guide."

"Lucky for you, the only other thing I would be doing is laundry." He glanced down at his dirty shirt and shrugged.

Edie shook her head as she laughed again. "Sure. I'll meet you here. I owe you a drink at least. But the tattoo I do on my own."

"Your loss. I'm an excellent speller."

Edie laughed again as he turned to walk away. "Oh, my name is Edie," she called out.

The man didn't stop walking, but turned to smile at her over his shoulder. "Tris. I'll see you tonight, Edie."

Edie sat back down with a happy smile on her face. She checked on the now-sleeping Carolina as a feeling of excitement coursed through her until large shadows fell over her.

"Who was that?" her brother asked seriously.

Edie turned to see Walker, Layne, Dylan, and Abby standing there, watching Tris disappear into a crowd.

"Tris," Edie said, unable to stop the smile that came at

the thought of him. "Your little angel here threw food on him and ruined his shirt."

Walker grinned. "That's my girl. Keep those men away from Aunt Edie."

Layne smacked Walker on the arm and shook her head before smiling at Caro. "That's my girl. Getting a handsome man like that to stop and talk to wonderful, deserving-of-a-hot-passionate-European-affair Aunt Edie."

Edie knew without a doubt that her cheeks were now bright red as Abby agreed with Layne while Dylan and Walker frowned at her.

"Ooh, a European affair sounds so sexy and sophisticated," Edie said enthusiastically, just to torture her brother. She had no plans to have one, but it was fun to dream anyway. She actually hadn't had any sexual thoughts of a man since Shane, but she'd been thinking some very sexy things about Tris.

Walker's jaw clenched and she saw him take a deep breath to calm himself down. "Do you think that's the best idea?"

"Sounds like a pretty good idea to me. The knitting club will love the stories from it," Edie said as she stood up. Layne was already moving to get the stroller. "So, what are all you doing now?" Edie asked, changing the subject.

"We were done at the beach and decided to do a little shopping and ran into Walker and Layne walking back from lunch," Abby said, holding up a bag. "We thought we'd do a little walking around before dinner."

"Would you mind a late dinner?" Walker asked Edie, but Edie knew better. This was to make sure she didn't have dinner with Tris.

"Not at all. How's eight?" Edie threw out. She knew that would give them enough time to eat and get back to the resort. Normally they ate a lot earlier because Carolina was in bed by seven.

"Let's do seven and Caro can sleep in the stroller," Layne said, looking at Walker as if he were crazy.

"Works for us. See you then," Dylan said as soon as they decided on a restaurant.

"Are you going back to the resort?" Walker asked as Dylan and Abby took off.

"No. There are some things I want to do and see and then I'm going to head to the beach." Edie had a bathing suit in her large tote bag and had been planning on taking Caro if Walker and Layne wanted more alone time.

"Be aware of everything and everyone."

Edie rolled her eyes at her brother. "You are becoming paranoid in your old age."

"Ha-ha." Walker leaned down and placed a kiss on her cheek. "Love you. Now, go have fun."

"Love you too," Edie smiled up at him before walking away.

Tristan watched the group from his hiding place. They were his key to getting to know his target better. He watched her and the large men around her and frowned. They carried themselves with military bearing but that hadn't been in the file. Of course, the file had only said she was married and had shockingly few details about her life. It didn't say much about who was with her either. Tonight, he'd get Edie alone and see what else he could find out.

Edie. That had been a surprise. He hadn't expected to talk to her. He'd been trying to get into position unseen when a spoon to his midsection had stopped him in his tracks. No, Edie turned around and those big blue eyes the same color as the Mediterranean were what stopped him in his tracks. He hadn't known she was a widow. That had also given him pause, but he wasn't after a relationship so there was no reason for it to matter to him. Then why did he ask her to join him for drinks? It had been dumb. He should have stayed invisible, but when she smiled and the darkness fell from her eyes, he was mesmerized. Her every smile seemed to go straight to his heart while her melodic laugh went straight to his loins.

While it wasn't his standard stakeout MO, it would be okay. He told himself it was good since he'd get the information he needed to make the determination if Pastor was overstepping and going after an innocent. Then he'd make a plan for coming out of this alive.

Tristan watched until the group walked off in their own directions before moving from his hiding place and strolling after her. He noted everything she did, everyone she talked to, and how she kept glancing over her shoulder as if she could feel him watching. He'd have to figure this all out. He couldn't let Pastor kill another innocent. Now, if he could only prove Pastor was committing these crimes, he could get his country and his life back.

## 3

---

Edie felt lighter every day she'd been on vacation. Tonight, though, she felt different. There had been a shift, or more specifically, an awakening. Her body felt alive again. Anticipation ran through her veins and straight to her core. She felt a little bit guilty for finding Tris attractive, but there was no harm in flirting.

*European Affair.*

Damn, that did sound fun. She'd been shut down for so long that she felt almost overstimulated just at the thought of being with someone. She'd been lonely for so long and longed for that human connection. Maybe it was just what she needed—a one-night stand with a stranger she'd never see again. It would be the equivalent of ripping off a Band-Aid or jumping into cold water. Then she could get over the roadblock of grief and guilt that kept her from even thinking of a man other than Shane.

Edie opened her closet door and stared at the mini dress she'd bought that afternoon. For dinner earlier she'd worn a cute sundress but tonight wasn't dinner with family and friends. It was her first night out as a woman again. It sounded strange, but tonight was a big night for her. She hadn't gone to a bar like this since Shane died. The bar in Shadows Landing didn't count. There everyone knew her, knew of Shane, and no one ever thought to flirt with her. Here, she was stepping out simply as Edie. Then she was going to get the tattoo she'd been thinking about since she talked to Shane's headstone. She knew exactly what she wanted it to look like. It was important to her and only then could she fully move on, because she'd be taking a little of him with her.

Edie stripped out of her sundress and caught a glimpse of herself in the mirror. She'd been athletically curvy before Shane's death but had lost quite a bit of weight since then. Food, like life, hadn't held much appeal for such a long time. However, eating her way through France and now Millevia was helping. Her curves were starting to fill back out. Her stomach was no longer hollow and actually looked quite touchable. Her skin glowed. Her brown hair had some blonde highlights from the sun and shone in the light. Her cheeks had filled out some and her face now looked her age instead of ten years older. Yes, this vacation had been sorely needed and tonight was the night to step out on her own.

Edie unhooked her bra and let it drop to the floor before reaching for the mini dress. She slid it on over her head and wiggled it over her hips. The blue dress matched her eyes and fell to mid-thigh. Thin spaghetti straps held up the V-neck top and a white ribbon tied at the waist, accentuating her curves.

Edie was taller than average, standing five foot seven or 1.7 meters here in Europe, so she usually wore flats. However, Tris was plenty tall so she slipped on a pair of cute heels that made her much taller. Now, what to do with her hair?

The knock on the door had her pausing. "Who is it?"

"It's Layne."

Edie frowned. She wanted to have this night to herself and if they asked her to keep Caro, her plans would all be ruined. She also worried Layne would tell Walker she was going out and he'd ruin it.

Edie walked to the door and looked out the peephole. At least it was just Layne with no baby and no husband. Edie opened the door just a bit and stuck her head out. "Yes?"

Layne took in the cracked door and a huge smile split her face. "I knew it. You're going out with the hottie."

"Shh!" Edie hissed before opening the door and yanking her sister-in-law into the room.

"Oh my gosh, Edie! You look smoking hot!" Layne cheered and even though it embarrassed Edie, it made her feel good too.

"Thanks. I thought you all were going to bed." Edie looked nervously at the door hoping Walker wasn't going to come and try to stop her from her going out.

"Walker and Dylan are watching Caro. They got some sports thing on and are happy as can be. Abby and I are meeting downstairs at the bar and I told Walker I was going to invite you, but I hoped you're going out on your own. So, tell me everything!" Layne sat on the edge of the bed as Edie glanced at the clock. She didn't have much time.

"He asked me to meet him where we met today. Then he's taking me to a bar that is close by," Edie told her as she moved to brush her hair.

"You know Abby and I will go with you if you want. You won't even know we're there. We can hide at a table in the back in case you need a rescue." Layne got up and took the brush from her. "Let me."

"I don't think he'll hurt me in the middle of a crowded bar. No rescue is necessary."

Layne laughed as she began to do some intricate braid. "It's not like he's a murderer. I meant, rescue you if he's really boring or only wants to talk about his previous girlfriends or how great he is. Or maybe he owns twenty cats and lives with his mother."

Edie laughed then. "You know, that's actually not a bad idea. I mean, I am in a foreign country and I haven't dated in so long. How about we walk in together, you two meet him, then you all take a seat somewhere else."

"Smart plan. After an hour, we'll stop by the table and tell you we're heading back to the hotel. If you need an out, you can say you want to walk with us. If not, then have fun, but text me where you end up so I know you're okay."

"As if my brother doesn't have a tracking app on my phone." Edie stared at Layne in the mirror who suddenly became very focused on braiding instead of admitting that Walker had probably done just that.

"There! You look beautiful," Layne said a moment later. "Now, let's get going. Abby's in the lobby."

"I can't believe I'm doing this," Edie muttered to herself as they rode down in the elevator.

Layne turned to her suddenly looking very serious. "Edie, you don't have to unless you want to. There's no timeline on grieving. I know people have been pushing you to go out again, but it's not their choice. It's yours. Are you ready?"

Edie took a deep breath and as she did her mind flashed to Tris. "Yes, I am. I don't know if I'm ready for a relationship, but to spend an evening with a sexy man who doesn't act as if I'm broken? Most definitely."

"You're not broken," Layne said, grabbing her hand.

"Your heart was broken, but not you. There's a very big difference."

"Thank you, Layne. I need that reminder sometimes. I'm ready to start taking charge of my life again."

"Then the first thing to do is to stop babysitting Caro," Layne teased. Edie had to admit she had been using Caro as a buffer to not be alone. "I'll make sure Walker backs off and gives you space to do what you want to do on the rest of this trip. And *who* you want to do."

Edie and Layne were laughing when they met up with Abby.

"I'm guessing Edie wasn't planning on a girls' night dressed like that. That's an 'I am woman, hear me roar or at least make me scream' type dress."

"We're going with her to a bar and meeting Tris," Layne told her as she filled Abby in.

"This is going to be so much fun. Do you want me to interrogate him? I can do this human lie detector thing to make sure there's no wife or girlfriend in the picture. And you know, to make sure he's not a murderer."

"Oh my gosh! No! When did a night at a bar with a guy become so complicated?" Edie asked as she wondered if Abby was joking or not. "And how do you know how to do that?"

Abby smiled innocently. "Just a little trick my dad taught me. I don't get to use it much since I'm working a desk job because of BunBun here." Abby rested her hand on her rounded belly and smiled down at it.

"I was a little confused by that. Why would you have to quit working on the farm for your dad? I didn't know horse breeding was physically demanding like that."

"I did a lot of riding. Lots of travel to visit other farms and sometimes horses can get temperamental, especially when breeding. So now I just work the phones and email," Abby explained smoothly. Edie caught Layne rolling her eyes and wondered about it. Dylan had been in the military before retiring to move back to Keeneston, Kentucky, and those types of husbands could be a bit overprotective. That was probably why Abby was on desk duty.

"There he is," Edie whispered as she saw Tris rise from the bench in front of the gardens where he'd been waiting.

"Good evening, ladies." Oh my, that deep voice just turned her to mush.

"Hello, Tris. I hope you don't mind, but my friends wanted to meet you and have a drink as well. It was going to be a girls' night," Edie said, sounding like she had to explain.

Tris smiled and didn't seem the least bit upset. "It's no problem, Edie. I'm happy to meet your friends."

"Tris, this is my sister-in-law Layne and our friend Abby," Edie introduced as Tris shook hands with Layne first and then with Abby.

Abby didn't let go, though. "Is Tris your real name?"

"Tristan. Is Abby yours?"

Abby smiled. "Abigail. Are you married or have a significant other?"

"No. I wouldn't meet another woman at a bar if I did. Are you married?"

"Yes," Abby answered. "Are you going to murder my friend here?"

"I'll try not to."

Abby dropped his hand and laughed. "Funny. Truthful, but funny."

Tris was the perfect gentleman and asked them all sorts of questions as they walked to the bar.

"Oh, look at that drink special. Come on, Layne, let's see

if they can make that a virgin for me," Abby said, pulling Layne into the bar and leaving Edie and Tris outside.

Edie felt as if she'd just witnessed a cross-examination as Layne and Abby walked inside leaving her and Tristan outside alone. "Sorry for my friends. They asked a lot of questions."

"It's okay, Edie. They're looking out for you. What do they do? Interrogate people for a living?" he asked with amusement.

Edie smiled at him and shook her head. "No, Layne is a doctor of physical therapy and Abby works at a horse farm in Kentucky."

"Kentucky? I thought you were from South Carolina. Are they close together?" Tris asked as he gestured toward the door of the bar.

When Edie walked past him, he fell into line beside her. "No. We're about eight hours away from each other by car. However, that's where my brother and Layne live and are friends with Abby and her husband, Dylan."

Inside was crowded and she felt Tristan's hand come to the small of her back to help escort her through it to an open table. Edie glanced around and found Abby and Layne sitting at the bar. Layne winked and Abby gave her two thumbs up.

"Why don't you also live there?" Tris asked as he pulled out the high-top stool for her.

"After my husband died, I moved back to my hometown and bought my childhood home. I've fixed it up over the past three years. While I like visiting Keeneston, Shadows Landing is my home."

.   .   .

Tristan flagged down the waitress and they placed their drink orders. He couldn't believe his luck. Edie had come, but she'd also brought others, which made it a lot easier to ask questions when Abby had so nicely opened the door to them.

"If you don't mind me asking, how did you lose your husband?" Tris asked after the waitress left.

He hated to see the frown on her face, but he liked Edie and wanted to know the good and the bad. "He was in the Navy and died during a mission three years ago. His team leader was a traitor and killed him along with the rest of the team. My brother was the sole survivor."

"That must be very hard to understand and accept. Was the man responsible caught?" Tris felt this story to his marrow. If he failed at this mission, he had no doubt Jean would try to kill him. Government assassins, or *assets* as the government liked to call them, weren't known for their loyalty to each other, only to their country and even then, some assassins would sell out for money in the private sector.

"He was caught and he paid for what he did," Edie said.

"I'm glad. So," he said, changing subjects, "tell me about your family and friends. Are you all enjoying Millevia?" Tris started his own interrogation. He liked Abby's direct style, but Edie needed finesse, not a jackhammer.

He listened as she told him that her brother worked at a military training facility now, along with Dylan. That made perfect sense after having seen them for all of three seconds. They constantly scanned the area, probably knew all the exits, trouble areas, and where the nearest cover was. Then she told him how Layne and Walker had met before she told Tris about Abby and her connection through her father to the Rahmi royal family. "Ahmed and Abby work together now at the farm. If you can't tell, she's pregnant and was annoyed that her father pulled her from more active duties around the farm to work at a desk." Edie gave a little laugh and he'd loved her narrative until the name Ahmed sunk in.

*Oh merde*. That wasn't in the files he got on everyone. How on earth was that not in there? Whoever did the background intelligence on this group seriously screwed up. There was only one Ahmed from Rahmi who worked with Prince Mohtadi in America and this Abby was his *daughter*? This little group of tourists had two former elite military men, a doctor, a world-renowned soldier's daughter, and a museum director all together. What a mix. It didn't change his job, but it sure as hell made it trickier.

"Wow, friends with a prince. That must be cool," Tris said, taking a sip of his beer.

"They're not like that. They're just Mo and Dani. Their kids are Zain, Gabe, and Ariana. In Keeneston they're just part of the town."

"Really? The president here isn't like that. Everyone has to stop and bow their heads," Tristan told her.

"Really. The whole royal family is so nice. We're going to visit Rahmi in a couple of days, but first, we fly to Bermalia the day after tomorrow. The Keeneston group has some friends there they want to see. Then we fly to Rahmi before heading home."

"You're not touring Italy?" Damn. Even the itinerary Proctor had given him was wrong.

"Not this time."

"What an experience you will have with all your travels. Tell me about Shadows Landing and why you love it so much. I've never been to America."

"You haven't? But your English is so good. You hardly have an accent."

Tris nodded. He and David got that a lot. "I grew up in an orphanage and we only had one television, but it wasn't hooked up to cable or satellite. Some charity had given us old videos of all these American movies and shows. That's all we watched so the accent kind of stuck with us."

Tristan felt a jolt as Edie grabbed his hand. Damn, it felt amazing. Awareness he couldn't even explain brought every cell in his body to attention. "How did you end up in an orphanage?"

"My parents were murdered during a political upheaval thirty years ago," he told her. He should never tell her the truth, but he realized he was treating this more like a date than research. "I had a very boring upbringing. Tell me more about Shadows Landing. Is it big? Who are your friends there?"

Tristan sat back and listened as she told him of the strangest little town he'd ever heard of. Alligators, pirates, ghosts, her friends, and something about the new wife of one of her friends taking a picture of him naked in the shower and two old ladies putting it on a banner, all for apple pie.

"Hey, you two," Layne called out as she and Abby walked toward them. "We're heading back to the hotel. Ready, Edie?"

No! Tristan's stomach dropped. He didn't want her to go. "Do you want to join us for a moment while we finish our drinks? Then I would be happy to walk you back myself. Millevia is pretty safe, but I wouldn't want anything to happen to three young women walking alone."

"That's very chivalrous of you, Tris," Abby said with a hint of mischief in her eye. "But we'll be okay."

"You two go ahead. I want to finish my drink, and there's one more thing I want to do before the end of the night. I have my phone with me, though." Tristan felt his whole body relax when he learned Edie was staying with him.

"Text me as we agreed," Layne told Edie as if a warning to him. "I'll see you when you get back."

"Have fun," Abby said before she accidentally dropped her purse. "I'm such a klutz."

Tristan slid from the high stool and stooped to pick up the purse at the same time Abby bent down to get it. "Hurt her and I'll hurt you, got it?" Tristan's eyes shot up to hers, then dropped to her belly. "Don't mistake being pregnant for being weak."

Abby stood and smiled down at him as he held up her purse. "Here you go."

"Thank you. You're so kind. Behave, you two," Abby said to both of them but her eyes were only on his. Ahmed's daughter wasn't a pushover. He should have known and would have known if that had been in the intelligence report. Now his mission was a hundred times harder.

## 4

---

"You don't have to do this," Tristan told her as Edie stared through the large windows of the tattoo parlor.

"No, I want to do it. But you don't have to do this with me. It's pretty private after all." Edie fidgeted with her fingers as she watched a man getting a giant tattoo on his chest. She wanted both Tristan with her and him to go. It felt weird doing this with someone else there with her.

"I can wait out here if you'd like and walk you home after."

Could this man be any more perfect?

"You'd do that?" Edie asked with hope because that would make her feel a lot better. It was after midnight and she would be walking back to the resort alone.

"I will. Go on. Do what you need to. I'm a grown man and more than capable of entertaining myself for a couple of hours. Unless you're getting a giant tattoo. Are you getting a full back tat or something? Then I'd go home and come back in the morning," he teased.

"No, just something small."

"Then I'll be right here." Tristan sat down and pulled out his phone. "Go on. I won't leave without you."

"This is really nice of you. Thank you." Tristan smiled back at her. She took a deep breath and opened the door.

A woman stood from an empty chair in the back and walked forward. "*Oui?*"

"Oh, um, do you speak English?"

"*Je ne parle pas Anglais*," she said, shaking her head. The head shake told Edie more than whatever it was she said.

"One second," Edie said, holding up her finger to indicate she should wait. Edie turned and hurried out the door.

Tris immediately looked up and frowned. "Is everything okay?"

"You don't happen to speak French, do you?"

"I do. And Italian. Millevia is a melting pot of the two countries after all."

"I guess I do need you to come in if you don't mind playing translator."

Tristan stood up and held the door open for her. Soon he and the woman were talking in French and she saw him gesture toward her before talking some more. Then he finally turned to her. "That's Viv and she's a tattoo artist. That book has some of her designs in it if you'd like to look at them."

"I know what I want." Edie pulled out her cell phone and scrolled through the photos until she got to the one of her and Shane on the beach. "Can you do a small version of that hawk on my left wrist?"

"Is that your husband?" Tristan asked gently as he lowered his head and stepped in front of her to make it appear they were in a more private setting.

"Yes, that's Shane. His nickname was Hawk and he loved

red-tailed hawks. You'll think I'm crazy, but before I came on vacation I went to his headstone and talked to him, asking for a sign that it was time to start living again. A red-tailed hawk swooped by. I feel very strongly that this is the last piece of my journey of mourning my husband. So, please ask her if she can do it but she has to be completely sure of herself or I'll wait until later."

"Edie," Tristan said softly, "that is beautiful. He was a very lucky man to have you as his wife. I know I'm not your husband. I would never presume to speak for him and I know my thoughts on this don't matter to you, but that would mean a lot to me."

Edie reached out and touched his arm. "No, you're wrong. That matters quite a bit. Thank you for telling me."

Tristan gave a little nod of his head before turning to talk to Viv. She nodded, her eyes teared up, and she suddenly hugged Edie.

"She agrees that it's a beautiful story and a great way to honor your husband," Tristan told her. "Can you show her the photo?"

Viv stepped back and Edie turned her phone around. "This one," she said, pointing to the hawk tattoo on Shane's chest. "Can you make it smaller and put it here?"

Tristan translated and Edie pointed to her wrist.

"She says absolutely," Tristan said while Viv turned to a book and began to leaf through the pages. "She wants to show you one she did last month."

Viv turned the book around and pointed. It was another bird, a phoenix rising from a broken heart. She spoke and Edie looked to Tristan to translate. "She says you're the phoenix. If you don't mind me saying, I agree. Not the broken heart, though. Your heart is hurt, but it's not broken.

If you feel like it, I think a small phoenix on your other wrist would be just as meaningful."

"Who are you and are you real?" Edie blurted out and then laughed when Tristan blinked in confusion. "I mean, you're so nice to a perfect stranger and I really appreciate it. Fate's funny."

"How so?" he asked.

"She put you in my life when I didn't know I needed you the most." Edie rose up on her toes and placed a quick kiss on his cheek. He wrapped an arm around her and simply held her against him for a moment.

"I'm glad I met you too. You and your friends are very nice. It makes me want to go to America. Now, let's get these tattoos." Tristan let go of her and began to talk to Viv as she led them to her chair in the back.

She started with the hawk first. It took her about an hour and Edie cried at how perfect it was when it was finished. Tristan talked to her through the whole process. By three in the morning, they were walking back to her resort with a small bandage on each wrist.

Edie felt alive and so much lighter. It was as if she were soaring like the hawk and phoenix. She sent a text to Layne and Abby that she was back at the resort even though they hadn't made it past the lobby yet. The night had been so perfect she didn't want it to end.

Tristan noticed that they both seemed to slow their steps as if they didn't want the night to end. This mission had gone sideways the first moment he'd read the file. His target was an innocent woman and didn't deserve to be used to leverage a trade deal and she certainly didn't deserve to die for it.

"So, tomorrow is your last day here?" Tristan asked, knowing the clock was ticking.

"Yes. We leave on the four o'clock train to Nice and then catch the red-eye to Bermalia."

Tristan watched as she slowly shuffled her feet until they stopped walking all together by the elevators. He was screwed. It had been an accidental meeting. He'd planned to use her for information, but he'd gotten to know Edie and damned if he didn't like her. A lot. She was stronger than she looked, she was funny, she was sexy, she was brave, she was smart, and so sweet that he had an overwhelming urge to protect her at all costs.

She told him about being in a knitting club and for some reason that struck a chord he hadn't known was in him. He wanted to experience what it would be like to have a family, and Edie was telling him not only about her family but about her very strange town that acted like one big family. He was drawn to it and to her and couldn't get the image out of his head of her knitting him a scarf, of all things. He would come home and she would be sitting by a fire with her knitting in her hands. She'd see him and smile just for him. It was doing something to Tristan that was driving him crazy with longing for a future he knew would never be his.

Tris didn't know what to do, but he had to make sure they got on that train and out of Millevia. Then he had to run for his life. He never thought his country would turn on him, but with Pastor in charge, the second he didn't complete this mission, it would. He couldn't kill an innocent woman. He had to save them. Then he'd have to run.

Edie pushed the up button on the elevator before she looked nervously up at him. "I'm being brave." Edie sounded like she was trying to convince herself.

"No, you *are* brave," Tristan corrected. "What are you being brave about?"

"I got my tattoos. I went to a bar on a date. I mean, it's wasn't a date," she sputtered, and he reached out to run his hand down her arm.

"Edie, it was a date."

Tristan watched as her eyes went wide. He was helpless to just stand there. He raised his hand to cup her cheek, giving her time to pull back if she didn't want him to kiss her. He felt the rapid flutter of her pulse and the way her eyes seemed to soften with desire when they looked at his lips.

Tristan was about to lean down to kiss her when she rose up on her toes and pressed her lips to his. It was awkward, but it was the permission Tristan needed. He angled his head, slid his hand to the nape of her neck, pulled her tight against him, and kissed her properly. Edie drank it in as if she'd been starving for him.

The elevator door pinged its impending arrival and Tristan reluctantly pulled back. He was breathing hard, his body was electrified, and the last thing he wanted to do was stop kissing Edie. However, it was clear from the kiss she hadn't been with anyone since she lost Shane and he wasn't the kind of man to take advantage.

"Tris," Edie said his name and if he wasn't already hard, he would have been with the longing in her voice. "I, um, would like it if you came upstairs with me."

"Are you saying what I think you are? I'll happily spend as much time as I can with you, but don't think for one moment we have to do anything you don't want to."

The elevator door slid open and Edie reached out for his hand. Silently, he followed her onto the elevator and watched as she pressed the seventh floor. Tristan used his thumb to trace little circles on her hand as they rode in silence.

He followed her to her room and waited as she opened the door. Edie walked inside and turned nervously toward him. "I understand if you don't want to do this. Most men get nervous about what to say or do around me and that's just after they flirt and find out I'm a widow. I don't want you to have to do this, but I would like to. Tonight, I feel at peace. And don't worry," Edie rushed to say. "I don't expect anything from this, from you. This is just a one-night thing, but I trust you with it. Does that make sense?"

Tristan closed the distance between them and reached for her. His hands cupped her hips as he pulled her toward him. "It's an honor and I've wanted you since I looked up from the gelato spoon attack you blamed on your niece. Maybe it was really you, and you wanted my attention."

Edie laughed and he heard some of the nervousness fade. Good. Edie had been honest with him about Shane, about what she wanted, about who she was, and he wasn't the least bit intimidated.

"Before I kiss you, Edie, I need you to know something. I'll go as slow or as fast as you want. If you want me to stop at any time, just tell me. I'll stop instantly with no hard feelings. I want you to soar, my little phoenix."

"Then come fly with me."

Edie was so nervous she didn't know how she'd managed to say a word. However, she didn't feel guilty. She felt alive. Tristan was just the right kind of man to hold her as she leaped... or flew.

His fingers tightened on her hips as he bent to kiss her. The moment she felt his tongue slide into her mouth, she closed her eyes and gave in to the sensations. She ran her hands across his shoulders and drew them to his chest. She felt his muscles tense and then release under her exploratory touch.

He was sinfully sexy and handled her with such tenderness she melted under his own exploration. The nervousness she'd felt before vanished when his hands cupped her breasts and his thigh moved between her legs. Blood pulsed through her body and Edie was tired of waiting.

She yanked his shirt from his jeans and reached for his zipper as he pulled the straps from her dress down and freed her breasts. "Edie," he whispered almost reverently before dropping to his knees while shoving the dress to the floor. She felt like a goddess as he worshipped her.

Tristan didn't handle her as if she'd break. He'd gone slowly to let her get comfortable, but not anymore. When he lowered her down on the bed and stripped, Edie didn't want slow. She wanted him.

Edie held out her arms as Tristan covered her body with his. He pushed up on his elbows. When he looked into her eyes, her heart beat so fast she thought she'd explode from the heat in his eyes. Heat for her.

Tristan kissed her hard when he thrust inside her and, like a phoenix rising from the ashes, she let the flames consume her.

## 5

Tristan didn't sleep that night. Instead, he savored every minute of holding Edie in his arms before slipping from the room. She wasn't what he'd expected to come into his life right now. He didn't need a romantic entanglement. While she wasn't offering one, he couldn't help but want it. Holding Edie in his arms gave him a glimpse of a life he'd never known he wanted. Home. Family. Love.

But, in order to keep her safe, he had to leave her. Slipping from her bed and from her life was the hardest thing Tris ever did. He kept to the shadows of the dark streets as he made his way to the small neighborhood that housed many of the Millevian soldiers. Tris knew where every camera was and avoided them so no one could track him or who he talked to.

The sun would be rising in the next hour, so he had to hurry. Tris entered his house and repacked his go-bag. He got his passport even though he knew he couldn't use it. Growing up in an orphanage had instilled the habit of hiding things so others wouldn't take them. That led to having several stashes of cash around his house that he cleared out. In less than thirty minutes, he was packed and heading through his postage stamp-sized backyard to enter David's backyard.

Tristan tapped on the bedroom window and was met with a gun in the face. David rolled his eyes and dropped from view. A moment later the back door opened. He took a look at the large duffle bag and frowned. "What's going on?" he whispered.

"I can't do it. She has nothing to do with trade deals or ships. I can't use an innocent like that."

"Damn. Pastor is going to send me after you."

"Let her send you. Come find me and bring Jean along. We'll find out who the real traitors are together," Tristan whispered.

"I won't kill you," David promised.

"I'm counting on it," Tris said with a small smile to his best friend.

"We can't have any contact. How will I know where you are? How will you know when we're coming? I can't let Jean catch you off guard and take you out before we're certain he's truly on Pastor's side."

Tristan stared at David in disbelief and shook his head. "As if Jean could sneak up on me. Plus, we'll find a way. We always did at the orphanage."

"What's your plan?" David asked, knowing Tris had one.

"Pastor is going to want an update today. I'm going to give her one. I'm going to tell her I turned her and I'm helping her escape her traveling partners at the train station. I'll tell Pastor I'm going to put her in a safe house and tomorrow I'll bring her to Pastor. By then, they'll be safely out of Millevia and I'll have left your boat in Monaco on my way to my own safe house, waiting for you to do what you do. Find me."

"What do you want me to do?"

"Just do your job. I can't let any suspicion fall on you."

David nodded and then reached out to clasp his shoulder. "Be safe, brother. Until we meet again."

Edie shouldn't have been surprised to wake up alone, but as she wheeled her luggage into the lobby to meet everyone, she was still dwelling on it. Tristan hadn't asked for her number or email, hadn't said goodbye, and hadn't given her the chance to say it either. But then again, she'd told him it was just a one-night stand and that's exactly what she got. However, the saying *be careful what you wish for* was running on a loop in her mind. Because, when Edie woke up to find Tristan gone, her heart had broken a little. She didn't know how, but Tristan had brought her back to life.

"I still can't believe you got two tattoos," Walker muttered as he shook his head at her. He grabbed her carry-on bag and tossed it over his shoulder along with Layne's. "What were you thinking?"

"Walker, I'm a grown woman. I can get a tattoo if I want. Do you want to see them?"

"Please don't be something stupid or something spelled wrong," he said before stopping and turning to look at her. "Let me see them."

Edie stared him down before she peeled back the bandage of the hawk and then the phoenix.

"Okay, those are cool." Edie heard the way Walker's voice caught. He understood what they meant.

"Yeah, you must have had a very interesting time last night," Abby said innocently, but the gleam in her eyes was far from innocent.

"Very. I'd never been to a tattoo parlor before," Edie said as they began to walk down the street toward the train station.

"Hopefully you found the new experiences from last night very satisfying," Layne said over her shoulder as she pushed Carolina's stroller before giving Edie a wink.

Dylan's head turned, but he didn't look at Edie. He looked behind them at the hotel and frowned.

"What is it?" Abby asked him.

Dylan took one last look and shrugged. "I thought I heard something, but I guess not."

Edie glanced behind her, but didn't see anything. She could admit to herself she hoped to see Tristan running after her, but reality was sinking in. She'd never see him again and just thinking about that hurt her heart.

Tristan wiped the bloody knife on the dead man's shirt. He was one of President Pastor's men. The gun in his hand had been pointed at the group and Tristan knew without a doubt he'd have fired if Tristan hadn't killed him.

The train station was three blocks away. Now all Tristan had to do was keep them alive until they got on their train and it left the station.

Tristan pulled the bill of his baseball cap down and stepped confidently from the side of the hotel. He walked with purpose to the gelato cart as he watched the group laughing and talking while they made their way toward the train station.

He paid for a cone as he watched them pick up a second tail. It was another of Pastor's men. Tristan moved the cone to his left hand as the hunter became the hunted. He scanned the area and saw a third man waiting by the station entrance.

Tristan hurried his steps as he approached the man trailing the group from the side. He tightened the grip on the tactical knife in his right hand and lowered his head as he walked right into the man.

Tris shoved the gelato into the man's chest and before the man could look up from the gelato, Tristan struck. Blood ran down the man's shirt, mixing with the gelato as Tristan kept his left hand over the man's mouth and yanked him behind a tree. It only took a couple of seconds for the man to stop moving as Tristan set him against the thick tree trunk, wiped the knife, and strode out to the street as if nothing had happened.

Tristan caught Walker, Dylan, and Abby turning and looking back every now and then. They knew they were being followed, but couldn't see evidence of it. They were smart. He knew once the group was on the train and out of Millevia, they'd be safe.

The man from the station slid in behind them and Tristan cursed as Abby and Edie broke off from the pack. He sure as hell hoped the daughter of the famous Ahmed knew how to defend herself because when they walked into the bathroom, Tris knew he could never get to them in time.

"I can't believe how much I have to pee," Abby said as she rushed into the stall. "I love being pregnant, except for the peeing."

Edie smiled from her own stall as the door to the bathroom opened. She stood, flushed, and was adjusting her skirt as Abby continued to talk about her pregnancy.

"So much better," Abby said before the toilet flushed.

Edie opened the stall door and came face to face with a man standing by the sinks. "This isn't the men's room," Edie said as Abby opened the stall door.

A gun appeared in the man's hand. Edie gasped in surprise and Abby leaped forward.

"Trying to rob the pregnant lady," Abby muttered as she knocked the gun from his hand. "Real gentlemanly of you." Abby ducked a punch and slammed her fist into his chin, sending his head snapping back.

Edie stared as Abby grabbed the man's hair and slammed his head into the sink. His body crumpled to the floor and Abby tossed the gun into the trashcan before washing her hands. "Don't tell my husband, but I needed that so badly. It has been way too long since I got to punch someone."

"What just happened?" Edie finally asked as Abby dried her hands.

"I had a feeling we were being followed. Probably just a thief thinking tourists are easy targets." Abby put her hand on her slightly rounded belly. "Did you hear that nice uppercut Mommy used? I'll teach you how to do that too," she said to her baby belly before looking up with a smile. "Ready?"

Edie looked down at the man lying on the ground and nodded. "You do look happier. Maybe you should punch people more often?"

"From your lips to Dylan's ears. I've been telling him this for weeks, but after my dad freaked out about me being pregnant, Dylan got all weird about letting me do stuff. I think my dad convinced him pregnant women need to be coddled. However, let me tell you about these hormones. They're crazy. I either want to kill someone or have sex *all the time*. There's no in-between."

"Hence the constant look of contentment on Dylan's face?"

"Exactly," Abby said with her own smile.

"You all ready?" Dylan asked, slipping his arm around his wife.

"Yes. Let's go visit Draven, the king of the golden dildos," Abby said with a laugh before launching into stories about the king of Bermalia who was married to their friend, Addison, from Keeneston.

Edie laughed at the stories of the royal-member-obsessed king as they got on the train. She took her seat by the window as Walker picked up the story about Addison and Draven's wedding.

Edie looked out the window as the train began to pull away from the station and sat up straight when she was sure she saw Tristan standing by a pillar.

"Edie? What is it?" Walker asked.

Edie turned and smiled at her brother. "Just your story. Are there really replicas of his penis in every room? Has he calmed down now he's married?"

"Oh yes, he's turned out to be the best husband," Layne answered, but Edie turned to look back at Tristan only to find him gone. He might not have actually been there but still, it felt like a happy memory was saying goodbye.

# 6

Edie had to admit she wasn't ready to leave Rahmi. They'd had fun in Bermalia with Draven and Addison and Edie felt as if she had two new friends. However, Rahmi was an island paradise and she wasn't ready to leave yet.

Edie had met more Rahmi soldiers than she could name and had realized she was no longer uncomfortable talking to them or even flirting some. She'd spent nearly every night at the dance club, loving every moment of dancing to the loud, pulsing music. It was somehow freeing to let all her emotions out on the dance floor. She screamed lyrics, jumped to the beat, and tossed her head back with carefree abandon.

Everyone in the group noticed her becoming more at peace and blooming in her independence. Walker had even hugged her that morning and told her how happy he was to see his teasing younger sister again.

This trip was exactly what she'd needed, but sadly it was time to head back to Shadows Landing. Edie hoped she took the lessons she'd learned from Tristan, from Draven and

Addison, and from Rahmi with her to apply to her daily life in Shadows Landing.

"Good thing we went to Millevia when we did," Walker said as they got into the palace limousine.

"Why do you say that?" Edie asked, feeling as if they knew something she didn't.

"Apparently a warning was issued saying that Americans are at risk there," Abby said with a shrug.

"I didn't think it was dangerous," Layne said with the same surprise Edie felt.

"Their president is more of a dictator, and I've heard she's a vengeful one. Can't be surprised when they take power with the military's backing and not the people's approval," Dylan said as they drove to the airport.

Edie nodded. She remembered Tristan saying something about that. Tristan was her best memory from the trip, and the tattoo of the phoenix would always make her think of him.

"Thank you for bringing me on this wonderful trip," Edie said to Walker and Layne as she held hands with a sleeping Carolina in the car seat next to her.

"I'm glad you came. It was fun spending time together again." Walker smiled at her and Edie felt closer to him than she had in years. "There's always room for you in Keeneston."

"I know, but I'm happy in Shadows Landing. However, I will visit more. Someone needs to spoil my niece," Edie said as Layne rolled her eyes.

"My father spoils her enough for all of us combined," she said about Miles Davies.

Edie listened to stories from the four about their parents and in-laws and laughed at their antics. But soon enough they were on the plane and Edie would be home the next day.

"Edie!"

Edie turned to the woman screaming her name. Tinsley Faulkner Kendry was jumping up and down and waving from behind a row of people standing at baggage claim in Charleston's airport. Harper Faulkner Reigns stood next to Tinsley rolling her eyes at her cousin's excitement. However, when she saw Edie, her smile was just as bright.

"Edie!" Tinsley squealed as she ran forward and slammed into her friend, wrapping her in a tight hug. "Oh my gosh! I've missed you. I can't wait to hear everything!"

"I want to hear how you ended up with a tattoo," Harper said as she joined them before giving Edie her own hug.

"Two tattoos," Edie corrected as she held out her wrists.

"Wow! I would never have guessed you'd get a tattoo. I can't wait to hear the story. All the stories! You can't leave out a single detail," Tinsley ordered as she grabbed Edie's hand and dragged her to the baggage carousel.

"I hope you don't mind, but everyone missed you so much they've ordered us to take you straight to the bar so they can all hear about your trip," Harper said as Edie grabbed her bag.

Edie had wanted to go home and sleep, but no. The New Edie was a woman about town now. "I'd love that."

"You would?" Harper asked as they walked toward the car.

"Yeah. I went to a bar and tattoo parlor in Millevia. There was this great dance club in Rahmi I went to every night. And . . . I even met someone." Edie dropped that bombshell before Tinsley started driving to avoid the possibility of a crash.

"You met someone?" Tinsley's head practically spun like in the movie *The Exorcist*.

"I did. In Millevia. We went out on a date and everything."

"And everything?" Harper asked with a grin fully knowing what Edie meant.

"And everything."

"Ooh, I bet Walker hated his sister getting laid," Tinsley said with a giggle.

"I felt like I was in high school," Edie admitted. "Abby and Layne covered for me."

Edie laughed and talked about her travels on the drive back to Shadows Landing. Sure enough, the entire Faulkner family and several of her other friends were packed into the bar waiting for her.

Gavin, the eldest of the Faulkners, and his wife, Ellery, were the first to welcome her. "How was my best friend? Was he a pain in the ass?" Gavin asked of Walker.

"Only slightly," Edie said, feeling lighter than she had in years.

"Well, not only did we miss you, but so did the museum," Darcy said, giving her a hug. "Wade and I are onto a new treasure."

"What kind of treasure?" Edie asked as Wade Faulkner beamed.

"The kind that arrives wrinkled and crying in about seven months," Darcy said with a grin.

"You're pregnant?" Edie gasped.

"Shadows Landing is in bloom," Savannah Faulkner said as her husband, Ridge, came to hug her. Savannah was in full bloom by the looks of it. Her due date was in a week or so if Edie remembered correctly.

"You're telling me," said the huge man in overalls and a giant hat that read COCKS on it.

"Is Bubba being ornery?" Trent Faulkner asked. "And sorry, Edie, Skye is shooting a movie right now. She'll be back next week, but I'm to report back with all the stories from your trip."

"Not ornery," Gator answered wearily. Gator was the town's alligator wrangler. "Horny. It's alligator mating season."

Paxton, Tinsley's husband, coughed and Tinsley slapped him on the back while she hid a smile. Apparently horny alligators were funny.

"I'm glad you're back," Ryker Faulkner said, stepping up to her when everyone started talking about alligator mating season. "You look good, Edie."

"So do you. It appears marriage is a miracle worker." Ryker had understood Edie more than anyone, having lived the past fifteen years in the shadows of life until he met Kenzie.

"To the right person, it's just that."

"Maybe to a man from Millevia," Kenzie said with a wink. Tinsley and Harper had apparently already shared her travel stories.

Ryker frowned. "Millevia is a corrupt country."

Kenzie rolled her eyes at her new husband. "That doesn't mean the men can't be just what Edie needs."

"Men?" Ryker asked as his frown deepened.

Kenzie shook her head and Edie laughed.

"Wait, you met someone?" Ryker said, crossing his arms over his chest. "Give me his name."

Edie laughed at one of the most powerful businessmen

in the world. However, here in Shadows Landing, Ryker was just a friend she'd known her whole life. "It was just a date, Ryker. I don't even have his number."

"Hm. I guess dating is okay, but without Walker here I feel the need to play big brother," Ryker said, trying to relax and failing at it.

"Thanks, Ryker, but I'll tell you what I told Walker. I can take care of myself. But, if I ever need a boyfriend background check, you're the first person I'll call." Edie yawned and Tinsley jumped into action.

"Okay, it's bedtime for our jet-lagged Edie. But before Dare drives you home, you have to give us a quick rundown of your travels," Tinsley said with a nod to Harper's husband, Dare.

Edie smiled and pulled up some of the photos on her phone as she began to tell them of her travels. The shortened version took twenty minutes, and soon she and her luggage were in Dare's car and her home was in sight.

"Sorry they ambushed you," Dare said. "I'm pretty sure they counted down the days until you got home."

"They're good friends," Edie said as Dare pulled into her driveway.

"Hey, did the house next door get sold?" Edie said, noticing the "for sale" sign was down and lights were on in the house.

"Rented for the next couple of months," Dare said as he lifted her luggage from the trunk. "Rumor in the knitting club is a guy rented it in return for fixing it up to sell. I guess there had been a lot of things that needed repairs, but old Mr. Keese couldn't do it himself."

"Aw, I miss Mr. Keese. He was a good neighbor."

"Miss Mitzi said she heard he's happy down in Florida," Dare said, carrying the luggage to the front door. "Anyway,

Tinsley brought over some groceries for you, and Wade put all of your mail on the kitchen table."

"Thanks, Dare," Edie said to the ATF agent. He was a bit rough around the edges, straight to the point, but also very kind. And he was in knitting club with her.

"Call if you need anything. Welcome home, Edie. And I like the tattoos," Dare said with a wink and a flash of one of his.

Edie laughed and unlocked her door. She waved to Dare before glancing next door. She saw a figure in the window and had to admit it was nice to have a neighbor again. She'd go over tomorrow to introduce herself but first, sleep called to her.

Edie dragged her suitcase inside and locked the door. She didn't even bother unpacking before stripping out of her clothes and crawling into bed. Blissful sleep overtook her in an instant as she dreamed of Tristan and Rahmi nightclubs.

## 7

Edie lifted the plate of chocolate chip cookies and walked out her door. She'd slept for ten hours and awoke feeling refreshed and ready to jump into her new life. That included meeting her new neighbor and heading into town for the farmers' market. They were going to have flats of spring plants today and she wanted to plant bright colorful flowers all around her cute cottage house.

Edie walked up the stairs and knocked on the front door. She heard footsteps and then the door was open.

"Hello, Edie."

Edie blinked and blinked again. She must still be sleeping because this wasn't real. "Tristan?" Tristan smiled and she about fainted. What was her one-night stand doing in Shadows Landing?

"Surprised?"

"Are you stalking me?"

Tristan raised his eyebrows. "No. Should I be?"

"Not that I'm not happy to see you, but what are you doing here? You live in Millevia." Edie took a step backward. This whole situation was weird. Right?

"I lost my job the day you left. Sorry, by the way. That's why I had to leave before you woke up. I had hoped to see you before you left, but when I came back you were gone. Anyway, I lost my job and you talked so beautifully about Shadows Landing. I figured there was no better time to visit than now. I didn't have your phone number or any contact info or I would have called beforehand."

"Oh," Edie said with a frown. That actually made sense. "I'm sorry about your job."

"It's okay. My boss was a real dictator. She liked to control everything and tell me what to do and when. I couldn't even question her when I knew her orders were wrong. That's what got me fired. I wouldn't do something that was wrong. So, I looked up Shadows Landing and saw this house. When I talked to Mr. Keese, I was sold. I just had to help him out. He's a very nice man."

Edie nodded. "I'm sorry, I'm still just really surprised to see you here. I actually don't know what to say."

"How about you tell me if you're not happy to see me?" Tristan asked.

Was she? Heck no. She was thrilled, but . . . "Are you sure you're not a serial killer here to murder me?"

"I'm pretty sure. Abby already cleared me of that."

Edie laughed and took a deep breath. She'd dreamed about him last night and here he was. It had to be fate and who was she to question it. "No, I'm very happy to see you. I live next door. I brought you cookies."


Tristan opened the door wider and took a step back to welcome her inside. "Next door? Wow, just like in the movies, this *is* a small town. Thank you for the cookies." Tristan hated lying to Edie, but he didn't have many options.

What would he say? That he was here to hide from his own country while they hunted him as he tried to figure out how to prove the president was a murderer? "The tattoos look great. Come in and tell me about the rest of your trip."

Edie walked by him, and he smelled her perfume. He took a deep breath, remembering being intimately connected to that smell as he kissed his way down her naked body. He'd thought about her constantly since he'd seen her safely on the train.

As soon as her train left the station he'd headed to the marina. There, he'd taken David's boat to Monaco and used his connections to come up with fake travel documents. Then he'd taken a public bus to Switzerland before changing buses to Liechtenstein. From there he took the train to Amsterdam, tossed his fake travel documents, even though he hadn't had to use them yet, and picked up new ones. He knew how easy it was for him to track someone so the more layers he had protecting his real identity the better. From there he'd caught a ride on a fishing boat to Oslo. Then he'd finally flown to Atlanta. He bought a nondescript car with cash and drove to Shadows Landing. It took three days, but he made it and his trail would be hard to follow.

Hopefully he'd have time to come up with a better plan while David and Jean tracked him. He'd left a message for David in the boat, but he didn't know when he'd get it.

"You cut your hair. It looks nice," Edie said as she walked into the house under renovation.

He'd almost buzzed it down to try to change his appearance. "Thanks. You had said Shadows Landing could get warm so I thought I'd cut my hair. I've really enjoyed Shadows Landing so far. I've been eating at the barbeque restaurants you told me about. I haven't gone into

Charleston yet, though. I was hoping we could try that one night if you'd like."

"Like as a date?"

Tris heard the hesitancy and knew not to push it. "I thought more like since I had shown you some of my town, I hoped you wouldn't mind showing me yours. That way I can know not to make any faux pas, but I have a lot of work to do so there's no rush."

"Oh." Did she sound disappointed? He hoped so. It was clear he needed to give Edie time to adjust to him being here and that was fine by him. He needed to keep a low profile, which was why he suggested Charleston instead of Shadows Landing. "Sure. I can take you some time."

"Great. Now, how was the rest of the trip?"

Tristan listened to her talk about the trip to Bermalia and frowned. "Wait, the people you are friends with are the King and Queen of Bermalia?" Pastor's target was beginning to make more sense. She was highly connected to the international political scene.

"Yeah, Draven and Addison," Edie said with a smile. "They're so nice, even if Draven has a thing for his royal member."

"His what?" Tris asked before he just shook his head. "No, is that what he calls it?"

Tris found himself laughing as Edie brought her trip to life with stories of Bermalia and Rahmi. "So, your brother and his friends are safe back in Kentucky?"

Edie nodded. "I talked to them this morning. They're all jet-lagged but happy to be home."

"I'm glad you had a nice trip, Edie. And while I love hearing about it, I'm sorry, but I have to get back to work. I'd love to see you again soon, neighbor."

Edie laughed. "Yeah, I'm sure we'll be seeing each other a lot. Welcome to Shadows Landing, Tristan."

Tristan stood from where they sat on the couch and walked Edie to the door. It was hard to do, but he let her walk out of his house. It was all in her hands now. He just hoped the spark they felt in Millevia was enough to have her come back to him.

"Your one-night stand moved in next door to you?" Layne questioned as if Edie hadn't just said it—twice. Abby's eyebrows rose and even over the video chat it was obvious she didn't know what to think about it. Neither did Edie, which was why she'd called Layne and Abby the second she returned home.

"What's his last name? I'll run a background on him," Abby finally said.

Edie froze.

"You don't know it, do you?" Abby asked.

Edie shook her head. "I don't think it ever came up."

"Is there a rental agreement or some mail you can steal?" Abby suggested.

"It sounded more like an over-the-phone agreement with the house's owner who lives out of state. I can't steal mail, can I?" Edie asked.

"You don't steal it. You just take a peek at it," Layne offered.

"Is it wrong that I was so happy to see him?" Edie asked them as she tossed in a load of laundry. She had two weeks of clothes to wash before going back to work tomorrow.

"That's sweet," Layne answered with a big smile.

"Unless he's a serial killer," Abby said dryly.

"I know what you need to do," Layne said suddenly. "Get to know him better and then take him out to dinner in Shadows Landing. Let my cousins at him. You know Ryker will find out who he is."

"That's not a bad idea," Abby agreed. "And you'll be in public so he's less likely to kill you."

Edie groaned and slid down the front of the dryer to sit on the floor. "Why? Why is the first guy I have feelings for an ax murderer?"

"To be fair, I only said serial killer. Hardly anyone uses axes anymore, too messy, and I don't think he's trying to kill you. I would have picked up on that when I met him."

"Not helping, Abby," Layne said to her friend. "Edie, maybe he feels the same way? Maybe he came to Shadows Landing to explore what you two had in Millevia?"

"It's kind of romantic, though, right? Coming all the way to Shadows Landing to see if your romance can bloom into something deeper," Layne said with a sappy smile on her face.

"So, is he a serial killer or a romantic?" Edie asked.

"Maybe he's a romantic serial killer?" Abby suggested with a shrug. "Your church teaches those self-defense lessons, right? Just take a knife with you, ask him to dinner at Harper's, and then call us after your friends interrogate him."

"Okay," Edie said, liking the plan. "I can do that, but I'm not ready yet. That takes brainpower and right now I just want to plant some flowers and figure out how I feel about Tristan being here. I'll let you know what I find out."

"If you need us, we're a short flight away," Layne told her. "You know Walker will be coming the second word gets back to him that you're out with a guy anyway."

"Great. Just another thing for me to worry about."

"I got you, sis!" Layne said. "I'm my father's daughter after all."

"I'm not entirely sure what that means, but thank you both."

Abby and Layne wished her luck before hanging up. The real question was whether Tristan moving in next door was the best or the worst thing to happen to her? Edie stood up and took a deep breath. There was only one way to find out. She would ask him to join her for dinner tonight at Harper's bar.

# 8

Edie stabbed the dirt with her trowel. Sweat ran from her hairline down the side of her face as she dug yet another hole for the now overwhelming number of plants she'd bought. What had she been thinking, getting so many? Each little pack had far more plants than she'd thought they would.

"Do you need help?"

Edie froze, the trowel buried deep in the ground. She looked over her shoulder and fought off the desire to run and hide. Tristan was sweaty and gorgeous. His T-shirt was damp and seemed to cling to every ridge of his abdominal muscles, drawing her attention like flashing lights. Meanwhile, she was sure enough dirt had mixed with sweat on her face to make mud.

"Hi, Tristan. No, thanks. I bought them all and I can plant them all."

"I came armed," Tristan said. Edie yanked the trowel from the ground ready to defend herself as Tristan reached behind his back. She almost screamed when his arm came forward, but then she saw it wasn't a gun in his hand, but a trowel of his own. "Just tell me where to dig."

Edie shook her head under the pretense of getting a wet piece of hair off her forehead but it was really to bring her back to the present. The idea that Tristan was a serial killer was ridiculous.

"Here, let me," Tristan said as he stepped forward until she was looking up at him from her position on the ground. He reached down and brushed the hair from her forehead and tucked it behind her ear. Edie hadn't even realized she'd leaned into his hand until she saw the smile on his face. "I've missed this too."

Edie's heart seemed to rev up in her chest as if it were the engine of a car that hadn't started in three years. "You did?"

"I did." Tristan bent at the knees but didn't move his hand from where he cupped her cheek. "I realize we didn't know each other long, and please believe I'm not telling you this to push you. But my time with you meant something to me. It felt different from other dates. Was I wrong? If I read too much into it, I can leave right now."

Was he wrong? No. Edie had felt that excitement and recognition the first time she saw him. "No, you're not wrong. It's just that it's so fast and it's been since—"

"Shane. I understand," Tristan said tenderly. "Which is why I think we should move very slowly. How about we become friends first and then see where it goes?"

Edie gave a little laugh until she saw his frown. "No, I'm not laughing at your suggestion, just at the fact we're going about this all wrong. Normally it's friends, then a date, then sex. We did it date, sex, then friends. But I really would like that, Tristan. Thank you for not pushing me."

Edie almost followed as Tristan removed his hand. She

missed his touch almost instantly. "No, thank you for giving me a chance. Now, tell me where to dig."

Tristan worked side by side with Edie all afternoon. They talked, they laughed, and it was just as if they were back on their date in Millevia. He hadn't been lying. He'd missed this. He'd missed her. When they were together it was just so *right*.

Edie was different from the women who hung out at the military bars in Millevia. She had experienced love and loss. She might be healing, but she was confident in who she was and wasn't trying to come off as anyone but herself. That was incredibly appealing to Tristan.

"What do you think you'll do about your job?" Edie asked as she planted the last of her flowers.

"I'm not sure yet. I've been working my entire life. It's nice to take a break and just build stuff. I've been working on built-in bookcases in the living room and look how great your flower beds look. As I work with my hands, I can think more clearly too," Tristan told her.

"Me too. It's why I like knitting. It lets my mind relax and I can come up with plans and ideas I normally would be too stressed to come up with. But do you think you'll go back to Millevia?"

Tristan frowned. "I don't know, that depends on my boss. If she's replaced, I may be called back."

"But if you don't work there anymore, can they really call you back?" Edie asked.

"I guess I'll find out. In the meantime, it's been nice just being here with you. Now, wait here. I've discovered this new drink. I'll be right back with it."

Tristan got up and walked across their front yards and

into his house. He filled two glassed with ice and poured his new favorite drink.

"Here you go," he said as he walked up Edie's front stairs to the swing on her porch.

"Thank you." Edie took a sip and then laughed. "This is just sweet tea."

"Yes! Isn't it wonderful?" Tristan asked as he took a sip.

"It is. It's a favorite around here. One evening I'll make you my favorite drink with sweet tea, vodka, and lemonade." Edie laughed at the face he made. "Trust me. It's wonderful."

"I trust you," Tristan said instantly, and he thought he did, but could he trust her with the truth? "I'd better get going. I'll see you around, Edie. Stop by anytime with that slightly gross-sounding drink."

Edie laughed as he raised his glass in a silent salute before leaving. He never wanted to leave Edie, but he'd had more time with her today than he thought he'd have. Edie had been deeply hurt by her husband's death. She'd most likely been hurt when Tristan left her after sleeping with her too. Now he needed to move slowly and let her decide if she was ready for more. Maybe then he'd tell her the truth. Until then, there was no reason to upset her.

Edie laughed as she took a sip of her cocktail. Somehow over the past week, she and Tristan had started their own habit of evening cocktails together. It had begun the next night after Tristan had helped her plant her flowers. She'd mixed a pitcher of sweet tea, lemonade, and vodka and taken it over to his house after dinner.

Now, a week later, they were sitting on his porch, sipping

a drink from his hometown and talking about their days, their dreams, movies, books, and everything in between. They'd get together every night after dinner. It was never planned but they'd seemed to fall into a schedule already. Some nights she came to his house and on others he came to hers.

Each night they tried a different cocktail as they spent a couple of hours together, talking and learning about each other. At first, Tristan had given Edie lots of space and sat on the stairs or on the other side of the sitting area, but tonight they sat side by side on his newly hung porch swing.

Her thigh was pressed against his. His arm rested behind her back and when she leaned against the swing, she felt his thumb brush her upper arm. Warmth and nervous energy filled her as they gently rocked and talked the night away.

Those nightly talks became the high point of Edie's days. She worked just to get through the day until she got to see Tristan again at night. What she appreciated was that he didn't shy away from talking about her past. He liked hearing stories of Shane, hearing the way they were still figuring out marriage when he went off on his last deployment, and he had held her when she'd cried as she told him the full story of his murder. Tristan never made her feel as if she were cheating on Shane's memory or dwelling on the past. Instead, he welcomed her and her memories of Shane into his life.

However, Tristan had not made a move to kiss her again. She hadn't felt his lips on hers since Millevia. Tonight, the warmth of the liquor mixed with the warmth of his touch, and she wanted that kiss again.

She turned her head and was just inches from his face as he talked about growing up with his best friend, David. His lips were right there and all she wanted was for Tristan to stop being such a gentleman and kiss her as he did in Millevia.

"Tristan," Edie said softly, almost without thinking. It had been in her mind to silence him and just kiss him, but she was as surprised by her voicing his name as he was.

Tristan stopped talking mid-sentence and shifted in the swing so that he was facing her. "Yes, Edie?"

Edie felt her heart fluttering faster than a hummingbird's wings as she looked into his eyes. "Kiss me."

Tristan's eyes heated instantly and his slow smile made her think of a wolf about to pounce, but right now she was begging to be his prey. "About time. I wasn't sure how much longer I could wait."

Tristan didn't give her a chance to ask him what he meant. Instead, his arm wrapped around her and drew her chest to his. His lips came down on hers and as she surrendered to his demanding kiss, his other hand squeezed her thigh, setting her pulse to pounding throughout her whole body.

"God, I've missed this," he whispered against her lips when he broke the kiss. He looked down at her and Edie saw the question in his eyes. He had done what she'd asked. He'd kissed her. Now he was waiting for permission to do so again.

"Then why stop now?"

That was all Edie needed to say. Tristan took command of the situation instantly, pulling her onto his lap as his kiss deepened. He grabbed her ass with both hands and pulled her tight against him. Edie felt the power and command in his touch and gave in to it. He used his hands to guide her to rock her hips against him as his tongue surged into her mouth.

Edie moaned and wrapped her hands around the back of

his neck, angling herself so she could take control of the kiss. She felt his erection pressing against her as she rocked against him. No longer needing him to guide her, Tristan moved one hand from her hip to her thigh. He moved confidently but slowly up her leg, giving her time to stop him. Stopping him was the last thing on Edie's mind, though. Well, until she heard the sound of a throat being cleared.

Edie squeaked because at the same time she heard it, Tristan turned so fast all she could do was hang on to his shoulders. It was then she realized he was using his body to shield her from whoever was in the front yard.

"I am going to tease you about this *forever*. Payback is finally mine!"

Edie rolled her eyes and shook her head. "Don't worry, Tristan. She's a friend."

"Are you sure?"

"Yes, but I hope you have a sense of humor." Edie looked around Tristan's strong shoulders and smiled. "Hi, Darcy."

"Imagine my surprise when I got back from a little treasure hunting trip and decided to finally come meet the new guy on the street to find you two rocking the swing so hard it was about to fall down."

"At least the whole street wasn't listening to me having sex," Edie said as she teased her friend. "Tristan, meet my friend and boss, Darcy Faulkner."

Tristan easily lifted Edie from his lap and turned to look at the woman with a huge grin on her face who seemed not the least bit ashamed of the sex joke. "It's nice to meet you."

"Oh, you too. I can't wait to tell everyone that sweet, quiet Edie is the new street slut. See, it had been me but I'm now passing on the torch. Maybe we should get a dildo or something to pass between us, to Edie."

Edie was laughing so hard she was almost crying. Poor Darcy and Wade's bedroom was situated at the right place on the street so that if a door or window were open, the whole street could hear them enjoying each other's company. "I do have a golden one from King Draven we could use."

"Wait. That was you early this morning?" Tristan asked, causing Edie to grab onto the swing's chain to stop from falling out from laughing. "I had heard the town is haunted. I heard the moaning and thought it was the ghosts I keep hearing about."

"Want that dildo back? My reign as street slut was short. I bow to the queen," Edie said before Darcy flipped her off and they both laughed.

"Well, now you know what you were getting into when you moved here," Darcy said to Tristan as she walked up onto the porch. "Have we scared you off yet?"

Edie's heart melted when Tristan reached over and took her hand in hers. "Nothing could scare me off."

"I wouldn't be so sure of that," Darcy said, leaning against the railing. "Edie has been noticeably absent from her normal evening activities this week. Dare called Wade and asked him to check on her since she missed knitting club tonight. However, lucky for Tristan, I came to check on you. Dare might have shot you. Now, I understand you've been *doing* more interesting things, but unless you want the entire town to put out an APB on your whereabouts, you might want to make an appearance at the Faulkner Friday dinner tomorrow. And probably bring Tristan with you." Darcy directed her conversation to Edie, but Edie heard the challenge to Tristan in it too.

"I'd love that. I've heard so much about you all that I'm

looking forward to meeting everyone," Tristan said smoothly.

"That's good, because we haven't heard a word about someone who was rounding second base with our best friend on the front porch."

"Darcy!" Edie gasped, realizing the teasing was over. Darcy was now ready to know exactly who Tristan was and Edie knew everyone else in town would want to know that too. Especially Gavin, Dare, and Ryker. Yikes.

## 9

Edie worked all day Friday and put up with Darcy's teasing comments about exhibitionists and if the sexy new neighbor would survive Harper. Edie had been worried about the men, but Darcy was right. Harper was just as dangerous to potential dates and that was exactly what Tristan was.

Tristan was the first man she'd dated since she met Shane years ago and certainly the first man she'd even liked well enough to date. Tonight, he was meeting her family, so to speak, as the town had really become her extended family. However, that didn't mean Edie wasn't going to prepare for the worst. And by worst, she meant the probability that Harper would be armed.

Edie may have moved away for a while, but she was still a Shadows Landing girl at heart, which meant she lived and breathed its unique history. Shadows Landing Church was founded by the pirates who founded the town. When the pirates would leave for their raids, they left their women in charge of protecting the town. To do so, they armed them with crossbows, knives, cutlasses, boarding pikes, and all the weapons a pirate could ever need.

The pirates may have gone, but the practice of arming and training the women in Shadows Landing was not. They met weekly in the church for arms practice. Some thought it was silly and never did it, but it was open to any female living in Shadows Landing over the age of ten.

When Edie had moved back to Shadows Landing, the man who had killed her husband had come after her as a way to draw her brother, Walker, out of hiding. Edie had fought and survived, thanks in part to some of her childhood training, her sister-in-law, and the rest of her Keeneston friends. However, after the attack she came back to weapons training full time.

The fact that she was sliding a dagger into her cowboy boot for a date in which Tristan met her family didn't escape her mind. She knew it was ridiculous, but that was the Shadows Landing style. They embraced the ridiculous and ran with it—literally every Sunday at church when there was a race to barbeque at the end of the service.

It was time to sink or swim. Edie could protect Tristan to a certain degree, but then she thought about Layne and her overprotective family. She'd always said she knew Walker was the love of her life when he didn't run, but embraced her family. Edie's feelings for Tristan had grown every day until she couldn't imagine not having him in her life. He made her happy. He made her laugh. He made her feel safe. He made her feel valued. He made her feel desired. However, now it was time to see how he fit into her life beyond their respective porches.

Edie opened the door at Tristan's knock and smiled at him. She tried to hide her nerves, but she didn't think she was doing it well enough when his smile slipped a little.

"Look, if you're not ready to introduce me to your friends, we don't have to go," Tristan said. "I can say I got sick or something."

Edie forced her lips back into a full, confident smile. "No, I want you to see Shadows Landing and to meet everyone. If you don't mind a little walk, we can enjoy this spring night and walk to town."

"Sounds perfect. Millevia is such a walkable country that I have found I miss walking." Tristan took a step back as she went onto the porch and locked the door.

Tristan took her hand in his and pulled her closer to his side as they walked down the sidewalk toward downtown. It felt so natural to touch him, to love him, to . . . Edie took a deep breath. Whoa there. She was getting ahead of herself. She had deep feelings for Tristan, but could she really already be thinking of loving him?

The guilt she expected to feel didn't wash over her. Instead, she smiled as they talked and thought that Shane would like him. They'd have been friends and that let her open her heart up to him. Did she love Tristan? Quite possibly, but first Edie wanted to see how he fit in with her friends.

"I remember you telling me the town was founded by pirates. What a neat history," Tristan said as they strolled toward town.

"It really is. My friend Harper owns the bar we are going to tonight. The bar itself was owned by the pirate, Black Law. He, Blackbeard, Anne Bonny, and other famous pirates all congregated here in Shadows Landing. If you're really interested in it, my friend Skeeter is the town's pirate expert. He even has a small pirate ship he takes tourists out on for tours of the area."

Tristan smiled easily and Edie began to relax. She had to

trust her heart and her heart told her Tristan was perfect for her. Her friends would see that too.

"This is where I work," Edie told him as they stopped in front of Darcy and Wade's museum. "I grew up with the Faulkner family, and while Wade is still in the Coast Guard, he and Darcy still hunt for sunken treasure together. Inside are just some of the pieces they've found together."

"I'd love for you to give me a tour. I had read about a ship they found a couple of years ago. I just didn't realize it was here in Shadows Landing. And I'd love to talk to them about their adventures. The treasure kind, not the nightly kind," Tristan said teasingly and Edie's confidence in him being able to survive the initial meeting of her friends grew.

"Across the street from us are the courthouse and church. Down the street a bit is Harper's bar and across from it is her cousin's art gallery. Tinsley is so talented. I have several of her paintings in my house."

"I'd love to see them," Tristan said as he smiled down at her, but not with kindness. With hunger. For her. Edie felt her body heat and was seriously rethinking dinner. Tristan had been the perfect gentleman for well over a week. He'd never asked to go inside her house. He'd never pushed her. Instead, he'd waited for her to come to him and right now the idea of dragging him home and up to her bedroom sounded much better than dinner.

"From the noise I gather this is the bar," Tristan said with a smirk as if reading her thoughts. Then his lips fell from a smile into a frown. "Are these bullets in the door?"

"Oh, those?" Edie said, trying to figure out how to explain them. They were from not one, but two different shootouts. "Harper thinks they add something to the pirate history. Let's go inside."

Edie opened the door. Noise, warmth, laughter, and

community washed over her. Harper was behind the bar with her young bartender, Georgina. Georgie, as everyone called her, had been shot during the last shootout. She was fully recovered but had become a little jumpy when the door opened.

Her face relaxed as she waved. "Hi, Edie! Welcome back!"

"Hi, Georgie. Meet my new neighbor, Tristan."

"Neighbor?" Tristan whispered with amusement. "Is that what we're going with?"

Georgie held out her hand over the historic wood bar and shook Tristan's hand. "Nice to meet you."

"This is my bar," Harper said, not bothering to hold out her hand or introduce herself as she tapped the blade of a knife on the bar top. "What are you doing here with Edie?"

"She's showing me around town. She told me the history of the place. It's fascinating. Hi, I'm Tristan."

"This is Harper," Edie filled in when Harper didn't seem keen to speak up.

"And I'm Harper's husband, Dare." Jeez! Edie about jumped out of her skin when Harper's hulking husband slipped up quietly behind them. "I'm also Edie's very good friend. Are you the reason she's been missing knitting club?"

Dare and Tristan were close to the same height as Dare tried to intimidate Tristan with a glare that left Edie frowning and Harper smiling. "I love you so much," Harper whispered to her husband before giving him a wink.

"Edie!" a woman called out from the side table, breaking the tension between Dare and Tristan. "Welcome back!"

"Olivia!" Edie called out, rushing over to hug her friend. Not one, but two large men stood on each side and glared at Tristan, who had followed Edie over to the table. "Olivia Townsend, meet Tristan. He moved in next door to me."

Bookends of Townsend men stepped forward. Olivia rolled her eyes and shoved at one of them. "Damon, Stone, knock it off."

Olivia was Ryker Faulkner's lawyer. While Harper thought she was a ball-buster, Harper had nothing on Olivia. She looked fresh off the pages of a fashion magazine with her picture-perfect blonde hair, her makeup always flawless, her suits fitted, and her heels high. However, she dismantled every lawyer she went up against with the ruthlessness of a mafia boss.

"Hello, Damon. Hi, Stone. How are you both doing?" Edie asked. They made her slightly nervous, but she had figured since everyone else was giving them wide berth she might as well be nice. They made their sister's life a nightmare and made Walker look like a pimp compared to how they scared off any man who got near Olivia. But they clearly loved Olivia and that counted for something to Edie. Over the past month or so, Edie had become brave enough to talk to them a couple of times. She found them to be intense, yet under that intensity were two gentlemen.

"We're well, thank you, Edie," Damon answered while never taking his eyes off Tristan.

Tristan didn't run like several of the other men in town, though. He stepped forward and held out his hand to Olivia. "Nice to meet you."

"Wait until Hunter gets here," Stone said with a scary amount of threatening glee. "He'd cut that arm off in a heartbeat."

"Wait, what?" Olivia gasped in alarm. "No, not Hunter, too. You told me Kane would be the last brother to move to Shadows Landing."

"He misses his sister," Damon said. "We *all* do."

Edie heard the door open behind her, but didn't think

anything of it until the slow, deep, commanding, and very dangerous voice of Ryker Faulkner vibrated through her.

"Who the hell are you and what the hell are you doing with Edie?"

Edie saw Damon and Stone smile. They'd moved here thinking Olivia was having an affair with her boss, Ryker, because Olivia bought a weekend home in Shadows Landing. However, after Ryker married Kenzie, Ryker appeared to have grown on the Townsend men. There was now a mutual respect between them. A recognition of other alpha leaders, but Edie wouldn't go as far as saying a friendship.

"Ryker," Edie groaned similarly to how Olivia had done to her brother. "Be nice. This is Tristan. He's my new neighbor. Tristan, this is my friend, Ryker Faulkner."

That elicited a raised eyebrow from Tristan. Apparently, even in Millevia they'd heard of Ryker Faulkner, billionaire businessman. When Edie had told Tristan about her friends, she might have left that out.

"How do you do?" Tristan extended his hand. Ryker didn't take it.

"Tristan what?" Ryker asked instead. Well, *ask* was the wrong word. Demanded was more appropriate.

Edie saw Tristan pause as she held her breath. She needed this last name to give to Abby. It was sad, but she'd forgotten all about getting his last name after they'd gardened together. Although now it looked as if Ryker would do the background check for her.

Tristan was screwed. He could give the fake name on his documents, but someone like Ryker Faulkner had the means to do a better background check than Tristan had been able to do in Millevia.

He came here to Shadows Landing for a reason and maybe having Ryker on his side would be a good thing. The only way to do that was to be honest. Tris took a little breath and then let it out. "Durand. Tristan Durand. It's nice to meet you."

"We'll see about that." Ryker's threat was clear. A flash went off and then Ryker was sending his picture and a text. Tristan was screwed. Very, very screwed. He just hoped the background check didn't alert Millevia of his presence here.

If Tristan were still in Millevia, he'd have fired whoever ran the background check on this "little group of tourists" for gross incompetence. While Edie and Layne might not have any red flags, everyone else Edie knew did. He didn't know what the Townsend men did, but they held themselves as men of power and authority. Her friend Ryker was one of the most powerful businessmen in the world. And her friend Abby was the deadly Ahmed's freaking *daughter*. This whole mission has been a shit show from the beginning.

Tristan frowned as an idea began to nag at him in the back of his mind. What if that was the whole idea?

Tristan looked up and saw Ryker watching him. Not just Ryker, but the Townsend men, and Dare too. Harper casually twirled a knife in her hand, a nice combat one at that.

A large man with a beard came over and stopped in front of Tristan, drawing his attention away from Harper's impressive knife skills. He hooked his thumbs in the straps of his overalls and sucked in between his teeth as if he had a piece of food stuck there. He pulled out the largest knife Tristan had ever seen and used the tip to pick at his teeth.

Beside him, a little guy came to stand on one side, and on the other a skinny man in clothes at least two sizes too big joined them.

"We're right neighborly people here in Shadows Landing," the short one said.

"But you're new and you're with our Edie. We're right protective of our Edie," the man in overalls said.

"The pirate ghosts can't get a read on you," the one with baggy clothes said and Tristan swore he felt something brush against his backside. Baggy Clothes rolled his eyes. "I'm not saying that, Anne. But she thinks you're hiding sumptin'."

"Guys, stop. Tristan is new to town. You didn't put Olivia through this. Or her brothers."

"Heck no. They could scare the soul from a ghost," the little man said.

"I'm not scary enough?" Tristan asked with a hint of disbelief mixed with amusement. "That's a first." Although, he hadn't been trying to intimidate. He'd been trying to be patient and gentle with Edie. However, in the past people had always just been able to pick up the dangerous vibes from him. It was as if they knew he was a predator and gave him a wide berth.

"Tristan, this is Turtle," Edie said of the short man. "And Gator," she said of the man in overalls. "And lastly, Skeeter. He's the one I told you about who knows the pirate history of town better than anyone."

"Who is Anne?" Tristan asked Skeeter.

Skeeter rolled his eyes as if Tristan were an idiot. "Anne Bonny, the female pirate."

"What didn't you want to tell me she said?" Tristan saw the skinny guy blush and then Tristan would have sworn he felt that cold breath of wind brush his backside again.

"You're a believer?" Skeeter asked suddenly with surprise.

"I'm from Millevia. We have more ghosts than you can ever imagine. Every building there is at least four hundred years old."

Ryker froze, his frown somehow deepening even more. "Millevia? You don't speak with much of an accent. What exactly are you doing here, Tristan Durand?"

The door burst open and Tristan automatically grabbed Edie and shoved her behind him and into Ryker's arms. Luckily, it wasn't Jean or any of the other guards there to assassinate him. It was a man in scrubs and right behind him was a pretty woman in matching scrubs.

"Who are you and what are you doing with Edie?" he demanded.

"Gavin, knock it off," Edie snapped. Tristan looked back at her and saw her face filling with color as her eyes narrowed. Tristan didn't claim to be an expert in women. The orphanage he grew up in had only boys and then he joined the military. He'd had some casual relationships, but they usually failed because of the secrecy and his time away on missions. But you'd have to be blind not to see that Edie was about to lose it.

"Stop it! Stop it right now!" And there she went. Edie stalked forward and grabbed Tristan's hand in hers. "You all want to know? Fine. Tristan and I had a one-night stand in Millevia and now he's moved in next door. We're kind of dating, but Abby and Layne said I need to determine if he's a serial killer or not so I can decide if I want to have a meaningful relationship with him. I mean, I want to, and I really like him, but I'm not sure if he'll kill me so we've been taking it slow. See? I'm more than capable of deciding these things for myself. I am not fragile. I am not going to break.

And I have the right to be happy again, dammit, to love again, to have a family, after all the dreams I had died with Shane. But y'all are messing it up by interfering!"

"Edie," the guy in the scrubs said, "we're just looking out for you."

"We only want what's best for you," Harper said from behind the bar.

"I know, but you have to let me be me again. It's my choice if I date a serial killer, who I don't think he is since he has managed not to kill any of you all tonight," Edie huffed and Tristan opened his mouth to talk, but he wasn't fast enough.

"Serial killer in the psychopath way? No. His psych evaluations show he's of sound mind when he kills people," Ryker said into the silence and Tristan knew his time was up.

"Ryker, what are you talking about?" the woman in scrubs asked even as Edie was already pulling away from him.

"I'm saying Edie's one-night stand is an assassin for the president of Millevia. Let me guess, you're here to try to kill me," Ryker said, looking amused.

Tristan didn't answer Ryker. His attention was solely on Edie.

"You're not denying it?" Edie asked softly as the woman in scrubs rushed over to put her arm around Edie.

"No, I'm not denying it. I'm a trained government asset," Tristan told her. He either needed to make a run for it or stand his ground and fight for Edie. The look in her eyes told him it would be one hell of a fight, but she was worth it. He'd fallen for her in Millevia. But after a week of spending every evening with her, he knew she was the only woman for him. He wasn't really sure what love was, but he knew

Edie had become the most important person in his life. He loved every moment with her and he was going to fight for her. Even if that meant baring his secrets to her friends and begging her to understand that he'd never hurt her.

"Are you here to kill my husband?" the woman in scrubs asked.

"I don't know who your husband is, but no, I'm not here to kill him."

The woman looked thoughtfully at him even as she frowned. "I'm Kenzie Faulkner, Ryker's wife. Are you here because of Edie?"

"Yes."

"Are you going to kill her?" Kenzie asked even as Tristan felt the entire bar closing in on him.

"No. If I were, I would have done that in Millevia before she ever saw me." Tristan ignored the desire to downplay who he was. He wasn't the soft and cuddly man she thought. Edie needed to hear the truth, even if that meant she'd hate him because they only had a future if she could love him— the real him. The truth was out and now it was up to Edie to decide if she could live with it or not.

Behind him, he felt a pair of hands grab him, but he didn't fight it. "Let's just put you in handcuffs for this little chat."

Tristan looked over his shoulder at two men with sheriff's badges on the waistbands of their jeans. There was no reason to fight. He could get out of the cuffs in a flash if he wanted. It seemed to make them feel more at ease to have the illusion of power, so Tristan gave it to them if it meant they'd listen to him.

"Is one of you the sheriff?" Tristan asked before he was shoved onto a chair.

"I am," the one in the cowboy hat said. "Granger Fox and this is my deputy, Kordell King."

"Are you going to question me?" Tristan asked, trying to hide his amusement.

"No, she is," Ryker said with a grin that sent shivers down Tristan's back as he nodded to Olivia. Tristan was suddenly very worried he'd made the wrong choice.

---

## 10

Edie kept her grip on Kenzie's hand. Kenzie was an emergency room nurse and was always calm and collected. Right now, Edie needed that calm energy. Edie watched Ryker hand his phone to Olivia as the rest of the Faulkners rushed to the bar. Gavin had already called into Keeneston and had Walker on video chat.

"Shh, take a deep breath," Kenzie whispered to her.

"While I appreciate all they're doing, it's really pissing me off, too," Edie admitted.

"Everyone back up and be quiet!" Kenzie yelled suddenly.

"Sweetheart," Ryker began to say, but Kenzie put her hands on her hips and glared at her husband. Edie would have laughed since nothing scared Ryker, but she was too shocked at Kenzie raising her voice to do so. "I mean it. Everyone but Granger, Kord, and Olivia need to back up. Sit down. Shut up. If you can't do that, then go outside and wait."

"We're staying," Damon Townsend said, crossing his arms over his wide chest.

Kenzie's eyes narrowed and one hand snapped up from her hip to point to the back of the room. She didn't say anything. She just glared at him and kept her finger pointed to the back of the bar.

Damon stared back and everyone was quiet as they watched what would happen. Kenzie began to tap her foot irritably and finally, Damon blinked and muttered something about leaving Olivia unprotected.

"You'll be twenty feet away. Anyway, she'll have Granger and Kord with her," Kenzie said with a roll of her eyes.

"Exactly," Stone said as he gave a look to the two single men.

"This is my bar," Harper said, interrupting the stare down.

Kenzie's head snapped in her direction. "Do you not see how upset Edie is? Do you want to make her more upset?" Kenzie waited as they muttered that they didn't want to hurt Edie. "Then sit over there and be quiet."

"Yes, ma'am," Gator replied as everyone got up and crammed into the back of the bar.

Edie watched as each person gave her varying looks of pity and worry as they walked by her. Finally, the table Tristan was seated at had cleared except for Kord, Granger, and Olivia Townsend. Kord released Tristan from the cuffs before standing directly behind him, hand on the butt of his service revolver.

"Edie," Tinsley said pleadingly.

Edie shook her head. "Please, this is between Tristan and me."

"Okay then." Tinsley grabbed Harper's arm and pulled her backward. "We will all be waiting over there. Just yell if you need us."

Edie kept her eyes on Tristan. Before Olivia could speak, she did. "What's going on, Tristan?"

"Everything I told you in Millevia is true. I believe President Pastor killed our previous president and is using my latest assignment as a way to possibly get rid of me since she knew I was loyal to her predecessor, President Gastaud. I've questioned her authority too many times to go unnoticed, and she probably found out I have been trying to look into President Gastaud's death."

Olivia glanced to Edie for permission to take over questioning him and Edie nodded. "Why do you think President Gastaud's death wasn't a riding accident?" Olivia asked.

"Gastaud's daughter, Emily, said he'd never take that path when riding. He stuck to the same path every day. He wasn't a jumper, and certainly not in heavily wooded areas with a stone fence that tall. Furthermore, the horse he was on wasn't a jumper and came back with not a scuff on any of its hooves. Pastor was head of the military and had ridden with Gastaud many times. She knew what route he took. She knew the exact time he rode, which horse was his, and she knew he didn't take guards with him since he stayed on his property. The second he was dead, Pastor swept in, fired everyone, and used the military as her way to gain control of the country. She hasn't taken just a page, but the whole book from Putin."

"You'd have us believe you're the good guy who is trying to take down a corrupt leader?" Granger asked.

Olivia gave a slight gesture with her chin and Granger walked over to where she stood. Shoulder to shoulder, they stood as he read what was on the phone.

"I have a clean record. I have commendations. I wouldn't

go after a sitting president without reason," Tristan answered.

"Ryker said you killed people. Who did you kill and why?" Granger asked.

"I'm not very different from Edie's brother, or even you, Sheriff. I've never killed someone without a good reason. It was all in the line of duty. The last person I killed before Gastaud died was a man by the name of Luka Anapoli. He was an Italian who trafficked women and children through our country's waters. I was charged with rescuing a boatload of women and children. My team and I tracked his boat, saw where it was going, and boarded it the second it hit our waters. Anapoli went after me with a knife and I killed him in self-defense. The mission was never to kill him, but to rescue the victims and arrest Anapoli. Gastaud had several layers of checks and balances in place to prevent rogue agents. I was never given one name and told to kill that person unless it was a life-or-death scenario. There had been one involving a terrorist plot at the train station that was a shoot-to-kill mission. Otherwise, it was capture first, kill only if necessary. Pastor sent me on her assignments as soon as she took power, which were completely different."

"How were they different?" Olivia asked.

"There was no threat to our country that I was trying to stop behind those missions that I could find. She also emphasized the kill order instead of the capture order. I tried to capture a political dissident—someone who opposed Pastor. Jean, my teammate, preferred the kill order. I had the dissident in custody and Jean shot him without my permission. That's when I started to become suspicious that Pastor was looking for a way to take me out."

"Take you out how?" Granger asked.

"I was given my mission and told if I didn't complete it, she'd send my own team after me to kill me."

Edie gasped in surprise. "She told you that?"

"Yes. I know my team is hunting me right now." Tristan thought about David and hoped like hell he'd play along. If his friend were killed because of Tristan, he wouldn't bother looking for evidence to remove Pastor from office. He'd kill Pastor and she'd never see it coming.

"So, you do kill people?" Edie asked again as she saw Olivia frown while she looked down at whatever records Ryker had found.

"Yes. Capture or kill. It's my job and I am good at it."

"Your files show that," Granger said as he looked up from the phone.

"Tristan," Olivia asked, "why are you telling us this? You could have lied about your name. You could have moved anywhere but here. Why are you in Shadows Landing?"

Edie had to sit as she waited for him to answer because her nerves left her shaking so much, she feared she'd fall down.

"I wasn't supposed to ever meet you, Edie." Tristan turned to talk to her and not Olivia. "But then I did and I couldn't stop thinking about you. I met your friends Abby and Layne, and I knew the mission was bullshit. It was a test. Kill an innocent to prove myself to Pastor, or refuse and prove I was against her.

"I knew the moment I met you I could never hurt you. I've thought through about a hundred scenarios. I could travel to anywhere in the world, but it's another catch-22. Stay away, but how can I protect you if Pastor finds out about you? Stay with you and put you in danger if they find me here? I probably should have stayed away, but I couldn't.

I haven't stopped thinking of you since your niece hit me with that gelato spoon."

"Your very own Cupid's arrow," Kord said with a grin.

Edie's throat was tight because she wanted to tell him the same thing. That she hadn't been able to stop thinking about him either. However, there was one big issue. "You were supposed to kill me then?"

"I wasn't supposed to kill anyone," Tristan said passionately, almost willing her to believe he was telling the truth. Edie didn't know what to think. Her head began to spin.

"Exactly what, or who, was your mission?" Olivia asked.

Tristan didn't take his eyes off of Edie's. She could see him willing her to believe him. "There was a trade agreement for shipping in place with President Gastaud that fell apart when Pastor took power. She wanted revenge for it. I was to capture my target, torture her, and send pieces of her to an address in order to get the contract back up and running. Those were Pastor's exact words."

A shiver wracked Edie's body at the cold-blooded order. "You were going to torture me to get Ryker to fulfill some contract?"

Tristan shook his head.

"I don't understand," Edie said into the silence. "Layne is a physical therapist. Abby works at a horse farm. What would they have to do with this?"

"I was to turn Abby since she's friends with the Rahmi royal family, specifically Princess Ariana. It was Rahmi that refused to support Pastor's presidency and dropped out of all proposed trade deals with them when she took power. Pastor thinks it makes her look weak so she wanted to hit them where it hurts—with their pretty princess. I met Edie while I was surveilling Abby. Then I got to meet Abby herself. I didn't realize she was the daughter of the famous Ahmed until Edie mentioned it. I knew then that if I ever touched her, my life would be over. Plus, she was cool. She's not a political player and probably had no knowledge of this contract to begin with. She's happily married with a baby on the way. Not some pawn for a country she didn't even live in. That's when it really hit me that Pastor had found me out and this was a test to verify it."

"You think so?" Edie asked as she listened to Tristan explain the situation.

Tristan now looked to Granger and Olivia. "My country's intelligence service allegedly ran background checks on everyone in the group but they left out Dylan's military past. They left out Walker's military past. And they left out the fact that Abby is Ahmed Mueez's daughter. Tell me if that doesn't sound like a setup."

Granger's frown mirrored Olivia's and that told Edie everything she needed to know. "We need to warn Abby," Edie said, reaching into her purse to pull out her cell phone.

## 11

Tristan knew his chance with Edie was over. She was lost to him forever but he could still do the right thing and keep her and her friends safe. Edie lived in a town with only a couple of full-time members of the sheriff's department. From what he'd learned, Granger and Kord were on duty days, then two men filled in part-time on nights. It wasn't exactly an army.

"Hey, girl, you figure out if that Tristan guy is a serial killer yet?" Abby asked as a way of answering the video call.

Edie's eyes shot to his and he couldn't help but give her a small smile. Under different circumstances he'd be best friends with someone like Abby. She actually reminded him of a female version of himself. Silly, though, since she worked on a horse farm and he killed people.

"About that," Edie said as the entire bar seemed to lean forward to hear the video call. "Everyone is here." Edie panned the phone so Abby could see the full bar. "Apparently you were half right. He's killed many people, but he's not a serial killer."

"You need to explain. Better yet, just give me his name."

"Tristan Durand," Tristan answered for Edie.

"One sec." Abby was quiet as Tristan heard her work on a laptop and then she laughed. "I knew I liked you, Tris."

Tristan blinked as she smiled at him. That was not what he was expecting. Edie's wide eyes said the same thing. "Excuse me? Did Ryker send you my file?" Tristan asked.

"Kinda. My brother did. Don't you love how they say *asset* when they mean assassin?" Abby said with a little laugh. "Hey, Dylan. Come look at this. This is the guy from Millevia who moved in next door to Edie."

There was silence as Dylan walked over and looked over her shoulder to the computer screen and then Tristan saw Dylan smirk. "Ha! Edie fell for an assassin. That's great. Wait, why are you in Shadows Landing?" Dylan asked with a look that felt threatening even from hundreds of miles away.

"That's why we're calling," Edie said. "I'll let Tristan explain."

Edie turned the phone toward him and Tristan fell into his military reporting tone. Heck, he was even standing as if he were giving a report to his team. "Abby was my target."

Abby snorted with amusement. Dylan frowned.

"How does Millevia know who Abby is?" Dylan asked.

"They saw her picture as Princess Ariana's bridesmaid. They thought Abby was close enough to Ariana to force the princess to get the trade deals back on track by threatening her," Tristan explained.

Tristan frowned when Abby began laughing so hard she had to hold her belly with both hands. Tears ran down her cheeks as she laughed so hard she had to take deep breaths to calm herself. Even Dylan had to turn away from the camera, but not before Tristan saw a smile.

"I thought you'd be more upset," Edie said, feeling the same confusion as Tristan.

"Someone trying to kill me is a normal Saturday night," Abby said as she tried to stop laughing. "Of course. The guy in the bathroom in Millevia wasn't a thief but an assassin. He was probably sent when Tristan didn't do his job. But, if he didn't do his job, then he's in Shadows Landing in exile."

"Wait, what guy in the bathroom?" Dylan wasn't laughing now but she waved him off with a shrug.

"It was nothing. If that's the quality of Millevia's assassins, there's nothing to worry about. Thanks for the heads-up," Abby said with a smile for Tristan.

"You don't work on a farm, do you?" Tristan asked, already knowing the answer.

"What? Of course I do. I'm also the daughter of Ahmed and Bridget Mueez. I have certain . . . skills."

The door behind Abby was shoved open and a man with a dog strapped to his chest like a baby rushed in. "What is happening? Your heart rate increased."

"Dad! Did you put another health monitor on me?" Abby asked as she started to pat down her clothes and then frowned as she took off a bracelet. "You've been tracking my vital signs?"

"Of course I have, I am your father."

Tristan was in awe. The real Ahmed. He was certainly scary—even with a dog sitting in a baby sling. The rust-colored dog yawned and snuggled in closer to Ahmed.

"Look, you woke up Nemi. Now what is going on?" Ahmed demanded. "And who are you and what are you doing next to Edie?"

Tristan immediately snapped to attention, his spine straighter than an arrow. There was no doubt in his mind that Ahmed could reach through the phone and kill him in a blink of an eye. "Sir, it's an honor to meet you."

"We haven't met. Who are you?"

"Tristan Durand, sir."

Ahmed looked at the computer screen. "Asset," he said with a roll of his eyes. "Assassin. Why don't they just say it? What are you doing with Edie?"

"He was supposed to kidnap and torture me so that Ari would make Rahmi reenter some trade contracts with Millevia," Abby answered for him and almost managed to keep a straight face. Almost.

The dog's head shot up and Tristan would have sworn the animal laughed. Even Ahmed's lips twitched before he frowned and turned to the phone. "When would you like to die? I'm busy tomorrow, but I can kill you the day after tomorrow. What time works best for you?" Ahmed asked in a way that Tristan took as being very serious.

Tristan swallowed hard. There was a literal time limit on his life now and it was counting down. He wasn't worried about Jean. Ahmed Mueez, however, was a completely different story.

"Dad," Abby said with a roll of her eyes. "He didn't do it. He loves Edie and they called to warn me."

Ahmed's eyes narrowed even further. "Does Walker know?"

"Yes, sir!" came a loud call from the back of the bar where Gavin was holding up his own phone with Walker's face on it.

"Do you want my help in killing him?" Ahmed asked.

"No, sir. I'm more than capable of killing him myself. Thank you, though," Walker answered back as Edie groaned.

"No one is killing anyone," Edie yelled.

"Look, I know you're upset," Abby said. "But don't ruin the fun for the rest of us."

Who were these people? Tristan would love to hang out with them if they didn't actually kill him.

"What's the plan?" Dylan asked.

"I've been working on that. I'm trying to find a way to prove that Pastor killed President Gastaud. The best information I have is from his daughter, but there's no physical evidence. I had to flee after I refused orders to capture Abby," Tristan said. "So now I'm stuck trying to find evidence from halfway around the world."

"We'll look into it and get back to you," Abby answered. Ahmed and Dylan nodded their agreement.

"We won't kill you for now," Ahmed said. "But if you hurt Edie . . ."

The dog growled and Tristan didn't need Ahmed to finish the threat. He understood completely.

"Thanks for filling us in," Dylan said before he and Ahmed took a step back.

Abby leaned forward and dropped her voice. "I like you, Tris. Don't mess this up." Then the video call ended and the bar erupted in discussion.

Kord worked to keep everyone back as Granger and Olivia stepped close to him and Edie.

"I'm not as scary as Ahmed," Granger said. "But I can kill you just the same. You will not come to Shadows Landing and hurt one of ours. Understand?"

Tristan was amused, but he wouldn't disrespect the sheriff by showing it. Ahmed could intimidate him. A small-town sheriff? Not really. But he did care for Edie and that was all that mattered. He made it through the elite military school as a charity case. He could put up with some threats if it meant he got his way—meaning he got Edie.

"Can I talk to you outside for a moment?" Tristan asked her as Olivia began to explain the international political ramifications of all this.

Edie nodded and headed for the door as Kord lost control of the crowd. They all surged forward but Edie just shook her head and walked out the door.

"What do you want, Tristan?" she asked as she rubbed her hands along her arms as if to warm them.

"You. I've wanted only you since you hit me with the gelato." Tristan would rather face Ahmed in hand-to-hand combat than to have this conversation, but Edie was worth it. "You're the only woman I've ever wanted like this, Edie. I love our talks. I love our time together and I want more. I have no experience with romantic relationships, but I want to try with you. I understand I hid what my job really is, but can you accept it? Can you accept me and give us a try?"

Tristan held his breath as he saw Edie thinking. He saw the unshed tears in her eyes and his heart sank. He didn't want to hurt her. He should just leave.

"You're going to go after Pastor, aren't you?" Edie asked.

"I have to find out if she killed Gastaud and give my country back its freedom," Tristan answered.

"Why you? Why does it have to be you?" Edie struggled to keep from crying.

Tristan wanted to reach for her, but it was clear she didn't want his touch right now. "It has to be me because no one else will do it. What kind of man am I if I don't try to free my country? It's the right thing to do, Edie."

Edie lost her battle as the tears fell. She sniffed and nodded her head. "Shane would have said the same thing. I'm sorry, Tristan, but I've already lost one man I loved. I can't lose another."

Edie rushed past him and hurried down the street. Wait,

did that mean Edie loved him? Tristan felt the impact of that more than any bullet. Edie loved him! He stood straighter and smiled with a warmth he'd never felt before. Until the full impact of what she said hit him. She loved him, but because of who he was it was over before it fully began. It was over and he couldn't tell her he was falling in love with her because she had just ended it.

## 12

---

Tristan frowned as Edie walked away from him. He knew better than to follow, but that didn't mean he would leave her on her own. He opened the door to the bar and scanned the crowd. "Sheriff," was all Tristan had to say to bring the lawman outside.

Tristan had gotten a feel for the people of Shadows Landing during his interrogation. They were protective of their own, which showed great character. He knew Granger would help him because, while the town might underestimate Edie, they loved her.

"What is it?" Granger asked. The lawman clearly didn't approve of Tristan and that was okay. In fact, he doubted anyone here did. It didn't matter. Only Edie's opinion mattered to him.

"Edie's upset that I'm in danger. She's comparing what I'm doing to Shane. Can you please see her safely home?" Tristan asked as they both watched her walking down Main Street.

"You know about Shane?" Granger asked.

Tristan nodded. "I was with her when she got the tattoo

in his memory. I've heard a lot about him and what a great man he was. Please, Sheriff. Will you make sure she's safe?"

"You can call me Granger. We'll talk more later."

Tristan felt a rush of relief when Granger jogged after Edie. Well, until the kick to the shin came.

"You made Miss Edie cry. You're a meanie!"

The little girl with a ponytail kicked his shin again before the door to the bar opened fully and children poured out at full attack.

"Leah, don't kick the mean man," a young woman called out as she hurried out the door behind seven children.

"Fine, I won't. Lindsey can," Leah said, crossing her arms over her chest and glaring at him as another little girl let out a kick a pro footballer would be proud of.

"You're a mean, horny man!" little Lindsey yelled, her pigtails swinging.

Tristan choked on a laugh even as his shin throbbed.

"Lindsey!" the mother gasped.

The oldest boy, who looked to be near thirteen, rolled his eyes. "*Ornery.* Jeez, Lindsey. How many times do I have to tell you all that?" Lindsey didn't seem to care that her brother was lecturing her. She looked ready to give Tristan another kick.

"And you are a mean, ornery man to lie to Miss Edie like that." Then the oldest boy pulled back his hand and landed a decent punch to Tristan's stomach.

The mother rolled her eyes as if this weren't something new as suddenly seven children were in various stages of trying to murder him.

"Landry, Lacy, Levi, Leah, Lindsey, Lyle, Leo! Stop this right now! Even if he does deserve it," the mother added to be sure the message was getting through to him.

*Pffft. Thunk.*

Burning pain shot through the side of Tristan's arm. Did one of the little darlings stab him? Tristan looked at his arm to see blood seeping out of a deep scratch, but then remembered the second sound. He looked to the thick wooden door and saw a fresh, smoking bullet lodged in it.

"Get down!"

Tristan didn't wait to see if they followed his order. Instead, he held out both arms and plowed all seven kids and their mother to the ground right as a string of silent bullets *thunked* into the wooden door.

The mother and the kids screamed as he struggled to cover them all with his body.

"Landry?" little Lindsey's tone was demanding. "Is he horny or ornery right now?"

"I'm very, very ornery, Lindsey. Now, will you all stay here so I can let the bad man know he's made a very big mistake by making me ornery?" Tristan asked.

"Tell him I'm pretty damn ornery myself," the mother yelled as Granger began to run down the street toward them.

The mother moved to cover her children with her body and Tristan moved up into a crouch at the same time he pulled a gun from the small of his back. Silencers were great, but they weren't completely silent. He could tell where the shooter was located from where the bullets had hit the door.

Tristan ran hunched over until he reached the hood of an SUV just down from the bar. He dropped to his belly and crawled past the front tire. He slowly military-crawled off the sidewalk and onto the street. Lying flat, he saw the feet of the shooter under a truck across the street.

Lying on his stomach, he put his arms out straight in front of him on the pavement and aimed. He fired twice, back-to-back, and was then up and running with his gun held out in front of him, ready to put a bullet between the shooter's eyes. He just hoped it wasn't David. He couldn't kill his best friend.

Tristan slowed as he came to the truck's tailgate. Keeping his gun out in front of him, he peered around the corner.

"I should have known it was you when you missed, Claude. I'm surprised they hired a mercenary. I feel honored they want me that badly, but kind of hurts that they sent the cheapest mercenary in Europe, who is a famously poor shot." Tristan held his gun aimed at Claude's head. He had to hold his gun several inches down from the top of Claude's head because of the giant man bun perched atop his head that was a mix of a bird's nest and a mohawk. It had probably taken Claude hours to get it just so.

"Piss off, Tristan," Claude said in his very posh French accent as he held his leg. Blood was running through his fingers, but he'd live. Claude was convinced that he was the best merc around, but he was actually the worst. What worried Tristan was that Claude had found him, somehow. "Now, give me your belt. I don't want to get blood on my ascot."

"It's a scarf, Claude. How did you manage to find me?" Tristan asked as Granger ran up to them with his own gun drawn.

"Eh," Claude shrugged. "Jean told me. I was already in this provincial little state on another job when he called. I said I'd handle it for him. Which I would have if you hadn't shot my leg. That's a real low blow, Tris. There's such thing as professional courtesy."

Granger stepped forward and kicked Claude's gun away as Tristan became aware of the growing number of people heading toward them from the bar. Leading the way was a very pissed-off mother of seven.

Granger cocked his head and used the barrel of his gun to poke Claude's man bun. "What is that?"

"It's art and you're ruining it. Some of us have real style instead of tacky cowboy hats."

Granger looked to Tristan and smirked. "Is this guy for real?"

"Brah, I am diggin' your vibe. Your hair is on fleek. You are slaying it."

Tristan groaned. "Oh god, there's two of them?"

"I'm Timmons," Man Bun number two held out his hands. He didn't look as if he were armed. He looked like he still lived in his mother's house.

"Uh-oh," the oldest daughter said as she watched her mother stalk toward Claude.

"That's her horny look," the littlest boy said. "She's really going to give it to him."

Landry groaned as if he were too tired from dealing with his younger siblings to correct him.

"You have a good punch," Tristan told Landry when he stopped to stand next to him.

"Thanks. I learned it from my mom. See."

Tristan glanced up to see Landry's mom deliver a blow to Claude's jaw that felled him like an oak.

"You." The mom kicked Claude in the stomach while he was down. "Could." *Kick.* "Have." *Kick.* "Killed." *Kick.* "My." *Kick.* "Children." She accentuated her displeasure with a kick to the balls that left Claude gasping for air.

Lindsey came up and tugged Tristan's pant leg as Kord held the mom back from beating up Claude further. Tristan wished he'd let her go. He wouldn't mind seeing what else she could do.

"Mr. Tristan, I know you're a meanie, but you're bleeding," Lindsey said as she pointed to his arm.

"Just a little. Don't worry, Lindsey. I'm not hurt." Tristan smiled down at the little girl who then wrapped her arm around his leg instead of kicking him. The acceptance was clear. He'd won them over by taking a bullet for them.

Granger had told Edie to go and stay in the diner, but when Lydia and the kids joined the crowd, there was no way she was staying behind. Tristan had been shot at. She's seen him shield Lydia and her children before taking out the shooter. At least that's what she assumed he'd done when Granger muttered a curse, shoved her into the diner, and took off down the street after seeing Tristan standing next to a truck holding out a gun she hadn't even known he had. It struck her how calm and confident Tristan was standing there, pointing a gun at someone. She didn't know how she felt about that, but her concern for Tristan overwhelmed any worry she had.

"Is everyone okay?" Edie asked as she ran up to join the throng of people surrounding the assassin while the mother cussed him out.

"Yes, Miss Edie. Mr. Tristan protected us," Landry answered.

"He has a boo-boo," Lindsey said from where she was wrapped around his leg. She pointed to his arm and Edie gasped at the blood dripping down his arm.

"Tristan! You're hurt. Gavin!" she yelled, searching the crowd for Gavin, the town doctor.

"What is it?" Gavin asked as he made his way around Lydia, who was threatening to cut off the shooter's balls and feed them to Bubba, the town's alligator.

"Tristan's been shot," she said as she rushed to get a better look at the injury.

"It's just a scratch. It's fine," Tristan said as he watched Granger handcuff Claude, who was now cursing at Lydia in French.

"You will not call me a bitch, you *petite chatte!*" Lydia screamed at the still horizontal Claude as Kord had to physically pick her up off the ground to prevent her from killing the assassin with her bare hands.

When Edie looked back to Tristan, Lydia's kids had him surrounded. Lindsey was hanging on to one leg. Landry and Lacy, the two eldest, flanked Tristan on either side. Somehow Leo, the youngest, had gotten Tristan to pick him up with his good arm. And Lyle, Levi, and Leah were standing in front of him.

"Okay, kids," Gavin said as he stopped in front of Tristan. "Let me take a look at our patient."

"He saved us," Lacy said solemnly. "Maybe he's not such a bad guy after all."

"Makes sense now why he was lying," Landry said, only moving enough to allow Gavin to see Tristan's arm. "He was trying to protect Miss Edie."

Edie was pretty sure it was a little more than that, but his actions in saving Lydia and her children spoke volumes more than anything Tris could have said. She had sensed he was a good man from the moment she'd met him. Shane was like that too. Good men who did the dark things their country required to keep them all safe. Shane had been allowed to tell her what he did for a living, but the individual missions he went on were classified. If they had met while he was on a mission, he'd have lied to her too.

Edie understood that. That wasn't the issue. The issue was whether she was strong enough to have the man she loved put his life in danger to do what no one else would—the right thing.

Tristan wasn't the problem. She was, and she knew it. It was the thought of loving and losing all over again. For three years, she'd felt as if she had died right along with Shane, and now to fall in love with a man being hunted by his own country? She couldn't risk her heart like that. She might not survive this time.

But her heart was already involved. Edie had already gone and fallen in love with Tristan over the past week. It would hurt just as much to leave him now. Walking away from him moments ago had hurt like hell. Her heart had practically seized in her chest at the idea of never seeing him again.

That meant there was only one thing she could do—help Tristan uncover the truth. Then they could finally move on, together.

"Gavin, how bad is it?" Edie asked.

"Just needs a couple of stitches. Nothing serious," Gavin said as he peeled off his medical gloves. "Come to my office. I'll have you sewn up in a couple of minutes."

Kord finally joined them with Lydia. She took a deep breath and brushed back her hair from her face. "I'm Lydia. Thank you so much for saving my children and me."

"I'm pretty sure they could save themselves. They're good kids. You have one hell of a right cross, ma'am." Tristan smiled kindly at Lydia and Edie knew she could never walk away from him again. He might be an assassin, but he was good, kind, and showed he would always do the right thing.

"Thank you. You should see what I can do with a dagger. Come on, kids. It's time to get home." Lydia gathered her children. The boys shook Tristan's hand and the girls each gave him a hug.

"I hope you're going to give him another chance," Lydia whispered. "You're a good, kind person always putting others first. It's time to put what you want first."

"Are you coming, Edie?" Gavin asked as he and Tristan began to walk toward the clinic.

"I'll be right behind you." She was going to put herself first, make what she wanted for herself the top priority. If that meant she had to fight an entire nation for what she wanted, she was going to do it. She hadn't had a chance to save Shane, but she had a chance now to help save Tristan.

Edie reached into her purse and pulled out the business card that had been tucked away for months. She dialed and the call was answered immediately.

"Mr. Abel? I don't know if you remember me, but this is Edie Wecker. I'm Walker Greene's sister."

"Of course I remember you. What can I do for you, Edie?" Sebastian Abel, billionaire businessman and best friend of the president of the United States had given her his card at Ryker's wedding. They'd recognized the loneliness in each other, although Sebastian had found love with Greer Parker from Keeneston shortly after.

"I need your help."

## 13

---

Tinsley was waiting for her when Edie hung up. She'd kept her distance as if knowing Edie needed her privacy, but it was clear she would not get away without Tinsley extracting every detail from her. How are you feeling? Pissed. How do you feel about Tristan? Went and fell in love with an assassin for a foreign government. She knew it was coming and Edie knew she'd answer because Tinsley was too damn sweet to tell her to F-off.

"How are you feeling?" Tinsley asked as soon as Edie began walking toward her.

"Pissed." Edie didn't stop walking. She wanted to get to the clinic and check on Tristan.

"I know Tristan lied, but—"

"I'm not pissed at him, Tins. I'm pissed at the people trying to kill him."

"Oh thank goodness," Tinsley muttered as they picked up Harper on the walk to the clinic. Or more like Harper ambushed them.

"We need to talk about Tristan," Harper said in her normal, no-BS voice.

"First, we need to talk about Edie," Tinsley said. She might be small and sweet, but Tinsley still had a backbone of steel and even her badass cousin wasn't a match for it.

"I'm good," Edie said, all business.

"That may be," Tinsley began. "But we aren't. We've been horrible friends, Edie, and I'm so sorry."

Edie stopped walking and looked at Tinsley with the same confusion evident on Harper's face. "What do you mean? You're excellent friends."

"If we were, we would have noticed that we were holding you back with our support instead of lifting you up. We were so overprotective and scared of anything hurting you again that we isolated you. We didn't let the men treat you as a grown woman. Instead, we all treated you as if you could break at any moment, and you definitely aren't going to break. You're one of the strongest women I know and I'm sorry I didn't support you as I should have." Tinsley then wrapped her arms around her and Edie felt a weight she hadn't even known she was carrying lift off her shoulders.

"Dammit," Harper cursed. "We did do that. I'm sorry, Edie. I was just going to tell you that after the events of this evening, I like Tristan for you."

"He totally supported her the way we should have. He took her to get drunk and get a tattoo," Tinsley said with a smile.

Harper grinned and Edie knew that look. She was up to something. "I have to go."

"I remember that look. That's not a good look," Edie called out as Harper jogged back to her bar.

"It is and it isn't. I just wonder if we'll be arrested this time." Tinsley said with a smile as they remembered the incident back in high school. "Here we were worried about Tristan, but you're the one with a criminal record."

Edie rolled her eyes. "My record was expunged. And you weren't even arrested. You sweet-talked your way out of it. It was just Harper and me in that jail cell."

"A girl's gotta do what a girl's gotta do." Tinsley didn't look a bit remorseful for hanging them out to dry—or in the previous case, leaving them sitting in jail. "Hey, who were you talking to on the phone a couple of minutes ago?" Tinsley asked, changing the topic as the clinic came into view.

"Someone with more knowledge of international relations than I have." Edie wasn't ready to say yet. Her plan wasn't fully formed. "Excuse me, I need to talk to Ryker."

Tinsley didn't push for more information and Edie was grateful for that. "I'll go check to see how Tristan is doing," Tinsley said before heading into the clinic.

"I wasn't expecting you to be here. Or do you care how Tristan's stitches are going?" Edie asked Ryker. He'd been a big brother to her ever since they were kids. Yes, Gavin was best friends with Walker and very much played the overprotective brother role, but it was Ryker who never pushed her to be anyone other than who she was and who had always been there with understanding when she'd needed it.

"I'm waiting for Kenzie. I grudgingly have an iota of a smidgen of respect for Tristan, so I hope it only hurts a little. Why aren't you already inside?" Ryker asked, cutting right to the heart of the matter.

"I had to make a phone call. I called Sebastian Abel." Ryker didn't say anything but his eyebrow rose with surprise. The two billionaires had become friends of a sort. At least that's what Edie gathered since Sebastian had been at Ryker's wedding and vice versa. "I've made a decision and I need your help."

"Anything you need, I can make happen." Normally that would come off as sounding arrogant, and, well, it still did. However, Ryker could back it up.

"Can we meet tomorrow morning? Just us?" Edie asked.

"The helicopter is picking me up for New York at six. I can meet you at five. Come to the house and we'll have coffee. Anything I should know before we meet?" Ryker asked.

"I want to know all about Millevia's current administration. Strengths, weaknesses, and more importantly what can be done to take the president down. She sent a mercenary to Shadows Landing. She wants to kill the man I have feelings for, and she almost hurt Lydia and the kids."

Ryker's lips turned up into a slow grin that would normally look menacing if it were aimed at her. However, there was just a hint of amusement in it for Edie to know it wasn't directed at her. "So, Jailhouse Edie is back."

"I was never gone." Ryker's eyebrow rose again, but he didn't argue. "I just lost touch with her for a while."

"At least this time you have Granger on your side so you probably won't get arrested."

Edie rolled her eyes. "That was Harper's fault. No one would have caught me if not for Harper."

"Like a thief in the night."

"They were my panties!" Edie stopped herself and smiled at the memory. "You're right. I'm back. I have been gone for a while, but I'm back now, *all* of me. I wasn't able to save Shane, but I sure as hell can save Tristan."

Ryker shook his head, but he was smiling. "I also most feel sorry for Tristan. He fell in love with a sweet, slightly shy woman, and now he's going to find out who you really are." His smile fell, though, as he shoved his hands into his pockets. "Don't do anything dangerous, Edie. We're not teenagers anymore, no sneaking into guys' houses or drag racing in fields. This is serious. Want me to call in some bodyguards?"

"No need. I have my own assassin to look out for me." Edie smiled up at Ryker with gratitude. He'd had his own hard times and was getting back to his former self just like she was. Well, Ryker kind of was. He still had the reputation of a brutal businessman, but he was smiling again. Laughing again. Loving again. He didn't even realize he was giving her hope for her own future with his love for Kenzie. "I better go check on the patient. Thank you, Ryker."

"Edie," Ryker said, putting his hand on her arm, stopping her from climbing the steps into the clinic. "You're the type of friend we'd all go to war for. We're here for whatever you need from us."

Edie gave him a small nod and headed into the clinic. Sadie, the nurse who also filled in for the secretary, was shaking her head as if she couldn't control the situation any longer and was giving up. The waiting room was packed, but that didn't mean Edie couldn't hear Turtle's voice booming above the rest. "Doc can add a good inch to your pecker. Or maybe it was the weight of the giant snapping turtle hanging from it that stretched it out a little."

When Edie made her way through the crowd, she found Tristan sitting on the edge of the exam table with Turtle acting out the time a snapping turtle bit his pecker and latched on tight. "I put a pot over it and banged it, hoping to scare it off," Turtle continued. He was jumping around pretending to bang his pecker. Edie glanced to where Gavin was stitching up Tristan. Everyone was smiling as Turtle went on about his pecker.

Edie stayed where she was and watched. When she

married Shane and moved away, she became part of the military family where the SEALS and then DEVGRU were stationed in Virginia Beach. Her friends here had never gotten to know him. She had Walker there with her but had left everyone else behind. Yet, here they were. They'd welcomed her back into their arms to grieve the loss of a man they'd never met. They loved her, they cared for her, and they supported her. Now, after protecting her from heartbreak, it appeared they were supportive of Tristan. The Faulkners and half of the town were crammed into the clinic to show their support. Would it be like this if she and Tristan stayed in Shadows Landing? Could she ever leave Shadows Landing for Tristan as she did for Shane?

Edie didn't have answers to those questions yet. The only thing she knew was she loved the assassin sitting on the table, not making fun of her friend for his outlandish, yet mostly true, story of a snapping turtle biting his pecker. She loved that Tristan's first action when attacked was to protect Lydia and her children. She loved that even though he gave Turtle his full attention, she knew Tristan knew exactly where she was and when she'd gotten there.

"He's all ready to go home," Gavin announced after putting a large Band-Aid over the sutures.

"I look forward to hearing more about your experiences with snapping turtles. And I'd love to watch you all wrestle an alligator," Tristan said as he stood up and stepped down from the exam table. "Again, I'm truly sorry for bringing trouble to your lovely town."

"Eh, it's better than what I brought to town," Kenzie said with a shrug before handing him a prescription for antibiotics.

"Don't tell my wife," Dare said, glancing around to make sure Harper wasn't there. "But I think she likes the bullets in her door. She says it adds character. It's why she won't take them out."

"What can we do to help?" Tinsley's husband, Paxton, asked. "You have the full resources of the FBI at your disposal."

Edie noticed that Tristan kept quiet. He wasn't pushing her or trying to take over. In fact, he looked hesitant. "Thank you everyone," Edie called out to the crowd. "It's time I take Tristan home and let him rest. We'll talk tomorrow."

A chorus of goodnights was called out as Edie turned to leave the clinic. Tristan walked a couple of feet behind her, thanking everyone as he followed her outside.

"Edie, I understand you're angry with me," Tristan said and Edie shook her head.

"I'm angry all right, but not at you. I was, but then you reminded me of Shane. He would have done the exact same thing as you. I just need to think, Tristan," Edie told him as Wade ran out, promising to grab the car for them. Her mind was spinning. What could she do? Could she really ask others to go to war for her? Because war was exactly what was coming if she went forward with the plan that was starting to come together in her head. Was Tristan worth putting her life on the line for? Edie looked at him and knew instantly the answer was yes. She was going to go to war to give their love a chance. Now, she just wondered if Tristan would let her, or better yet, if he could stop her?

## 14

Edie needed to think and he'd let her after she heard him out. At least she wasn't telling Tristan to get lost, so that had to be promising. "This is the worst timing, but if you're thinking about your future and whether or not I'm in it, then you need all the facts," Tristan said.

"What facts?" Edie asked.

"Here's the car," Darcy called out.

Tristan wanted to groan with frustration as they climbed into the backseat of Wade and Darcy's truck. Wade and Darcy talked the entire way, but Tristan couldn't tell you about what. His only concern was the woman beside him who hadn't looked at him the entire ride. She's only made some noises to indicate answers to the questions Wade and Darcy were asking. Otherwise, she kept her head turned and looked out the window for the short trip.

Wade pulled up and parked on the street between their houses. "Let me make sure your house is safe," Wade said to Edie. Darcy put her arm around Edie and off Wade jogged toward her house.

Tristan pulled his gun, checked the magazine, and walked toward his own house.

"Tris, wait," Edie called out. "You can't go in there alone."

"I'll be fine. I promise." Tristan liked that Edie cared enough to worry about him, but it wasn't necessary. She didn't appear to be worried for Wade and he wasn't nearly as deadly as Tristan was. Tristan jogged around to the back of the house. There was a large tree that provided the perfect entry to the master bedroom on the second floor. He scaled the tree, climbed out a limb, and dropped onto the top floor deck. Then he used his key to unlock the sliding glass door. He wanted the higher ground if someone was waiting for him downstairs.

Silently, Tristan stepped inside. He listened but didn't hear anything. Then he slowly cleared room after room. By the time he was done, he was sure the house was empty and secure. He glanced out the front window and saw Edie watching his house along with Wade and Darcy. He unlocked the front door and stepped outside. "It's all clear. Thank you for the ride."

"We're just right down there if you need us," Wade called out. It had been an offer for help, but it was also a dismissal.

"Thank you." Tristan closed the door and watched through the window as Wade and Darcy walked Edie home. Edie kept glancing back at his house, but she didn't come back to him. She walked into her front door and closed it.

Tristan frowned, but he knew this needed to be on Edie's time. His phone vibrated in his pocket five minutes later and he hoped David had found a way to contact him. Instead, it was Edie.

*Come to the back door. We need to talk.*

Tristan didn't hesitate. He strode out his back door, locked the house, and jogged over to Edie's patio. She sat waiting for him in the darkness. Tristan saw the bottle of bourbon sitting on the table and two glasses. One was to her lips as she took a sip. "My brother got me hooked. It's made in Keeneston. Want some?" Edie asked.

"Sure," Tristan said, taking a seat across the coffee table from her. Edie pushed the glass across the table and Tristan picked it up and took a sip. The amber liquid had a bit of a kick, but the burn quickly faded and caramel was left dancing along his tongue.

"You said I needed to know the facts. What are they?" Edie asked, getting right to the point.

Tristan took another sip and set the glass on his knee. He turned the crystal tumbler absently as he looked through the darkness at Edie. The lights from inside made the patio glow just enough to see, but the darkness afforded them a bit of cover that he knew made Edie feel freer.

"There are several facts," Tristan said before taking a deep breath. "I don't mean to scare you, but I am an assassin. I grew up learning how to kill people quickly and efficiently. It's what I'm good at. You have to know that's who I am. However, you also have to know I'm not an evil person. I don't kill for fun. I kill to protect. I can't tell you the number of terrorists, traffickers, and other assassins I've killed to protect my president, my country, and my people. I take that job very seriously. If I don't do it, who will?"

Edie didn't say anything so Tristan pushed forward. It would have been easy to try to manipulate her into believing he was a saint, but he wasn't. He was a killer. If they had a shot at a future together, she needed to know that and accept that.

"Next, I will move heaven and earth to protect you. I also

will understand if you tell me to leave Shadows Landing. The ball is entirely in your court. I will do whatever you want me to," Tristan continued to reassure her. He saw her stop drinking and stare down into the glass she was holding as if it had the answers. "The reason I will do that is because I am falling in love with you." Tristan had never been so nervous. Give him a shootout any day instead of laying his feelings bare. "Because of that, what's most important is for you to be safe and happy. There now, you have all the facts." Tristan leaned forward and put his tumbler back on the table before standing up. "I await your decision of whether you want me to stay or leave Shadows Landing. Whatever your decision is, I won't be angry. I only want what's best for you, Edie."

Tristan had his hand on the screen door when Edie stopped him. "I already have my answer, Tristan."

Tristan turned to look at her in the shadows but didn't press her. This was her call.

"I want you to stay because I'm falling in love with you, too," Edie said softly but clearly.

It took three large steps for Tristan to get to her. He stopped in front of her and then sat on the table so that his legs bracketed hers. He reached out and took the glass from her and set it on the table next to him before taking her hands in his. "Edie, I don't deserve it, but with your love I can do anything knowing you're with me. I swear, I'll protect you and make you happy."

"I swear the same, Tristan."

Tristan was going to ask her what she meant but Edie leaned forward and kissed him. It wasn't the slow tentative kiss from Millevia. It was confident and demanding.

"My room is upstairs," Edie whispered between kisses.

Tristan had been dreaming of this moment since he'd

left her bed in Millevia. Finally, they could be together again, this time with no secrets between them. However, knowing Jean was going to be after them added urgency to their kiss. It was as if they both knew the clock was ticking and they didn't have a moment to waste.

The first time he'd let Edie take the lead. He had wanted her to feel in control and comfortable, but this time he didn't want to hold back. He wanted Edie now, tonight, tomorrow, and forever.

Tristan slid his arms around her and, in seconds, was standing with her in his arms. "I love you, Edie. So damn much I can't stop touching you or thinking about you."

"I love you too, Tristan. Don't stop. Don't ever stop."

Tristan walked inside, closed and locked the door, and then turned with Edie still in his arms. She was kissing his neck and when she bit his earlobe just enough to sting before sucking it into her mouth and running her tongue over it, Tristan stopped trying to hold back. He took the stairs two at a time. "Which room?"

"End of the hall in the back," Edie said before kissing her way along his jaw.

Thankfully, the door was open and Tristan didn't stop until he had her lying on the bed and was covering her body with his. Their hips were already moving, trying to reach each other through the clothes that were only frustrating them.

Tristan straddled Edie's hips as he yanked his shirt off while she worked on the button of his jeans. Reluctantly, Tristan got up to push his pants off as Edie shimmied out of her clothes.

"You're so beautiful," Tristan said reverently as he crawled back onto the bed. "I didn't know I could ever be so lucky."

"Let me show you how lucky you can be."

Edie hooked her legs over his, ran her fingers down his back, and arched up into him. Lucky couldn't even begin to describe how Tristan felt as they loved each other, absolutely, honestly, and thoroughly.

## 15

---

Edie slid from the bed before the sun was even thinking of crossing the horizon. She tiptoed into the bathroom, got dressed, and wrote a quick note to Tristan before leaving the note on her pillow.

Edie lingered as she looked down at Tristan sprawled naked in her bed. It was strange for it not to be Shane, but it wasn't wrong either. It felt right. That feeling only solidified her purpose for sneaking out early that morning.

It took Edie eight minutes to get to her car, roll it out of the driveway in neutral so she wouldn't wake Tristan, and drive across town to Ryker's house. Most of the house was dark, but several lights on the first floor were on.

When Ryker had buzzed her through the gate at the end of his drive, he'd told her to come into the kitchen. The smell of fresh coffee led the way as she climbed up the back steps and entered the giant house that sat on the river.

"You look way too put together for five in the morning," Edie grumbled as she took the coffee Ryker offered her.

"I haven't been to bed yet. Kenzie got home at three this morning and made herself dinner before she went to bed not thirty minutes ago. I'll sleep tonight on the plane. What's going on?" Ryker asked while looking completely awake and powerful in his fitted navy suit and solid deep royal blue tie.

"I want to help Tristan," Edie said after taking a fortifying drink of coffee.

Ryker leaned against the stone countertop and crossed his arms over his chest. "Ask him what he needs then."

"What I need he can't give me, but you can."

"I'm a married man now, Edie."

Edie rolled her eyes and gave a little laugh. Ryker could deliver lines like that without blinking. He'd found his sense of humor again along with his heart when he met Kenzie.

"I want to take Pastor down. Now, a widow from Shadows Landing who works in a museum can't do that. But you and Sebastian can."

Ryker looked hard at her for a moment. "What do you want me to do?"

"Cut off all business with Millevia. Block their port, stop any influx of money, and use your international clout to put pressure on Pastor until they have fair elections." Edie held her breath and waited to see what Ryker would do. That was a lot to ask. It would cost him untold millions in revenue and put his reputation on the line.

"When you finally ask for a favor, you don't hold back, do you? You said you've talked to Sebastian. What did you ask of him?" Ryker asked.

"Information on Pastor. He's calling me back today. I didn't think I could ask him to put any skin in the game since I don't know him as well."

"You need to call your brother and you need to talk to Abby and Dylan," Ryker told her.

"No, I don't. Walker is the only one who could help, but

he's retired with a baby. I lost my husband on a mission. I'm not going to lose my brother too. Abby and Dylan? They can't do anything about this."

Ryker blinked at her and shook her head. "Don't you know who Abby and Dylan are?"

"Of course I do, but I don't see how they can help Tristan. Dylan is my brother's cousin-in-law and Abby works on her father's horse farm. I guess Abby could talk to Ariana and I can see if Rahmi can help, too. They are probably pissed off about Pastor wanting to torture Abby to force Ariana to make that contract happen."

"Edie," Ryker said carefully, as if she were an idiot. "Abby and Dylan are black ops. It's secret here, but the entire family and town of Keeneston know about it so I feel as if it's okay to tell you since you're practically family. They'd be a big asset here."

"Dylan isn't in the military anymore and Abby certainly isn't." Edie paused, remembering the bathroom incident. "She just knows how to disarm assassins because of who her dad is, right?"

Ryker slowly shook his head. "They're better trained and better-funded versions of Tristan."

"I take that as an insult, but it all makes much more sense now."

Edie screamed in surprise at the voice behind her. At the same time a coffee cup Ryker pitched as if it was a major league fastball flew past her head and smashed into the wall next to where Tristan was standing.

"How did you get in here?" Ryker demanded.

"Has no one listened to me? I'm a really good *asset*. It's literally my job to sneak up on people," Tristan said, leaning against the doorframe. There was coffee dripping down the wall next to his head, but he hadn't so much as flinched even when the coffee cup shattered. "As such, I'd really appreciate being looped into a conversation that appears to be about me."

Ryker was muttering something about a dude and typing furiously on his cell phone, leaving Edie to explain what she was doing here to Tristan. "You're just going to tell me no."

Tristan cocked his head, raised an eyebrow, and waited. The silence made Edie nervous as she tried to think of how to explain what she was up to.

"I'm trying to help you prove Pastor killed the former president and demand free elections for Millevia," Edie said quickly as she gave a nonchalant shrug, trying to play it off as if this wasn't a big deal.

Tristan's eyes moved to Ryker and then back to hers as he asked Ryker a question. "How exactly are you planning on doing that?"

"I've just ordered all my ships to evacuate the Port of Millevia and form a casual sort of blockade in international waters to make it difficult for any other vessel to get into or out of the port. Official report is some bug in the computer systems shutting the ships' navigation down. I also just transferred all my money out of Millevia's banks and halted all business dealings with anyone in the country, including the government," Ryker answered. "And I'm having my home security upgraded."

"You did all of that in the five minutes Edie has been here?" Tristan asked with disbelief.

"You should see what I can do in ten minutes."

"Bragging again, babe?" Edie saw Kenzie stumble into the kitchen rubbing her eyes and wearing a robe that was inside out over her pajamas. "What is going on down here?"

"Apparently my girlfriend and your husband are

personally overthrowing the Millevian government from the kitchen," Tristan said dryly.

"Is it Tuesday already?" Kenzie asked. "That's usually the day he reserves for political coups."

"Everything is okay, angel. Go back to bed." Ryker walked over to his sleepy wife and kissed her goodnight. She muttered something that sounded like "I love you" and shuffled back upstairs. Ryker turned back to Edie. "Let me know what Sebastian says. In the meantime, I printed up a report for you on what I could gather on Millevia and Pastor since we talked last night."

Ryker handed her a thick folder as the back door opened and Olivia strode in wearing a fitted light-blue pencil skirt suit and four-inch silver heels. Her hair was perfect, her makeup flawless, and she had a sickeningly wide-awake look to her.

"So, I see political coup is on the calendar for today. It's not Tuesday already, is it?"

Edie had to press her lips together not to burst out laughing. The look on Tristan's face was priceless. He thought they were nuts.

"Wait. Are you all serious? You really think you can help me do this?" Tristan asked. Edie saw the hope come alive in his eyes only to be reined in.

"Sure we can. Especially with help from friends and family in Keeneston," Ryker told him as Edie walked over to Tristan to offer her silent support. "Olivia and I need to get going. She's going to have a busy day with a lot of pissed-off Millevians calling. Keep us in the loop. We'll be back tonight."

"Thank you, Ryker," Edie said with all sincerity.

"I've been where you are. I'll do anything I can to help." The sound of a helicopter drew everyone outside.

Edie stood with Tristan and watched Ryker and Olivia fly away. The file in her hand was heavy. She'd have a lot of research to do today. Not counting some phone calls to make.

Tristan was in a state of mild shock as he watched the helicopter fly off. Ryker Faulkner had just declared economic war on Millevia for him. For a man he didn't even know. For a man he'd outed as an assassin just the prior night.

"Edie," Tristan said once the helicopter was out of sight. "What the hell is going on? I wake up to you closing the front door and chase after you only to find you plotting an overthrow of Millevia's government. Something I've been looking into doing for the past year with no luck. How on earth do you expect to do it when you're not even from there?"

"With a little help from some friends," Edie said, holding up the thick file. "I figured if Pastor was after Abby because of Rahmi's stalling of their trade deal, money is her weakness. Come on, I need to call my brother. I can't believe Abby and Dylan are black ops. Although," Edie said as she paused as if remembering something, "smashing that man's head into a sink without blinking should have tipped me off."

"Our intelligence was seriously off. Pastor was sending me to my death when she assigned me to my mission," Tristan said, thinking of his assignment to kidnap Abby.

"I didn't get the impression anyone knew about this. I'm guessing they really did think she just worked on a horse farm."

"Look, Edie. I don't know how I feel about you calling in

all this help," Tristan said as they walked to her car. "I don't want to put anyone in danger and now Ryker will be in their sights. What if they come after his wife?"

"They're already coming to Shadows Landing, right? Your teammate, Jean, he knows you're here." Edie paused and took a deep breath. "Tristan, I couldn't stop what happened to Shane. I love you, Tristan. I can't lose you now. I want to help. I need to help. I think you'll find that our pirate past has made the women of Shadows Landing a force to be reckoned with."

When Tristan had considered the idea of a wife before, he never imagined her as someone who was docile, but he certainly had never pictured a wife who would understand him and understand what he wanted the way Edie did. She understood love, loyalty, and was fiercely protective. He couldn't put into words the emotions he was feeling. Instead of trying, he reached out and pulled Edie into a kiss. He loved her so freaking much right at that moment and he had to show her how much.

The ringing of her phone interrupted their kiss. Edie pulled it from her back pocket and frowned. "That's strange." She answered it and put it on speaker. "Walker? I was just going to call you. Did Ryker tell you to call me?"

"Ryker? Dammit, Edie. You went to freaking Sebastian first and then Ryker and were only now going to call me?" Tristan hadn't talked to Walker personally before. He'd overheard him while Tris was surveilling Walker in Millevia and then at the bar, but Tristan didn't need to have ever talked to him to know the man was seriously pissed off.

"Walker," Edie said in a voice Tristan was beginning to learn was the one she used to calm someone down.

"Don't *Walker* me, Edie. I didn't interfere when Gavin called me about you dating a freaking assassin. Sure, I listened and threatened to kill him, but Layne swore he was good for you. But now I have to find out from *Greer* that you turned to Sebastian for help before me? I'm your brother, Edie. It's my honor and duty to protect you. But you turned to Sebastian and Ryker instead of me. And where are you? I know you're not home and you're not at Tristan's."

Tristan winced at the phone and the reprimand in Walker's voice. He pitied any boy little Carolina brought home someday when her father had a tone like that. He also wondered who the hell Sebastian was.

"How do you know I'm not home right now? Are you tracking my phone?" Edie asked with a trace of anger in her voice.

"No, we're sitting in your living room."

Tristan's eyes shot up to Edie's. She looked nervous and then mad. "We? Who is with you, Walker?"

"Everyone. Now get home. We need to talk, and bring Assassin Boy with you."

# 16

Tristan saw several black SUVs parked along the street as Edie pulled into her driveway. The lights in her house were all on, and he could see several people staring out the living room window, waiting for them. The front door was thrown open and Walker stormed out. Tristan sighed. This wasn't going to go well.

"Walker," Edie warned as she scrambled out of her car as fast as she could.

It didn't do any good. Walker brushed right by her as Tristan stood his ground. He saw murder in Walker's eyes and couldn't really blame him. Edie had already endured so much pain in her life and now she was smack dab in the middle of international espionage and a country she had no involvement with before meeting him.

"You asshole," Walker ground out between his clenched jaw a second before the punch sent Tristan staggering back.

"Walker!" Edie yelled in a gasp.

"Feel better?" Layne asked her husband dryly from the front porch.

"Not yet," Walker snarled as he pulled his hand back to punch Tristan again. "Why aren't you fighting back?"

"Because I'd do the same thing in your situation. I hate the idea of Edie in danger, and she's in danger because of me. Go ahead. I deserve it." Tristan waited for the next blow to come.

"Dammit!" Walker growled. "I can't hit a man who won't hit me back after being provoked. I thought you were some deadly assassin?"

"I am. But I'm not without honor," Tristan said bluntly.

"You're an assassin. I wouldn't talk about honor," Walker shot back.

"Exactly how is it different from what you did in DEVGRU or what Dylan and Abby do now?" Tristan asked. He loved Edie, but he needed Walker to know that he might let him land a punch, but Tristan would not be disrespected.

"He has you there, hon," Layne called out. "Come on, Walker, you can torture Tristan in a little bit. Now we have some planning to do."

Walker growled again and spun around to storm back into Edie's house. "Did you lock my door after you searched my house?" Tristan called out before following Walker.

"It's Shadows Landing. No one is going to steal anything. If you're worried about assassins, a locked door won't stop them," Edie said as she held out her hand.

"Good point." Tristan took her hand and together they walked toward her house. Tristan tried to prepare himself for whatever awaited him inside. At least he had Edie by his side.

"Sorry about my brother. He's pretty overprotective of me since Shane's death."

"I'd only be mad at him if he weren't." Tristan kissed her

temple before heading up the stairs to face his execution squad.

"Hello, Tristan. Good to see you again," Abby said with a smile even as her husband glowered at him. Walker joined Dylan, and together they crossed their arms and scowled. "This is my husband, Dylan."

Tristan gave a quick nod as a greeting. Dylan didn't say anything. He only sent a bone-chilling stare as if he were reaching inside Tristan and smothering his soul.

"You already know Layne," Abby continued on. "But you don't know our friends Sebastian and Greer Abel."

Tristan turned and then blinked in surprise at the man sitting in the leather chair. He was tall and brooding, even from a seated position. His eyes were like steel as they bored into him. Walker's punch had nothing on this surprise. "The Sebastian you asked for help is Sebastian Abel, the billionaire?" he asked Edie in amazement, who just nodded.

Sebastian slowly rose to his full height. He didn't look like any of the billionaires in Europe, that was for sure. He looked more like a soldier than a businessman. "Sebastian Abel, the friend of Edie's. You hurt her, you die. Got it?"

"I think between several men named after animals, her friends, her brother, and seven children who would tear me to pieces. You'll have to get in line to kill me. Billionaire or not." Tristan wasn't sure, but he thought Sebastian's lip might have twitched with amusement.

"I'm Greer. It's such a pleasure to meet you. Abby and my cousin Layne have told me so much about you." Tristan shook her hand and relaxed a little. Greer looked like a sweet, girl-next-door with her big smile and bouncy, honey-brown hair. "However, I can take you out from a thousand meters away. If you hurt Edie, you don't have to worry about my husband. You'll have to worry about me. I also have two older brothers so I'm not above knocking some kids out of the way to get to you first. Got it?" she asked perkily, but the hard glint in her eyes told Tristan she wasn't messing around.

"Only one thousand meters?" Tristan asked with a smirk. Greer's smile didn't fade. Instead, it grew.

"As if you could make that," Greer said with a cute laugh.

Tristan rolled his eyes. "Why does everyone ignore the fact that I'm a very good assassin?"

Greer's smile slipped and her brow creased as she thought of something. "Wait, are you the guy who took out the gun runner from Africa in Millevia two years ago?"

"I'm impressed. Millevia is such a small country. I'm surprised you know my work." Tristan had a moment of pride. These were people whose respect wouldn't be won easily and if they were important to Edie, he wanted them to accept him.

"The sniper boards were worse than a middle school girls' chat group over that shot. Everyone wanted to know who made it. Well, now I'll feel slightly bad if I have to kill you," Greer said with her full smile back on her face.

"No! Don't you go liking him, Greer," Walker said, shaking his head at her. Greer just shrugged in response.

"What exactly do you do, Greer?" Tristan asked.

"I used to be with FBI Hostage Rescue," Greer said with her signature sweet smile. She avoided the answer, which led him to understand that she worked for the government. Probably in the same capacity as Abby and Dylan.

"Well, now that you've all threatened me, should we get to the reason you're here?" Tristan asked.

"Wait," Abby said, looking down at her phone. "The last person just arrived."

"Who?" Edie asked as there was a knock on the front door.

Tristan watched Layne open the front door to find a man in a perfectly tailored suit that spoke of power. He reminded Tristan of Olivia in a way. He was completely confident in who he was as he leaned forward and kissed Layne's cheek.

"Always making an entrance, huh, Zain?" Dylan teased.

Tristan didn't need an introduction to know who this was. He bowed his head as Zain Ali Rahman walked into the room. "Your Highness." What the *hell* was a prince of Rahmi doing here?

"Assassin," Zain said dismissively as if Tristan's name wasn't worth knowing.

"We think we might like him," Abby said with a wink to Tristan.

"I'll reserve judgment." Zain walked in and kissed Edie's cheek. "It's good to see you again. Mila was very upset I didn't bring her with me to see you, but I was on my way home from London when Abby called and didn't have time to go to Keeneston to pick her up."

"Oh Zain," Edie said, upset. "I don't want you to miss spending time with your family. You don't have to be here," she said with genuine honesty.

"I think I do. It appears Rahmi is somehow involved in all this. I'm here representing the king on this matter."

Tristan was sure he'd wandered into an alternate universe this morning. Billionaires, royalty, and black ops all here in Shadows Landing to help Edie.

Sebastian leaned forward to place his hand on a folder sitting on the coffee table. He slowly pushed it toward Tristan. "As for why we're all here, Edie called me last night to ask a favor. She wanted information on Annette Pastor and Millevia's government. Here's everything I have."

"Thank you, Sebastian. But you didn't need to fly out to give me this," Edie said, picking up the folder that seemed just as thick as Ryker's.

"I was intrigued by your request," Sebastian said, leaning back in the chair. "I was friends with President Gastaud. Because of him, I invested in Millevia. Since his death, things have gone to hell. I have to bribe and threaten to get anything done. In the course of three months, Millevia went from a prosperous democratic country to an economically declining dictatorship. I have two hundred million dollars wrapped up in projects there, so my motives aren't entirely altruistic."

"I never knew your motives were ever altruistic," Zain said with a slight challenge.

Sebastian smirked. "See, we are starting to get to know each other."

Tristan wanted to alternatively sigh with relief and cheer with gratitude at Sebastian's analysis of Millevia. "That's exactly what's going on. Further, I think Pastor killed Gastaud."

Sebastian's jaw tightened briefly and he gave a slight nod. "I figured it wasn't an accident. I rode with Gastaud on his property several times, and he would never take a jump. He knew the risks, and riding his property at a gallop gave him the sense of freedom without the risk."

Zain looked thoughtful but then he turned his full attention to Tristan. "Now, tell me exactly how you met Edie."

Tristan grimaced as he looked at Abby. She seemed highly amused and not the least bit offended as he told of his mission. He thought Zain would be angry by the way he was pursing his lips, but then he burst out laughing. In fact, he was laughing so hard Tristan thought he saw tears.

"That's priceless. You, kidnapping and torturing Abby? Oh my gosh. I heard this story secondhand before, but I thought they were joking. It's even funnier hearing it from you."

"I did look into you further after I found out who you were," Abby said with a smile. "You're good. I might have had to actually try a little if you came after me. We'll spar after the baby comes. For fun, of course."

There would be nothing fun about it. She'd be sparring to make a point and he'd be sparring to make his own. However, that actually did sound fun. "I'd like that," Tristan said before turning back to the group. "So, what do you all think?"

Walker stepped forward until he was almost toe-to-toe with Tristan. "Do you love my sister?"

"Walker," Edie said again with admonishment and a bit of annoyance at constantly scolding a brother who was ignoring her.

Walker didn't look away from Tristan. "I do," Tristan answered honestly.

"Will you die to protect her?" Walker asked.

"Without hesitation," Tristan answered immediately.

Walker turned to look at his sister. "Do you love Assassin Boy?"

Edie rolled her eyes at her brother. "I do. I'm sorry. I know Shane was your best friend and—"

Walker cut her off by enveloping his sister in a hug. "Don't you dare apologize, Edie. If you love Assassin Boy, that's all that matters. I'm happy if you are, Sis."

Walker pulled back from hugging Edie, and Tristan saw tears in Edie's eyes. He gave a slight dip of his chin to Walker to silently convey his appreciation. Walker didn't hug him back or even smile. He might have snarled. "Now, tell me what you need to keep my sister safe?"

"Evidence to oust Pastor from power," Tristan answered promptly. "But I don't know how we're going to get that. I've been trying to find it for the past year, *very* discreetly."

"Who needs evidence? Why don't we just overthrow her?" Greer asked as she looked at her phone. "I can do next Wednesday."

Dylan looked up from his phone with a nod. "Wednesday works for me."

Edie laughed as if they were joking, but when they looked up from their calendars, they weren't laughing with her. Instead, Tristan believed they were completely serious.

"Is that too late? I can move some stuff around and do it Sunday," Greer asked.

Tristan leaned close to Edie's ear. "I know they'll probably kill me, but I really like your friends."

"Sweetheart," Sebastian drawled slowly to get Greer's attention. "As much as it turns me on when you overthrow a country, I think this time it might be good to make this an international united front. If that doesn't work, then you can make it look like an accident. A riding accident would have a certain flair of irony to it."

"What do you have in mind?" Tristan asked, seeing that Sebastian already had an idea.

"I've gotten reports that Ryker has pulled all his money from the banks and halted all projects. I'm going to do the same while placing the blame solely on Pastor and her government. I won't do it publicly, but I'll whisper it in all the right ears. By the end of the week, Millevia's tourism and financial industries will completely collapse," Sebastian said as if he weren't thinking twice about destroying a country.

"My people," Tristan began to say in alarm. "I want Pastor out, but I want the citizens protected. This will send the country into a deep depression."

"I know," Sebastian said as if he hadn't worried about that at all. "The idea is for a short period of pain and then prosperity. Once Pastor is out and democracy restored, the economy will come roaring back."

Tristan was torn, but then Zain cleared his throat. "Rahmi will pledge support to the people of Millevia. We won't let them suffer for Pastor's actions. Now, I need to know what evidence you have besides your word that Pastor wanted Abby in order to hurt my sister."

Tristan grinned as he looked around the room. "You didn't find it when you searched my house? Someone wasn't thorough. I'll be right back."

Edie stood silently as the front door closed behind Tristan. Zain and Sebastian were talking quietly. Greer, Abby, and Layne were grinning at her while Dylan and Walker were frowning.

Edie felt as if she'd run an emotional marathon in the past hour. When her brother had hugged her and freed her from the fear that he'd be mad at her for moving on, it had released the floodgates of emotions she'd kept bottled up.

"Oh, Edie," Layne said as she grabbed Edie's hand. "He's perfect for you."

"I must admit, I didn't see an assassin in your future. I thought school teacher or something," Greer told her. "But Tristan is so much better for you."

"You're alive again," Layne said simply. "Ever since you met him, you've changed. He's helped you find yourself and I have to support that. Plus, he's totally hot."

"I like his dry sense of humor. I agree. I love him for you," Abby added. "Now, we'll just handle this little coup and you can live happily ever after."

Edie shook her head. "I feel so stupid. I had no idea

what you did. Greer, I thought you were a policy advisor to the president. Abby, I thought you worked on the farm. I thought Dylan was just a retired soldier."

"Don't feel stupid. Keeneston only knows because we had to have a home base and, well, you've met the people from Keeneston. They would figure it out anyway so the president gave us permission to fill them in," Abby explained to her.

"Speaking of the president," Greer said as she pulled out her phone. "As soon as I see the evidence Tristan has, I need to call him. For all that I do, I am still one of his advisors. This is about to become a political pissing match and the U.S. will stand with its allies."

Edie took a deep breath to rein in the wild emotions she was experiencing. "You don't have to do this. You all are putting too much on the line for me. All that money, all the politics of this. It's too much."

"Edie," Layne said, grabbing her hand and forcing Edie to look up. "You might live in Shadows Landing, but you are very much a part of Keeneston too. You're family and we will always help family."

"But Sebastian," Edie began to say. Sebastian seemed to hear his name as he looked up from where he was talking to Zain and pinned her with his gaze.

"What about me?"

"You're doing too much. I can't ask you to put all that money at risk to help Tristan and me. You don't even know me well and you certainly don't know him."

"You have a silent strength I saw the night we met. I respect that. Plus, my wife thinks the world of you. That's enough in my book. As I said, I'm getting something out of this too."

Edie shook her head at him even as her heart swelled

with gratitude. "You try to pretend you're not, but you're a good man, Sebastian."

Sebastian winked at her. "That's our little secret."

The door opened and Tristan walked in with a folder and a laptop. He looked around and Edie saw that he appeared comfortable with her friends and family. He wasn't nervous, but instead he was confident in who he was. It was that quiet confidence that seemed to be rubbing off on her.

She noticed the first thing Tristan did was find her in the room. He gave her a look that asked if she was okay. She gave him a smile in return and only then did he talk to Zain.

"Here's the evidence on my mission. Further, I've been trying to collect evidence for the past year. Everything I have is on a Swiss cloud storage site," Tristan announced.

"I'll take the computer. Log me in," Sebastian said as Tristan handed the folder to Zain.

Abby came to sit on the couch next to Zain as Dylan stood behind them. Together they read the file. Edie saw both of their faces harden. Zain's jaw clenched and Dylan looked as if he were going to rip the couch in two. Edie knew whatever they were reading, it wasn't good.

"I'll kill her myself," Dylan muttered. "No one tortures my wife."

"Or hurts my sister," Zain added in a voice that would have sent someone to the gallows centuries ago.

Edie shivered. She'd only known them to be kind and loving but right now, the two men were deadly. However, Abby wasn't so affected. Instead, she'd calmly taken the file and was flipping through it.

"Strange," she muttered.

"Right?" Tristan said as if knowing exactly what she was talking about.

"What's strange, babe?" Dylan asked.

"They never mentioned my maiden name. A toddler could put together a better background search. Not only that, but a lot of this is just wrong. Look at the backgrounds on Dylan, Edie, Walker, and Layne. They're mostly wrong. There's no post-Millevia itinerary beyond the wrong information about a trip to Italy. And look at who's the contact he's supposed to send pieces of me to."

Zain looked at where Abby was pointing. Edie saw Tristan move over to look too. "Is that not who is in charge of Princess Ariana or maybe the foreign relations?"

"No," Zain answered with a frown. "That address is in Rahmi, but it isn't a government address. Hold on." Zain entered the address into his phone. "It's a rental house near the palace."

"Rental?" Tristan was already engrossed in looking at the map on Zain's phone when Sebastian asked for the address.

Edie moved forward with Layne to sit and wait for answers. She saw the way they were all working together and didn't want to distract them.

Sebastian's fingers flew over the keyboard of his own laptop. He was laser-focused as he worked. "Okay, I got it. It's one of those vacation rentals and the company doesn't have good security on their data. I got into their files. It was rented to a company registered out of Italy. Let me look into that."

"You forget he got his start by being a computer genius," Layne whispered to Edie, who just nodded. It was mesmerizing watching Sebastian work.

"Here it is. I had to dig a bit as whoever set this up tried to hide their name behind shell companies. But three companies later across three countries and a hack of a law firm, I have a name. Tommaso Pastor," Sebastian said, looking up at Tristan.

"Who is that?" Edie asked.

"President Pastor's husband," Tristan answered.

Edie's brow furrowed as she took in the statement. "But why would he be receiving the pieces of Abby, which, of course, you never sent?"

"I don't know," Tristan said slowly as if he were thinking of something else. "But I think we should find out."

Tristan was furious. Pastor was up to no good and now he had the evidence. However, he couldn't see any motive to make sense of it all. What exactly was her husband up to and why?

"How are you going to find out?" Edie asked him.

"I'm going to call in and claim to have hunted Abby down. Then I am telling them I'm sending in a piece of her to the contact Pastor gave me," Tristan explained as an idea formed in his mind.

"Not a bad idea," Abby said. "But I'm not giving you my finger."

"Send a fake one with a recording device in it. That way it can be used as evidence," Dylan suggested.

"That may prove whatever is going on is linked to President Pastor, but it doesn't prove motive. If we're going to take her down, we need motive," Zain said to the group.

Damn, he was right. It all kept coming back to motive.

"I need to get in contact with my friend. He's working on the team hunting me down. Maybe he's heard something," Tristan said.

"I can make that happen. I have some untraceable

software. We can spoof his own mother's number if you want," Sebastian told him.

"We don't have parents. We grew up in the orphanage together. But I know a number we can use that will get his attention but not raise any red flags." Tristan felt hope starting to build. No longer was he hiding and waiting. He was hiding and fighting now. With this unlikely team, he was going to free his country.

Tristan was giving the number to Sebastian when the front door was kicked in. Tristan would have laughed had his heart not stopped beating for a brief second as he calculated how to get between the intruder and Edie.

"Hello, Sheriff. What brings you over this morning?" Tristan asked, lowering his weapon as Granger took in the room with his own gun raised and at the ready.

"I was driving into work and saw all the black SUVs. I thought President Pastor had found you," Granger said, lowering his weapon. "Should have known it was the Keeneston contingent."

Tristan watched as Granger shook hands with the men and nodded at the women. Tristan had been observing the lawman since they'd met and concluded they were very much alike. They were damaged from their pasts. Tristan didn't know the damage Granger sustained, but it was there in his eyes. The tired weariness of the past and also in how he held himself apart. Yes, he was part of Shadows Landing. Yes, he had friends—very good ones. But Granger was always a little apart, just like Tristan.

"I take it something happened since you're all here. Or are you here to kill Tristan? It's alligator mating season. You could get rid of the body easily. Mean Abe would eat him up in a heartbeat." Granger gave Tristan a look that didn't give anything away.

Tristan smiled. They all cared about Edie and that made them good friends. "You know, my life has been threatened more in this small town than my entire time as an assassin."

Granger hooked his thumbs in his jeans' pockets and rocked back on the heels of his cowboy boots. "And here I thought we were going easy on you."

Walker chuckled and Layne shook her head. "No wonder you adapted to Keeneston so easily," Layne said with a roll of her eyes at her husband.

"So, what's going on?" Granger asked again.

Tristan headed over to Edie as Walker filled him in. He felt the need to be near her. She'd been quiet through this meeting as she let him work with her friends, but he knew she had ideas too.

"What are you thinking about?" Tristan asked her, putting his hand on her back and pulling her against his side.

"How did you know I'm thinking of something?" Edie looked up at him and he hated to tell her that it was written all over her face.

"I've gotten to know your facial features. I can tell when you're mad, annoyed, tired, excited, thinking, and when you're seconds away from climax." Tristan dropped his voice for the last little bit and enjoyed the blush that rose on her cheeks.

"Well, for your information, I *was* thinking of something." Edie paused and her lips turned down into a grimace. "How do you know your friend is trustworthy? I think it's a risk to call him."

"How do you know your brother is trustworthy?" Tristan asked back. "Because David is my brother in all ways except blood. I trust him with my life."

Edie nodded and then a little hint of mischievousness

sparked in her eyes. "I'm glad you have David in your life then. Now, I have another idea about the finger. We need to talk to Gavin and Kenzie. I think we should send a real finger, but bug the box it's sent in."

"That's not what I was expecting and a little gross, but I like it. Why?" Tristan asked as Walker finished up talking to Granger.

"If it were a fake finger, they'd know the jig was up right away. If they see it's real and think it's Abby's, we'll see what their end game is. I'd even text Pastor or whoever your handler is a picture of Abby tied up as proof you have her."

Tristan bent down and kissed her. "That's genius!"

"What is?" Sebastian asked, looking up from his computer.

"We have a new plan."

"I'm not giving you a toe either," Abby said instantly, and Tristan laughed.

"I don't need a toe, but I do need something from you."

## 18

So, this was what it was like being on a mission. Edie's living room was overflowing with people and it wasn't even eight in the morning yet. Papers were spread out on nearly every flat surface. Zain and Sebastian were strategizing. Gavin and Kenzie were debating the best place to get a finger. Tristan was working with Granger, Walker, Greer, and Dylan. And Tinsley was painting the staging area for Abby's ransom photo shoot.

A knock sounded at the front door and Tristan leaped up to answer it. "Relax. I don't think assassins knock, do they?" Edie asked as she stepped toward the door.

"Not usually, but I'll have to try it, seeing how readily you went toward your death," Tristan said as he strode past her.

Edie crossed her arms and rolled her eyes as Tristan checked who was out front before opening the door. "Hello, dears. We saw the cars and figured you needed some food. We brought breakfast casseroles."

"Oh, yeah," Edie said to Tristan as two large oven-proof

dishes were shoved in his hands. "Death by casserole. Thank goodness you saved me."

Miss Ruby and Miss Winnie looked at her strangely before giving Tristan directions on how to serve them. Then, they surveyed the rest of the room with interest.

"Winnie, do you know what I'm thinking?" Miss Ruby asked. The two old women were polar opposites in looks. Miss Ruby was the perfectly plump grandmother with her round face … and well, round everything else. Her naturally black hair had sprinkles of white in it while her reddish-brown skin was a bit wrinkled now but that only added to her charm. Winnie, on the other hand, was as scrawny as a soup chicken and as pale as a plucked one. However, both were treasures to the people of Shadows Landing. Both because of their sweetness and sass, but also because they made the best apple pie in South Carolina. Their pies made people's clothes fall off—literally.

"I'm thinking our next sign will win us the state fair blue ribbon," Miss Winnie replied. "We've never done a group shot before."

"Edie, dear," Miss Ruby whispered as she crooked her finger at Edie. Edie took a step closer so they formed a tight circle and bent her head. "How do you ask a prince to get naked?"

"I'd assume the same way you ask all the men you use for your banners to get naked," Edie said, struggling not to laugh.

"Who's the other hottie in the suit? I'd like to see him in nothing but his tie and my pie," Miss Winnie whispered.

"Did I hear something about pie? Edie, are you making a pie?" Tristan asked as he walked into the room right behind her.

"No! Don't even think of my sister's pie." Walker glared

at him and Edie blushed because she knew he wasn't talking about pie. Well, the kind you eat . . . no, that's not right either. He wasn't talking about the kind you bake.

"Walker dear," Miss Ruby said to him in the kindest tone possible, "that cow has left the pasture. Now, how do you feel about taking a picture for us? We have a blue ribbon at the state fair to win and we need to stand out."

"And a picture of me with your pie will make you stand out?" Walker asked with the amused grin of a man whose ego was just stroked.

"No, dear," Miss Winnie answered with a shake of her head. "We need to stand out. We need a group photo. Ruby?" Miss Winnie asked as if she'd just gotten an idea, but it was so clearly staged that Edie bit her lip to prevent herself from laughing out loud.

"Yes, Winnie?" Miss Ruby asked as if she had no idea what Winnie was going to say.

"I know a sure way we can win! Boys," Miss Winnie said, getting the room's attention.

"Yes, ma'am?" Dylan responded instantly.

"You want two sweet old ladies who may not be alive next year to win the state fair for their apple pie, don't you?" Miss Winnie asked.

Edie would have sworn the little old lady hunched her shoulders and sucked in her cheeks. Miss Ruby was no better. Her face fell as if her puppy had just been kicked. Then she placed her right hand over her heart and raised her left hand up into the air. "Lord Jesus, please give us the strength to live another year to make it to the state fair, and for these kind, caring men to help us fulfill our lifelong dream of winning best pie."

"Amen," Miss Winnie said as if they were in church.

"Of course we want you to win. What can we do to help?" Dylan asked.

"I can call the governor," Zain suggested.

"I can pay off anyone you need," Sebastian offered.

"I can disable your competition's ovens," Dylan proposed.

"I can shoot out the competition's tires so they can't arrive in time for judging," Walker added.

"I can't listen to this," Granger said, walking into the kitchen to get the casserole.

"Well, you know what I can do," Tristan said with a smirk.

"Good Lord, you'd kill them for us?" Miss Ruby gasped.

"No, I'd shoot their pies. I'd feel really bad about it too because I love pie." Tristan gave them a wink.

"What do you need us to do? We'll do anything to help," Dylan volunteered like the polite man he'd been raised to be.

Edie saw victory shining in Miss Ruby's and Miss Winnie's eyes. She *should* warn the men, but watching a prince, a soldier, a billionaire, a secret operative, and an assassin being taken down by two old ladies over pie was too priceless to stop.

"We just want to take a little picture with you holding our pies," Miss Ruby said innocently.

"A picture? That's it?" Zain asked.

"That's it. Just one little picture of you all lined up holding a pie," Miss Winnie said with the same innocence that Miss Ruby was using.

"I'm happy to help," Zain answered as the rest of the men nodded.

"Oh, thank you! We'll be back as soon as we bake a pie for each of you nice young men." Edie watched Miss Ruby and Miss Winnie transform back into their healthy selves in an instant and rush from the house as they made plans. Baby oil was mentioned and Edie swore she'd make any assassination attempt wait until she saw this. Heck, those two feisty women would probably make the team sent to kill Tristan strip for a picture as well.

"Tristan," Sebastian said, interrupting a discussion between the guys over Marcy Davies's pie and Miss Ruby's and Miss Winnie's. The conclusion was that Dylan's grandmother's and Miss Ruby and Winnie's pies all had magical powers. "We're ready."

The room was hushed as Tristan walked over to where Sebastian had set the computer. This phone call wasn't being made by a phone, but by using the computer to clone another number and call.

Tristan was a smart guy, but by the time Sebastian had finished explaining the program he developed to make calls untraceable, Tristan just nodded and pretended he understood. "What do I do?"

"I'll place the call. Then just talk as normal. The call will also be recorded, so don't worry about trying to remember every single detail. Just get whatever information you need," Sebastian told him. "Ready?"

Tristan nodded as he took a seat. Sebastian hit a couple of keys and then the sound of a ringing phone filled the room.

"General Bernard," David said as he answered the phone. "What can I do for you and the academy?"

The program worked. Tristan had advised Sebastian to use the head of the military academy's phone number since they were still in regular contact with their former headmaster.

"I'm calling about your old roommate. It's time for our annual charity drive and we need your help," Tristan said.

"Anything to help the school. Give me a minute to get that information for you, sir. I left it in the car," David replied and Tristan let out a breath knowing his friend understood the situation.

In the background, Tristan heard Jean and others talking. "I have to get something for General Bernard. I'll be right back," they heard David whisper before the background noise began to fade until there was silence.

"Tris! Holy shit, things have gone crazy here. Are you okay? They found you in South Carolina and have sent Claude after you," David blurted out in a hushed whisper.

"Of course I'm okay. There's a seven-year-old girl here who would be a better assassin than Claude. I know we might not have much time, but I'm here with Abby," Tristan began to say only for David to cut him off.

"You killed her? She's innocent!"

"David, her father is Ahmed Mueez." Tristan dropped that bomb and waited to hear what David would say.

There was dead silence on the line and then, in a strangled whisper, "He's going to kill you."

"Exactly. Thankfully, I didn't kidnap or kill her. She's helping me. Listen to what we've found so far and tell me what we're missing." Tristan gave a very brief synopsis and then waited.

"Pastor's husband? He arrived back yesterday. It was said he'd been on a diplomatic mission for President Pastor. You're telling me he was the one waiting to get the dead or mutilated Abby Mueez in order to pressure Rahmi?" David asked.

"Yes. We don't understand why this mission even exists and what Pastor's motives are. I can understand that she wants me dead. This had to be a test to see if I would do whatever she said, but what about her husband?" Tristan asked.

"It all makes sense now. Tristan, she's setting you up," David said suddenly.

"I know that. I just don't know why."

"No, no, no, not just to fail on a mission to prove that you are against her. She's setting you up as Gastaud's murderer. We both know there were rumblings about his death being a murder as soon as it happened. One reporter actually placed the blame on Pastor, but remember what happened?" David asked.

"He disappeared." Tristan remembered the incident. The reporter's source had been Emily Gastaud, the president's daughter. It was what had solidified Tristan's belief that Pastor was behind Gastaud's death because the day it ran, the reporter left his flat and was never seen again. Emily had called Tristan, frantic that she would be next. She fled Millevia for Italy and had been in hiding there ever since.

"The day after you left, Pastor called in all high-ranking officers in law enforcement saying new evidence had turned up that Gastaud's death might have been murder. She placed the blame on a conspiracy to weaken the country by throwing it into upheaval so there could be a coup."

Tristan shook his head. "That's exactly what *she* did."

"Yes, but hearing everything you have found out, I understand it all now. She's moving all the focus off of her and directing it at you. It's actually genius. With one setup, she's fixing all the problems caused when she killed Gastaud and stole his office. First, she proves you murdered Gastaud, therefore making her the hero who avenged a beloved president rather than the prime suspect. Second, with her name cleared, she'll look like the good guy internationally and win back the other countries' support. What you don't know is that not only has Rahmi refused to work with her, but now two major investors have pulled everything from Millevia. The banks are empty and all construction has stopped. Hell, there are boats blocking the port so we can't get supplies shipped in." Tristan looked up at Sebastian who showed no reaction to the news. "Further, there's talk that Rahmi is so pissed at Pastor that Princess Ariana is going to call on their allies to stand against Pastor at the next UN meeting."

"I know," Tristan said. "Rahmi is pissed that Pastor sent me to kill one of their own in order to hurt the royal family. And get this, Edie—"

"The woman you like? And how does Rahmi know? How do *you* know that Rahmi knows?"

Tristan smiled as Edie reacted with surprise to hear that he'd talked about her to David. "The woman I love. Yes, her. Rahmi knows because I've talked to the royal family."

"You need to tell them they're in danger, too," David said in a rush.

Tristan saw Zain lean forward and his lips pursed with that news. "David, I'm Prince Zain of Rahmi. How are we in danger?"

"This isn't the time to start joking, Tris."

"David, that really is Prince Zain. We're all here. Prince Zain, Abby, Sebastian Abel . . . we aren't alone anymore. We have people who believe us." Tristan felt relief and something else. Hope. He wasn't fighting alone anymore.

"Crap, Jean is watching me. I have to make this quick. Your Highness, I know because Pastor has her underlings spreading the word that Rahmi wants to take over Millevia for our port. The rumors are that Rahmi funded the coup against Gastaud, but that she prevented Rahmi's invasion by taking power upon his death."

It hit Tristan hard. It all came into view. "She takes them down with me, and not only does she win domestic favor, but she also looks the victim on the international stage. While she won't get the contracts with Rahmi, it'll make other countries work with her and prevent Rahmi's allies from standing against her presidency."

"Exactly. Look, they're waiting to hear from Claude and then we'll be shipping out if he failed. If you're going to do anything, you'd better do it now."

"How did you all find me?" Tris asked.

"They had nothing. Jean started looking into the people on your last mission. They sent someone to Keeneston first, but they didn't see you. Then they sent Claude to Shadows Landing. He reported back that he'd seen you. What are you going to do now?"

"I'm going to call Pastor and tell her I have Abby. We need to buy some time to set up her husband and have the proof we need to take Pastor down. Thanks for your help, David."

Tristan hung up with his friend and calmed his racing heart just like he did when lining up a shot. "I need a burner phone that she can call back on if needed."

"Sure thing," Dylan said, walking over to a bag and pulling one out. "I always have a handful with me."

Tristan called the number he'd had memorized since the first day on the job. The line connected and Tristan gave his code name and authorization number and requested to speak to Pastor. He could imagine them scrambling to tell

Pastor he was on the line. It didn't take long for her voice to answer the call.

"Durand. I thought you'd fled the country."

"Madam President, I would never betray my country. I'm sorry for the delay, but the mission has finally been accomplished."

"You have Abby Davies? I want proof." Pastor demanded with clear shock in her voice.

"I do have her and I'll send you a photo. I'm sorry it took longer than anticipated, but I was attacked at the train station. I'm embarrassed to admit they got the jump on me. I staggered onto the train after them, but my injuries were too much. I was stabbed and passed out. I didn't wake up until a couple of days ago only to find myself in a Paris hospital. My phone and ID were gone, but you know I'd never leave a mission unfinished. I had to get new documents and raced to the United States to find the target. I went to Keeneston first, but she wasn't there. Next, I went to Shadows Landing where she was visiting and grabbed her. I've taken her to a secure location, followed your instructions, and mailed her finger to the address you gave."

Pastor was quiet for a moment. "Good job, Durand. Has she said anything yet about Rahmi's intent? We've received intelligence that Rahmi wants to invade Millevia."

"Not yet. She's stubborn, but I'll get the information from her."

"Threaten her baby. She's a woman. It'll have her talking," Pastor said with sureness.

"And if it doesn't?"

"Kill the baby and then kill her."

"Yes, ma'am." Tristan hung up before Pastor could ask him any more questions, like where specifically he was.

"I'm going to kill her myself," Dylan said between clenched teeth.

"Not if I get to her first." Abby was scary. She wasn't obviously enraged. In fact, she was remarkably calm, but her eyes . . . the blue in them had turned so dark he wondered if she was the devil herself.

While Dylan and Abby were so angry they were calm, Zain was livid. He had his phone out and was speaking very quickly into the other end before hanging up and taking a deep breath. "Well, Pastor was right about one thing. You are working for Rahmi, as of right now. Not to take over Millevia, but to neutralize a threat to Rahmi. You have full immunity, sanctuary, and authority to act in any way you deem necessary to protect Rahmi, the royal family, and our interests. The king will have the rental house under surveillance. The second Tommaso Pastor lands in Rahmi, he will be watched and recorded to prove his involvement in this plot."

"I'll have your cover story settled in a couple of minutes," Sebastian said. "There will be a fake news story about a stabbing victim on the train and a fake medical report at one of the Paris hospitals."

"Now, let's take a bloody picture of me missing a finger," Abby said. The teasing Abby was gone. Standing in front of them was Ahmed's daughter, and right now Tristan almost felt bad for Pastor. Almost.

## 19

Edie watched as Tristan snapped a picture of Abby. She didn't need to fake the pissed-off look on her face. However, the blood and the gory stump of a finger were all Tinsley's work as an artist. The blood was thinned-out paint mixed with corn syrup. The background of a gray cement holding area was all a painted canvas. Edie already knew Tinsley was a very talented artist, but she also had a future in makeup and special effects if she ever wanted it.

Tristan sent the text to Pastor and everyone waited.

To be safe, they took additional pictures with a few more fake injuries while they waited for a reply that never came. Probably to be able to deny involvement.

The knock at the door interrupted further thought of Pastor. Granger opened the door with his gun drawn. Tristan moved between Edie and the door, but she knew there was no threat when the gun was holstered and Granger eagerly held out both hands. "Let me help with that."

The smell of apples and cinnamon filled the living room

as Granger carried in a large basket filled with fresh-baked apple pies.

"What's going on?" Tinsley asked Edie.

"The guys agreed to take a picture with the pies for Miss Ruby and Miss Winnie," Edie whispered back.

"Do they know they'll be—"

"Eating the most amazing pie of their lives when they're done? No, they don't know that yet." Edie cut off Tinsley. It was devilish of her but she really wanted to see this play out.

Tinsley pursed her lips. Her face turned red with the effort it took to not laugh out loud.

"What's going on?" Greer asked.

"Tinsley, are you okay?" Abby asked. "You're an alarming shade of red."

"I'm just great. Let's go watch the photo shoot," Tinsley said, trying hard to hide the tears of suppressed laughter about to slip from her eyes.

"Why do I get the feeling I'm missing something here?" Layne asked as she joined the women in following the group of men outside and into the backyard.

"The only thing about to go missing are their clothes," Granger answered, joining them as Miss Winnie arranged the men in a line.

"That is an impressive lineup," Layne muttered as Miss Winnie walked by them with a hot apple pie at nose level.

"Okay, gentleman. Thank you so much for helping out two old ladies," Miss Ruby said, pulling out her camera. "This is a super-casual picture. The state fair doesn't need suits and ties. These are everyday-type folk. Can you ditch your shoes and socks and certainly your jackets and ties?"

Sebastian looked at Zain and frowned, but the men all kicked off their shoes, peeled off their socks, and then pulled their ties from their shirts. Their jackets were last to come off as they got back into line.

"We can't have them posing for a photo without trying our pies, can we, Win?" Miss Ruby asked and Edie about died at the manipulation going on. The guys looked so eager to try a bite they'd do anything.

"You're right," Miss Winnie said, pulling forks from the basket. "I happened to make a couple of extra pies to sample. Oh dear," Miss Winnie frowned.

"What is it, ma'am?" Dylan asked, full of concern.

"Our pie is very gooey and I'd hate for it to get all over your shirts." Miss Winnie looked as if she were trying to come up with a way to fix this.

"We can put on napkins," Walker suggested.

"I am not being photographed with a bib," Sebastian said.

"I know!" Miss Ruby said and everyone looked relieved as the pie was held under their noses. "Just take off your shirts. I'm sure the ladies would hold on to them so they don't get wrinkled. Right, ladies?"

"Definitely," Edie said helpfully, walking forward with her hand outstretched, hoping the others caught on.

"Your Highness, it would be an honor." Tinsley giggled as she did a mock curtsey in front of Zain and held out her hand.

"Come on, Bash," Greer said with a straight face. "I know how you are about your shirts being clean. Off!" Greer snapped and even though Sebastian looked confused, he began to unbutton his dress shirt.

Edie loved her friends and family. They understood what was going on and instead of being angry, were leaping into the farce with gusto. In less than a minute, the men were now standing shirtless.

Miss Winnie came forward with the pie. Walker took a bite and groaned. "This is so good and I know good pie. My grandmother-in-law makes an awesome apple pie. This is just as good, but slightly different."

"We use a different secret ingredient from Marcy Davies," Miss Ruby told Walker.

"Mmm. Caramel. It's caramel and it's really good," Walker said as he moaned over another forkful.

Dylan was next. Edie watched as he closed his eyes briefly and enjoyed the pie.

"Whoops!" Miss Winnie gasped as the pie hit Tristan right in the crotch. Gooey apple pie slid down his jeans and dripped onto the ground.

Edie watched the horror play out across the men's faces. She would have sworn a couple of them were eyeing the pie on the ground and thinking about the five-second rule.

"I'm so clumsy. I am so sorry, Tristan. I have one more pie so don't worry, you can still have a taste. Edie, dear? You'd better put some stain remover on Tristan's pants."

Tristan looked slightly panicked as Edie stepped forward and held out her hands once again. "Pants."

"You don't mean for me to strip naked in front of all these people, do you?" Tristan whispered.

"No, just to your boxers."

"Love, I was racing after you this morning. I didn't exactly have time to put my boxers on," Tristan whispered back.

Edie turned, walked over to Miss Winnie and Miss Ruby, and dropped her voice. "I get my own pie every month for the rest of the year."

"Deal," they hurriedly agreed.

Edie grabbed one of the pies and walked back to Tristan. She stood in front of him and smiled. "I got this. No one will see a thing. Go ahead and take them off." The other men snickered as Tristan hesitated. "It's nothing I haven't seen before," Edie whispered.

"But they haven't seen it," he whispered back, looking at Tinsley and the rest of the women standing ten feet away holding on to shirts and jackets.

"And they won't. I got this. Trust me."

"Come on, Durand, we have a plane to catch," Dylan called out, teasing Tristan.

Poor guy didn't know what he had coming, but it worked. Tristan shoved his pants down and Edie placed the pie precariously close to his package. "Hold it right here," Edie instructed.

Edie stepped back and her mouth watered, and it wasn't for the pie. Well, okay, the pie was part of the reason. A naked Tristan was definitely a sight to behold.

Then Edie frowned. "Now it doesn't look right."

"No, it doesn't," Tinsley said. "Wait, Miss Ruby. Don't take any pictures. From an artist's perspective, it just doesn't work."

"What is it that's not working?" Edie asked as the guys looked at each other as if trying to figure it out. "The pant legs. Of course."

"That's it," Tinsley snapped. "One bare-legged man and the rest look strange with multicolored pant legs. You have jeans, suits, and all of different colors. Y'all need to be uniform."

"You're so right," Greer said, nodding. "Sebastian, you look silly in just those pants. You and Zain look like stick-in-the-muds while Tristan looks ready to party."

Sebastian rolled his eyes. Zain narrowed his.

"Roll up your pant legs," Greer instructed them.

"This is a hand-sewn Italian suit. I'm not rolling up the

legs," Sebastian said, crossing his arms over his chest. "No pie is worth it."

"What he said," Zain said with a nod to Sebastian.

Miss Winnie brought the other pie over and held it up to the two men. "Try a bite."

Sebastian and Zain looked unimpressed until they bit down. There was moaning and pleasure-induced eye-rolling.

"Come on, hand them over." Greer grabbed two pies and walked over to the two men.

"Hand what over?" Zain asked.

"Your pants. If you won't roll them up to hide them behind the pie, then take them off. Tristan did and he's enjoying more pie." Greer looked over her shoulder at Edie and winked.

Edie grabbed the pie and hurried forward to spoon-feed Tristan a bite.

"It's worth being naked for, but can we hurry up? We do have a coup to pull off." Edie shoved another spoonful into Tristan's mouth as everyone looked at him enviously.

Zain caved first. He was wearing boxers that he rolled up to hide behind the pie Greer gave him. Greer rolled her eyes at her husband and tapped her foot impatiently.

Sebastian finally shrugged and shoved down his pants. Edie didn't mean to look but got a big eyeful before the pie was shoved into his hands. Apparently, Sebastian and Tristan had more in common today than she might have guessed.

"Hurry up, Dylan," Abby called out. "The baby smells the pie, and if you don't get naked right now so I can have some, I'm going to tell my father you're going to let me come with you on Plan B."

"Now, babe," Dylan stammered. "That's not right. You

know your father would cut off my balls. Are you feeling a little hormonal?"

"Aw, shit," Walker said under his breath. "You *never* say that to a pregnant woman."

Edie and every other person near Abby took a giant step away from her. She looked ready to explode. "*Hormonal?* I'm only growing your child inside of me and you're acting all prudish over getting naked? You never had that problem before. Do you need me to remind you of the number of times I've dropped my panties for you and now you can't do it one time to get me some freaking pie? I mean, get the *baby* pie. The baby needs the pie. If you don't get this baby some pie, I might just be *hormonal* until he or she goes off to college."

"Just don't tell Ahmed I would let you go with us on Plan B," Dylan said quickly as Abby shoved a pie in his hands the second his pants dropped, boxers and all.

"Are you taking note, Bash?" Greer asked.

"You're never hormonal, sweetheart. You're extra feisty, which is exactly how I like you." Sebastian said it so diplomatically that Edie, Greer, and the rest of the ladies shared a look as if they were trying to figure out whether it was an insult or not.

"Walker, dear," Miss Ruby called out. "You're holding everyone up. Tinsley, does this look better?"

"As soon as Walker takes off his pants it will be perfect. I love how y'all are all within the same height range. I think we should go dark to light hair color. That would really be artistic," Tinsley said with a cocked head as if she were examining a painting.

Edie nodded dutifully next to her. "Oh, you're right."

"Dylan, you and Tristan switch places. Sebastian and

Zain, you two switch and then we'll be good," Tinsley instructed.

The guys grumbled but moved while Walker took off his pants and pushed up his boxer briefs so they wouldn't show in the picture.

"Perfect. Now smile," Tinsley called out as Miss Ruby snapped away with the camera. "Now glare." The men narrowed their eyes and frowned. "Now kind of look at each other and laugh." The men really started to grumble, but they did it. "Perfect! One last pose. Now purse your lips and suck in your cheeks just a little."

"That's freaking duck face," Sebastian growled.

"Yeah, I'm not doing duck face. I'll take the knife to the balls," Dylan said.

"Princes don't do duck face," Zain said royally.

"Princes also don't have pants," Greer replied, holding up his pants before turning and running.

"Layne?" Walker called out, but when Edie looked Layne was right behind Greer.

"Toodles!" Tinsley gave a little finger wave before running off after them.

"Abby," Dylan's voice held a thread of annoyance to it.

"How's this for hormonal, babe?" Abby turned and sauntered off. She tossed the jeans over her shoulder and added a little extra swing to her hips.

Tristan was smiling. He thought he was the only one going to get his pants back. Edie smiled back at him, blew him a kiss, and then took off after Greer and the women. Behind her, she heard the cries of disbelief mixed with Granger's laughter.

## 20

Tristan stood, holding a pie in front of him and stared at Edie's retreating back. "Did they really leave us standing here naked with pie?"

"I'm a dead man, aren't I?" Dylan asked with real fear in his voice.

"So dead," Zain said with a laugh. "Ahmed is going to kill you if he thinks you're putting Abby in danger. And if he doesn't kill you, Abby will torture you forever. Wives have memories that put elephants to shame. Twenty years from now, she'll pull that back out and drill you with 'I guess I'm still hormonal.'"

Walker snickered. "I'm sorry. I'm laughing because it's so true."

"What do I do?" Dylan asked.

"I'd start by giving her the entire pie," Sebastian suggested.

"You've been married for all of a second," Dylan complained. "What do you know?"

"By the answer he gave Greer, I'd say he knows a lot," Zain replied.

"Damn, I really wanted this pie," Dylan muttered before stalking off.

Tristan fell in line as they walked naked across the backyard and into the house. There were definitely pictures taken of their bare asses as they walked past Miss Ruby and Miss Winnie. He'd better get more than one pie for this.

While the guys were dressing, Tristan wrapped a towel around him and ran for his house. By the time he came back with clean clothes on, the group seemed to be wrapping up. Dylan was begging Abby not to tell her father and that Dylan was really the one who was hormonal.

"Let me see your real phone." Greer ambushed him at the front door and held out her hand. She waited for Tristan to give her his phone and then her fingers flew over the buttons before she handed it back. "We have to go. It's been lovely meeting you, Tristan."

"You're leaving now?" Tristan asked Greer, not understanding what was going on. He'd only been gone for five minutes. What had he missed? Apparently, a lot.

"Yes, Dylan and I are. Sebastian and Abby are going to catch a ride back to Keeneston with Zain. You and your future brother-in-law are tasked with holding down the fort for a bit. And if you have a spoon handy, Layne will help out, too. All of our numbers are now programmed in your phone. I even started a group chat for you to keep us up to date."

Walker crossed his arms over his chest and glared at Tristan. After being naked with the man, Tristan had hoped they'd gotten over the overprotective brother thing. Edie rolled her eyes at Walker. Layne grinned at Tristan with excitement.

"What does a spoon have to do with anything?" Tristan asked as they all packed up.

"We're going to have so much fun," Layne said as she rubbed her hands together. "If you really want to get crazy, you should see what I can do with a spork."

"Where are you and Dylan going?" Tristan asked Greer, even as he was totally confused by Layne's comment.

"Plan B," Greer answered as Abby grumbled about being sent back to Keeneston.

"We don't have a Plan B, so what is this plan you've been talking about?" Tristan pushed.

"There's always a Plan B," Dylan answered for Greer before he tried to calm Abby down about being left at home and not mentioning the word *hormonal*.

"You're going to kill Pastor if everything goes to pot," Tristan said when the reality of the situation hit him. Dylan was like Tristan. Greer was an advisor to the President of the United States, whom she'd sent the phone conversation between Tristan and Pastor. Tristan could see it now. The same conversation that had Rahmi making a deal with Tristan and because Rahmi and the United States were very close allies, they'd have made their own deal. "You're not a political advisor. You're Dylan and Abby's handler."

Greer just smiled sweetly at him before kissing her husband goodbye. "Keep in touch, Durand. Let us know when the wedding is," Greer called out.

Greer hugged Edie and then she and Dylan strode from the house. Abby was still grumbling about pregnant women having the right to work while Sebastian packed up his things.

Zain slid his phone into his inside suit jacket pocket and looked at Tristan. "I can send you some backup if you need it."

"Tristan has Kord and me, as well as Walker," Granger said from the kitchen with an apple pie in hand.

"How did you get that? You didn't get naked," Zain asked as if the greatest injustice had just occurred.

Granger smiled and slowly took a big bite of pie. "Mmm. I was rewarded for keeping my mouth shut and not telling you what Miss Winnie and Miss Ruby were up to."

"You betrayed us men for pie?" Sebastian asked, joining in the glares Zain was sending Granger.

"Damn right I did." Granger took another exaggerated bite. "Mmm. So worth it."

"They're not actually going to use that photo of us naked, are they?" Zain asked and Tristan tried not to laugh at the royal. He suddenly looked very worried.

"No," Edie said. "They'll probably use all the photos of you naked. It's kind of their thing."

"And you went along with it?" Walker asked his sister, insulted.

Edie shrugged and grinned at her brother. "I guess that makes up for my junior prom."

Layne laughed and asked for details, but was interrupted by another knock on the door. Tristan and Walker were instantly on guard as he moved to open in.

He was met with a plastic bag, blood, and a finger.

"Don't ask me how I got this," Kenzie said, shoving the package at him. "What people do when they're on meth is beyond my comprehension."

"Did you cut someone's finger off?" Edie gasped.

"Cool," Layne said, grabbing the bag with the finger.

Kenzie rolled her eyes. "No, I didn't cut it off. She cut it off herself while high on meth. She thought her hand was possessed and trying to kill her. There was so much meth in her system. If Pastor touches this finger, she'll probably overdose."

Tristan took the bag from Layne and turned to Kenzie. "This is going to buy us time. Now I just need to get it to Rahmi."

Zain grimaced but held out his hand. "I'll take it. We have a diplomatic courier who can get through security. He'll take it to my uncle, who will send it with an undercover agent posing as a deliveryman. The chain of custody of the finger won't be in question. We can get video evidence of Tommaso signing for the finger and everything."

Tristan handed over the finger and soon the house had emptied of all but Edie, Walker, Layne, and himself. Layne went to call her father and mother to check in on their daughter, Carolina. Edie went upstairs.

That left Tristan alone with Walker.

"Do you think Pastor will send your friend to kill you?" Walker asked Tristan as he took a seat on the couch and leaned back.

"Yes," Tristan answered instantly. He might have delayed the attack, but it was still coming. Pastor couldn't miss her chance at framing him.

"How many people should we expect?" Walker asked.

"She'll most likely be testing David as well, so I'd expect her to send at least two teams. We have both three- and five-agent teams, so I'd expect around ten or so trained agents. Although David will be on our side," Tristan explained.

"That's all? No need to call in help from Keeneston. This will be a piece of cake."

"Don't get too cocky, Walker. My men are well-trained." Tristan tried to warn him not to take this lightly. "And you never know if Pastor will send more."

"Regardless, I got this. You can go home now, Assassin Boy." Walker dismissed him as Edie walked into the room carrying a tote bag overflowing with yarn.

"Where are you going?" Walker asked his sister.

"Knitting club. I missed the last two meetings. I have the guest room made up for you and Layne, but I need to go. I'll pick up dinner on the way home or you can meet me at Harper's bar in two hours," Edie told her brother.

Tristan didn't know if he were included in that invitation so he stood quietly, waiting to see how this played out. Walker was in full overprotective big brother mode and Tris was getting tired of arguing with him.

"You'll skip knitting club. You're in danger and can't go."

"I'm not in danger. Tristan is. Plus, Dare is in knitting club with me and we're pretty deadly with those needles." Edie didn't even look concerned when Walker glared at her.

Tristan smiled on the inside as Edie ignored her brother's order while she kissed his cheek. She turned and walked over to where Tristan was standing. "Dinner at Harpers?" Edie asked him.

"Sure. I'll see you there." Tristan took his life in his hands as he bent down and placed a kiss on her lips. He made sure it was quick, but it was still a statement.

Walker was grumbling under his breath when Edie closed the door on them. Tristan looked over to Walker to find his arms crossed over his chest, his eyes narrowed, and he was frowning.

"Take a seat, Assassin Boy. We need to talk."

## 21

"Sorry I'm late!" Edie hurried into the all-purpose room in the back of the Shadows Landing Church and grabbed the last available seat. She smiled at Dare, who was sitting to her right and tried not to show her surprise at seeing Stone Townsend sitting on her left.

The Townsend men were like boulders, massive and impassive. Wide shoulders, muscular legs, and sculpted faces that made you think they'd been chiseled in stone and brought to life. In Stone's thick fingers were yarn and knitting needles. His brow was furrowed as he glared at the needles, trying to scare them into working.

"Hi, Stone," Edie said tentatively. Stone grunted as Edie shot Dare a questioning look. Dare shrugged as if having no idea why Stone was there. She wouldn't say any of the Townsend brothers were nice and outgoing, but she was used to Walker, Shane, and the rest of the DEVGRU men. She spoke fluent grunting.

"I can't get this," Stone grumbled, and Edie was afraid he'd break the needles in half.

Miss Winnie, Ruby, and Mitzy hid their smirks by suddenly being very interested in their projects.

"You need to loosen your hold on your needles," Edie said to him. She reached over and tapped his knuckles. "They shouldn't be white."

Stone growled but loosened his hold on the needles as Edie gave him a little more instruction. "Like this?" Stone asked. He never looked up with his gray eyes, so Edie was looking over black hair on Stone's head that looked a couple of weeks past needing a haircut to see what he was doing.

"Yes, just like that. Very good, Stone."

Stone grunted.

"So, man," Dare said, trying to get Stone's attention. "What has you learning knitting?"

"My coach said I needed to find a way to relax. I tried it my way first, but apparently having sex with the women in the front office wasn't what he meant. After a fight broke out among the women, he told me his mother knitted for relaxation and ordered me to take a class. I have to make something by next Friday or I won't start the next game. Luckily, Olivia told me about this group, but you all seem to know what you're doing already."

"It's okay, we all were beginners once," Edie told him. "If you don't mind me asking, what coach? I don't think we know anything about the mysterious Townsend brothers."

Stone grunted and finally looked up from the knotted yarn that he'd "knitted." "I'm a professional hockey player."

"Do you play for the Charleston Gators? What position?" Dare asked, suddenly interested.

"Yeah, I was just traded to the Gators. I play center. Now, how do I do this? I have to be the starter for the playoffs."

Edie leaned over and unraveled the knotted mess he was working with. "Let me show you." Edie worked with him until he got the rows of garter stitch going on his own. "This can be a potholder if you'd like. Or if you really get the hang of it, just keep going and turn it into a scarf."

Stone grunted and finally looked over to the project on her lap. "Thanks. What are you making?"

Edie smiled as she held up the tiny green object. "It's going to be an alligator cozy for Kenzie's stethoscope. See, the town kind of has a mascot of our own, Bubba the Alligator. He also happens to love Kenzie because she feeds him jerky. I could make a gator for your hockey bag or something."

Stone grunted again, but she knew that grunt. That was a "yes, but I'm too manly to admit I want it" grunt.

"You're doing much better, Stone," Miss Mitzy said from across the circle a couple of minutes later.

"Thank you, ma'am. What are you knitting?" Stone asked.

"A sweater for my kitty," Miss Mitzy said with a smile. The little sweater had her cat's face knitted onto the back of it.

Stone leaned near Edie and dropped his voice. "Is Miss Ruby knitting a giant dick, or am I just seeing things?"

Edie smothered her giggle. "No, it's a giant penis. She's got quite a following on a big craft site for selling erotic knitting and embroidery." Edie raised her voice and asked Miss Ruby, "What order number is this, Miss Ruby?"

Miss Ruby looked up and smiled. "I've sold fifty-three of these suckers."

Miss Winnie nodded her head. "We started our own company. These dick dolls are selling almost as fast as our apple pies. Ruby knits the dicks, we stuff them, and I make clothes for them. People like to dress them up like dolls.

This one will be dressed in Regency attire. Meet the Duke of Dick."

Miss Ruby looked up as she finished a row and Edie was afraid Stone was going to catch flies with his mouth hanging open like that. "The alien orders are huge too. My next order is for a big blue alien with two peckers. Now, I just need to attach these balls to finish this order up. See, we fill them with two bags of dry beans to give it some weight so the pecker can stand up nice and straight. No one likes a floppy pecker."

Stone turned to Edie, wide-eyed and blinked. "She's messing with me, right?"

Dare and Edie were struggling not to laugh at Stone's shocked expression. Edie couldn't talk without a giggle escaping. Luckily Dare answered for her. "Nope. That's made her thousands of dollars this year already. You can make a ton of tit knit projects too. I made a scarf with boobs at the bottom last winter for my wife."

"Well, that would make interesting gifts for my teammates," Stone said as if he were slightly stunned.

"You can make winter knit caps too," Edie added just to mess with him. Although it was true. Boob caps were great. "Flesh colored cap and then you can even add a knit puff for the nipple for extra flare. It's very cute."

"This town is very strange, but I think I like it," Stone said slowly as if he were still undecided on his opinion.

"It's why Olivia likes it here," Edie said, trying to open up dialogue about his sister. "How many brothers are there? Are you all older or younger than Olivia?"

"Some are older, some are younger, but not by much. We are all born within a year of the next one. Mom wanted a lot of us in the shortest amount of time possible. Now, can you show me how to move to the next row again?" Edie knew that tone. Stone was done talking about his family. Maybe she could bribe him for more information by making boob caps for his teammates.

Edie settled into her knitting project while every now and then helping Stone as the group fell into a discussion about town gossip.

~

Tristan heard the door close and then he was alone with Walker. Layne was still on the phone with her parents and he could hear her cooing over video chat with her daughter.

"I don't like you." Walker got right to the point. "I respect my sister's feelings and I'm happy for her, but that doesn't mean I'm happy about you."

"I gathered," Tristan said. "But I also gathered you wouldn't like anyone Edie brought home."

"I liked Shane."

Tristan frowned. "Edie said he was your best friend. She told me what happened and I'm sorry. Having your own man turn against you . . . that's hard."

"You should know. Sounds like your men just turned against you too," Walker said and Tristan saw the moment he realized they were more alike than Walker wanted to admit. "Okay, Assassin Boy, enough of this. I only care about Edie not having her heart broken again, which is exactly what will happen at the end of this. I'll help you fix your country, but then I want you gone."

"You told Edie—" Layne began as she reentered the room.

"I know I told her I want her happy, but these are the facts. Tristan isn't going to make her happy when he's dead or leaves her here to go back to his country."

"Walker," Layne's warning seemed to echo across the room. "It would break her heart if he left her at the end of this, but it's not your call to make anyway. It's Edie's and Tristan's. Let them find their path, just like we did. He knows you'll kill him if he takes the wrong path, just like my father would have killed you."

Walker grunted unhappily. "I should call your father and have the uncles come down here. Then we'll see what Assassin Boy is made of."

"I'm pretty sure I can handle a few uncles," Tristan said, trying not to laugh at the idea of a bunch of senior citizens attacking him.

"You know Ahmed?" Walker asked and Tristan nodded warily. "Image a group of Ahmeds and that's the uncles."

Well, crap. Maybe he *couldn't* handle a group of uncles.

"Come on, let's head to the bar. We don't have Carolina and all the gossips of Keeneston watching us. You know how I like tequila." Layne grinned and looked like an excited college student after finals were over.

"And you know how I like you with tequila, too." Walker's wink told Tristan all he needed to know about that. Maybe it would be a good idea to let Edie spend the night at his house tonight.

"I'll buy the first round if you tell me what it is about you and spoons," Tristan said.

"Deal." Layne bounded out of the house, leaving the two men to follow.

"This does not make us drinking buddies," Walker warned.

"Whatever you say, bro," Tristan taunted before heading out after Layne and leaving Walker fuming. It might be fun having a brother-in-law like Walker. Now he just needed to survive long enough to marry Edie.

## 22

Tristan was next to Layne as the trio walked into town to have dinner at Harper's. He listened as they talked about their daughter, about their friends in Keeneston, and about Walker and Edie's time growing up in Shadows Landing.

They were almost to the bar when Tristan's pace faltered.

"What is it?" Layne asked, instantly catching on to his slowed pace, but Tristan didn't have to answer when the boisterous batch of kids caught everyone's attention.

"Hi, Lydia!" Walker called out down the street. "She's younger than me, but when you grow up in a small town, you know everyone. Her husband is deployed a lot. I think there's a kid for almost every time he's back home."

That explained a lot. Tristan grimaced as he heard the moment the kids spotted him. Instead of the battle cry he expected, the mom smiled and waved along with all the kids who came running toward them.

"I figured it wouldn't take you long to get here when you heard Edie had a man," Lydia said with a grin. "He's a good one, though."

Tristan felt inordinately proud of that as two of the little kids grabbed his hands and began talking at once.

Suddenly everyone fell silent at a strange sound that reverberated down Main Street. It sounded prehistoric and the answering bellow sent chills down Tristan's back.

"Landry!" Lacy, the oldest girl, cried excitedly. "Do you have your phone?"

"Already got it out," Landry said, sounding just as excited.

Lydia and Walker resumed talking as the kids eagerly looked around.

"What's going on?" Layne asked them.

"It's alligator mating season and . . . there!" Lacy said, pointing to an enormous gator close to the bar. The gator made a throat-chilling sound and now the bellow that answered was closer to them. "It's Bubba and Bertha!"

Landry shoved the phone to Levi, the second-oldest boy. "Don't mess this up!"

Tristan watched as Landry ran toward Bubba and Lacy ran toward Bertha. "Um, Lydia," Tristan said as Levi headed to the middle of the road and began filming. "Should the kids be playing with alligators?"

But the question came too late to stop them. "Now!" Landry yelled and all at once he and Lacy leaped on their respective alligators, which then charged toward each other in a mating-induced frenzy.

"Hmm?" Lydia asked, turning to look to where Tristan was staring in horror. "Landry, Lacy, how many times have I told you that you are not to surf the alligators?"

Tristan was trying to pluck off the little ones trying to ride on his legs so he could run to rescue the kids who were in danger of being eaten by giant, prehistoric carnivores. Landry's and Lacy's arms waved a little in the air as they kept their knees bent and looked as if they were surfing. Only it wasn't waves they were riding. It was alligators.

"If you're not off Bubba and Bertha by the time I count to three," Lydia yelled. "One." The kids didn't move. "Two." The gators were almost to each other. Jaws were wide open and guttural sounds filled the night air along with Lydia's threats. "Thr—"

Landry and Lacy leaped off right as the alligators clashed in what could only be described as a violent mating frenzy. Lydia rolled her eyes and turned back to finish her conversation with Walker.

"I am not allowing Carolina to do that no matter how cool it looked," Layne whispered to Tristan as they both stared in horror at the mating.

Tristan just nodded and noted that none of the kids were paying attention. Levi, Landry, and Lacy were watching the video of the gator-surfing, the youngest two were still clinging to Tristan's legs, and the middle two were arguing over some game they were going to play back home.

"Well," Lydia said, getting Tristan's attention. "Good luck with your coup. Let us know if you need any help. Lacy is quite talented with a dagger. Come on, kids, time to get home." She let out a piercing whistle and the kids fell in line behind her as they headed home.

"Those kids scare me. They're all cute and then they ride alligators and play with daggers," Tristan said, shell-shocked as they entered the bar.

"To be fair, Edie's pretty good with a dagger too," Layne said as they walked toward a table where Granger and Kord were sitting.

Right, Edie with a dagger. Edie was sweet as Miss Ruby's apple pie. She couldn't hurt anyone.

"Any updates?" Granger asked when they were seated.

"Not yet. Hopefully, we'll have some news tomorrow," Tristan said as the door opened and Olivia stormed in. She looked around, her eyes connected with his, and she stomped toward him.

"I'll pay you ten thousand dollars to scare my brothers away from Shadows Landing," Olivia said, pulling out her checkbook.

"What did they do now?" Layne asked as Georgie came over with a round of drinks. Tristan saw her share a shy smile with Kord as she set his drink down and wondered if the two were dating.

"I have a date tonight," Olivia huffed. "Sorry, *had* a date. Damon showed up at my office and intercepted him. The front office paged me to say that my date was there and three minutes later I came out and he was gone. Instead of my date, Damon was there, looking smug."

"You had a date? With who?" Granger asked.

Olivia tossed back a shot of whatever Georgie had put in front of her. "Doesn't matter now."

"I didn't know you were dating," Granger mumbled.

"I'm not! That's the problem," Olivia huffed. "You know why I'm not dating?"

"Your brothers?" Granger asked with a hint of humor.

Olivia narrowed her eyes. "No, because men these days are wimps. Well, except Tristan. He appears to be handling Walker's overprotective pissing contest pretty well. But he's in love with Edie so he's off limits."

Tristan thought Granger made a sound pretty similar to the one Bubba had just made.

"One, two, three," Olivia paused, "Okay, more than three intimidating brothers and dates just fold. Where's the chivalry? Where's the confidence to stand up and say, 'I want you and I'll fight for you'?"

Layne gave Walker a look that convinced Tristan that Edie was definitely going to spend the night at his house tonight. Layne apparently not only understood what Olivia was saying but agreed and found Walker's confidence very sexy. At least that's what Tristan guessed when she licked her lower lip at Walker.

"Or maybe it's women who are the problem." Granger shot back his drink and crossed his arms over his chest.

Kord's eyes widened in shock as he scooted away from Granger.

"Women? Tell me how are we the problem?" Olivia's eyes were narrow and hard and Tristan scooted closer to Walker.

"I've seen that look," Walker whispered. "That's not a look you want a woman to have."

Tristan nodded. He was pretty sure a toddler would know to run away from that look, but Granger only leaned forward, put his elbows on the table, and looked Olivia straight in the eyes.

"Maybe if women weren't so caught up on having the perfect man, they'd see what was right in front of them. That maybe the perfect man for them isn't perfect at all. Because who is? But no. They have to have that perfect man to snap pictures with and brag about. He has to have the right job, drive the right car, and own the right house. Tell me, did the women of the world cry in unison when Ryker got married? Because as far as I can tell, he's the only man who checks all the boxes. Regular, good, but slightly scarred men, who work hard, don't care about social media pictures, and only want a good woman to love seem to get shoved to the side." Granger sat back and recrossed his arms as Olivia huffed.

"That is not true!"

"It's as true as your assessment of men. If your dates are running after three minutes with one of your brothers, did it ever occur to you you're dating the wrong type of men?" Granger asked as Damon strode in looking like a cat that had just gotten the cream. Well, until he saw Granger sitting across from Olivia. Then his smirk fell.

Only Granger smiled at Damon for once. "Damon, tell us about the date you just ran off." Damon's stride faltered just a bit in surprise as he approached the table. "Tell us what he was like."

Olivia looked ready to explode.

"Five foot ten and a hundred and fifty-five pounds of investment banker douche. Drove a sports car. Red. Dates only blondes with C cups or above. Folded in sixteen seconds." Damon took a seat between Olivia and Kord. "My record stands."

"Record?" Granger asked as Olivia's face turned redder than he thought was healthy and her eyes narrowed so much Tristan didn't know if she could see out of them.

"Not a single one of her dates has lasted longer than forty-seven seconds with me before running." Damon gave a nod to Georgie who got a drink ready for him.

Granger smirked and didn't need to say "told you so."

Olivia stood up, placed her hands flat on the table, and leaned over so she was looking down at Granger. "Maybe the average Joes just need to stop being cowards and make a move."

"Who's Joe? What move?" Damon asked as Olivia stalked away after tossing down a gauntlet even Tristan could see.

Olivia shoved open the door and made a growling noise as her brother Stone stood there with Edie and Dare.

"Men!" Olivia said as if a curse.

Stone smiled as he walked inside, leaving his sister to storm off. "I take it your record is still intact."

"Sixteen seconds," Damon said and then Stone high-fived him. "How was your meeting?"

"Good," Stone said, not looking at Edie or Dare.

"Stone, dear," Miss Mitzy called out as she walked to the table. "Here's that knitting pattern we talked about. We'll work on it next class."

"Thank you, Miss Mitzy," Stone said, refusing to look at anyone sitting at the table.

It was quiet as Miss Mitzy left the bar. All eyes turned to Stone, who was very interested in putting the papers into the backpack he was carrying. Tristan noticed the open backpack contained knitting needles.

"Your hockey meeting was about knitting?" Damon asked, trying not to laugh and failing.

Stone gave his brother the middle finger. Tristan put his arm around Edie as they laughed at the brothers. It was surprising that Damon and Stone didn't leave right away. Instead, the group around the table only grew as more and more of the town filled the bar.

Various Faulkners joined the table. Skeeter, Gator, and Turtle stopped by to say hello before heading to the bar. Then Tristan got to meet the Olympic shooting brother-sister team of Gage and Maggie Bell.

The stress from the day seemed to melt away as they joked with each other. Now, if only Tristan could find a way to get Edie to himself tonight, it would be the perfect ending to a long, hard day.

"Hmm," Savannah said, quickly stopping the laughter at Miss Ruby and Miss Winnie's Dick Dolls company as she rubbed her very pregnant belly.

"Are you okay?" her husband, Ridge, asked, instantly concerned.

"Yeah, just got this quick pain across my belly. It's gone now, though." Savannah reached for another bite of her dinner and froze. Her eyes narrowed, then flew open as she looked down at her lap. "Uh-oh."

"Uh-oh, what?" Ridge asked, worriedly.

"My water broke," Savannah said as if in shock.

"Okay, then," Kenzie said with full command in her voice and a reassuring smile on her face. "Let's get you to the clinic. Can someone call Gavin and tell him Savannah is in labor?"

"I'm supposed to go to the hospital in Charleston," Savannah said a moment before she clutched Ridge's arm and let out a shrill scream.

"Yeah, we're not going to make it to Charleston," Kenzie said with her same reassuring smile. "Okay, let's get moving. Clear a path," she ordered.

"Gavin will meet you there," Darcy said as she hung up her phone.

Savannah gripped Ridge's arm again and groaned. It was low, deep, and primal. Tristan had never been so terrified. Ridge and the rest of the men looked ready to run in fear.

"I am not having this baby in a bar!" Savannah yelled between pants.

"We can use the beer dolly," Georgie said suddenly before vaulting over the bar and running to the back of the building. A second later, she ran forward with the dolly they used to transport the kegs.

"Short little breaths," Kenzie ordered as Savannah seemed frozen in place with one hand on her stomach and the other holding a death grip on Ridge's arm.

Georgie set the dolly near Savannah, but Savannah didn't move. Her eyes were weirdly focused on something Tristan didn't see. "Granger, Kord, help me." Tristan shot up and grabbed the dolly. He moved it as close to Savannah's back as possible. "Just step back," he gently instructed Savannah.

All she did was grab her husband harder and groan.

"So, the good news is you're going to have a nice quick labor," Kenzie said to Savannah with a reassuring smile. "The bad news is we need to move you or you are going to have the baby right here in the bar."

Granger looked to Kord and nodded. He took an upper arm and Kord took the other. "On the count of three," Granger said.

Tristan got the dolly ready to move. The second Granger reached the end of his countdown, Tristan shoved the dolly forward as Granger and Kord lifted Savannah up.

"Got it," Tristan said as he tipped the dolly back while Granger and Kord held Savannah in place.

"This better not be in the paper or I'll kill whoever writes it," Savannah said between clenched teeth a second before another contraction hit.

"Go!" Kenzie yelled.

Damon was up and holding the front door open as Stone cleared a path from the table to the door. Tristan looked at Granger and Kord, and then to poor Ridge, his arm was still in his wife's iron grip. "Let's go."

It wasn't graceful, but they made it outside as the entire bar followed behind them. "It'll take longer to get her in and out of a car. Let's make a run for it," Granger said. Tristan had already figured that as he didn't so much as slow down as they jogged down the sidewalk.

Guttural noises echoed down the street, but Tristan didn't stop as two large alligators strode forward and blocked the road. Gator, Turtle, and Skeeter sprinted by Tristan to wrangle the gators.

"It's Bubba and Mean Abe trying to fight over the ladies," Gator yelled back at them. Mean Abe didn't sound good and Tristan began to slow.

But then Savannah let out her own guttural cry as another contraction gripped her. The gators froze. Both heads, with jaws full of nasty-looking teeth wide open, turned toward them. Savannah cried out again. The gators' mouths snapped shut a second before they turned and ran.

"Look at you. You're the alpha bitch," Kenzie joked, but Savannah only cried out again. "Tristan, can you run faster?"

Tristan got the nod from Kord, Ridge, and Granger and kicked up the speed. Gavin came into view at the door to the clinic as Tristan took the ramp with Savannah. Granger and Kord didn't have room so they'd let go and ran up the stairs to meet them.

"This was certainly fast," Gavin said as he moved so Kenzie could hold open the door.

"She'd been complaining of back pain for the past twelve hours. Then her water suddenly broke," Ridge said as Savannah worked on remembering to breathe.

Tristan rolled her right into the exam room.

"Now, now, now!" Savannah yelled as her legs faltered, nearly cramping.

Granger and Kord caught her and kept her from falling. Tristan wiggled the beer cart away from her and out the door.

"Let's have the baby right here," Kenzie said with the unflappable happiness of a kindergarten teacher. "Everyone out!"

As Tristan left, Kenzie was laying disposable pads on the

ground as Gavin dropped to his knees ready to deliver a baby on the floor. Ridge was sitting on the floor with his back against the exam table and his wife between his legs.

The door shut and Granger, Kord, and Tristan shared a moment of shocked silence as Savannah let out a scream.

"Push!" Gavin ordered. "That's it."

The waiting room filled with people. It didn't take long for Tristan to find Edie. "This sounds worse than war," Tristan whispered.

"It sounds wonderful," Edie said on a sigh.

The sound of a long groan followed by a second of silence and then the wail of a newborn filled the clinic. The lobby cheered. Women hugged, men shook hands, and everyone waited for the door to open.

It took fifteen minutes, but finally the door opened. Ridge walked out with a little bundle in his arms. "It's a girl," he said with a tear in his eye. "Everyone, meet Scarlett."

## 23

Edie walked hand in hand with Tristan back to her house. Scarlett was perfect. Savannah was doing great. Ridge was overwhelmed with emotion and Savannah actually had to pry Scarlett from his hands so she could feed her.

It was a happy occasion, but Edie didn't feel happy. She felt sad. Sad for the children she'd never had with Shane.

"Did you and Shane want children?" Tristan asked.

He seemed to always know what she was thinking. It was both comforting and disconcerting. "Yes, two. We were going to start trying when he got back from his mission."

"I'm sorry you didn't get that chance with him."

Edie blinked her eyes quickly to stop the tears from forming. "It's okay. Sometimes things aren't meant to be."

"I wouldn't say you're not meant to be a mother. Maybe you just weren't meant to be a mother at that time. You have plenty of time yet to become a mother, if that's what you want."

"It might not be so easy. I had a fibroid removed before my trip. My doctor warned getting pregnant may take a while."

"Then maybe we'd better get started trying."

Edie laughed. "Funny. You don't even know where you'll be living in two weeks. You have a coup to execute, a new government to install, and a country to serve. A country that is not the United States."

"Dual citizenship is a thing." Tristan was beginning to sound as if he were serious.

"Wait, are you serious?"

"Edie, I love you. I've never wanted a future with a wife and children until I saw you wrestling a baby for gelato. I'm just saying this isn't temporary. This thing between us . . . it's real and I'm in it forever, babies or not, just as long as I have you."

Damn eyes. They were threatening to water again. "It's the same for me," she admitted as they stopped in front of his house.

"Edie, are you coming?" Walker called out from the front door of her house before Layne grabbed him and yanked him inside.

"Take your time!" Layne called out before slamming the door.

Tristan put his hands on her hips and pulled her to him. Edie looked up into his eyes a moment before they closed and his lips covered hers. The kiss was slow, deep, and held all the promise of a future together. If only they could live long enough to find out if they had one together.

"Sweet dreams, Edie."


Edie closed the door behind her and was met with an impatient Walker. He hurried over to her and locked the door. Then moved a side table in front of it. "Just want to make sure the house is locked up tight before we head to bed." He yawned. It was so fake. "Layne and I are so tired. She's already gone up to bed. See you in the morning!"

Edie watched Walker run up the stairs two at a time. Eww. She didn't want to know what her brother was going to be doing very shortly. Especially when she wanted to be doing that with Tristan but had just been locked inside.

Edie climbed the stairs. Walker and Layne were definitely not sleeping. She closed the door to her room and walked to the side window where she had a view of Tristan's house. She watched as he turned off the downstairs lights and a moment later the bedroom light turned on. She couldn't see his room but saw the light spill out onto his backyard.

Edie moved to the sliding door against the back wall of her bedroom and opened it. She stepped out onto her small deck and tried to see Tristan. She placed her hands on the top of the flower trellis and leaned out to see better, but he wasn't out on his deck.

Edie looked down at the trellis. No . . . hmmm. Could she? Edie shook the trellis and it didn't move. It was bolted tightly to the house. Yes, she could, but should she?

Walker and Layne made the decision for her. She was not going to listen to *that* all night when she could be fifty feet away having her own fun with the man she loved.

Edie was about to swing her leg over when she stopped. If she were going to seduce her man, she was going to do it right. Edie hurried back inside as she yanked off her clothes. "It's got to be sexy." Edie pulled open her drawer and yanked out her bras. Huh, she never realized how many sports bras she had. No, no, no, aha! Edie held up the old satin bra only to see the underwire sticking out.

The one she was wearing was a plain cotton bra and was as boring as her life had been before Tristan entered it. So were the plain cotton panties she had. Edie stripped out of them and went back to looking through her old lingerie. It was a pitiful collection. She owned nothing sexy, only sensible pieces.

Edie looked in the mirror. Well, maybe she didn't need fancy lingerie. Men were visual creatures. Why have clothing in the way? But . . . Edie glanced out the back door. She wasn't going to climb down a trellis and up the side of Tristan's house naked.

A robe! That would be quick and easy to discard. If she were caught, she'd claim she heard a kitty and was trying to rescue it. Edie grabbed her robe and cringed. It was *cute*. It was a fluffy pink terry cloth robe with gigantic colorful flowers on it. There was nothing sexy about this robe but it was the only one she had.

Ugh. Too many issues when she just wanted to get naked with Tristan. She'd go online tomorrow and order a whole slew of sexy things.

Edie grabbed the trellis and after taking a deep breath, she swung her foot over. The purple flowers of the clematis that covered the trellis were at least soft on her bare feet as she slowly navigated her way down to the ground.

Edie dropped down and pressed herself against the side of her house. She looked around and when it was all clear, she darted to the back of Tristan's house. It was a very similar floor plan to her house except it didn't have a trellis. There was, however, a tree. A tree with a very wide branch close enough to the house that she could probably jump onto his deck without any trouble.

Edie grabbed the lowest branch and began her climb. The bark wasn't nearly as kind to her feet as her flowers had been but the closer she got to Tristan's room, the more turned on she became, until she couldn't even feel her feet.

Edie shimmied out to the edge of the branch. Okay, now she was starting to think just knocking on the front door would have been the way to go. Except that wasn't seductive. No, she was going to seduce the clothes right off of Tristan, no matter what. She closed her eyes and jumped.

Her feet hit the wooden deck and she opened her eyes only to find a gun pointed at her head.

"Edie? What the hell are you doing?" Tristan asked, lowering the gun and setting it on a table inside the door. He was clad in a towel and nothing else. His hair was wet, and rivulets of water ran down the muscles of his chest, over the ridges of his abs, and into the towel that sat low on his waist.

Edie stood up like a phoenix rising. Instead of stepping from the fire, she stepped from her robe.

Her heart beat wildly as she waited for Tristan to say something. Only he didn't. He yanked the towel from his waist and in two steps had her in his arms. Her breasts pressed against his hard chest, and while his skin may be wet, it was hot as she melded to him. Tristan's lips took hers in a kiss so hot the water probably evaporated right off him. His hands grabbed her ass and lifted her up. She wrapped her legs around his waist, never breaking their kiss. She felt his erection pressing against just the spot to drive her wild with need.

Edie speared her fingers through his hair and kissed him deeper as he carried her into his bedroom. He didn't drop her on the bed like she expected, though. He sat on the edge of the bed so that she was straddling him.

Her eyes practically rolled back in her head when Tristan rolled his hips against her. Edie clung to him as he reached for a condom. She hated to put any space between them, even if it was only for a few seconds, but then he was back. He didn't wait either. Tristan laced his arms under hers and reached up her back so his hands were holding onto her shoulders, pushing her to him. He surged into her and Edie gasped as she buried her head into his neck and held on.

Tristan collapsed back on the bed with Edie landing on top of him. Holy smokes. That had been amazing. He had just gotten out of the shower when he heard something in the tree. He thought Jean was there to kill him only to find a pink puffball jump from the tree.

When Edie dropped the robe, all thoughts fled. He had happily given over to his lust and now they were basking in its glow. "Should I put a ladder up so you can get in easier? I'll happily have you climb through my window and seduce me anytime you want."

Edie giggled and ran her hand over his chest as they caught their breath. What had gotten her in the mood? They'd been talking about babies . . . "Should I have skipped the condom?" Tristan asked.

"Huh?" Edie murmured from where she had her head resting on his shoulder.

"Did the baby talk turn you on?"

"No, the loving me regardless of having a baby or not turned me on. Talking of a future together turned me on. You turn me on."

Tristan ran his hand down her back. The feeling was mutual. Edie turned him on. She was turning him on right now in fact. "When your brother leaves, we can spend every night together. We can have morning coffee and make a tradition to go to the Friday dinner at Harper's together. I am not, however, joining the knitting club."

"Oh, Tris. Keep talking dirty to me." Edie giggled as

Tristan rolled over with her in his arms so that she was now lying on the bed and he was on top of her.

"I can even bring some of my stuff to your house if you'll give me a drawer. We can go boating together, have date nights in Charleston, and have a show we only watch together."

Damn, this was turning him on. This time he was going to take his time. He grabbed another condom and moved to his elbows so that his head was close to Edie's ear. He moved in and out of her slowly as he whispered to her all the things he wanted for their future. A future he would do anything to have.

## 24

Tristan woke to the sound of his front door being kicked open. Edie's eyes popped open and he grabbed the gun and motioned for her to hide. He had the gun aimed at the door as he used the closet wall for cover.

"Tristan! If my sister is here, I'm going to kill you."

Tristan lowered his gun as Edie's head popped up from under the bed. "Walker?"

"Edie? I'm going to kill him." The master bedroom door was flung open and Walker stormed in, armed. "What the hell do you think you're doing?"

"Are you asking her or me?" Tristan asked.

"You're naked," Walker growled.

"Again, me or her?" Tristan asked as he walked over to the bed and set his gun down before tossing a shirt to Edie, who was hunkered down with part of the sheet over her and doing her best to use the bed to cover her.

"Would you please put on some clothes," Walker yelled.

"You really need to learn to be more specific. Me or her?" Tristan asked turning to face Edie's irate brother.

"Both of you! You took advantage of my sister and I'm going to beat the shit out of you."

"Walker, I love her. I'd never hurt her," Tristan said with annoyance. Had he ever given the impression he wanted to hurt Edie?

"Would you please put on some pants and if you say 'her or me' one more time, I'm going to punch you."

Tristan grinned and walked across the room to grab a pair of shorts from the drawer as Edie finally stood up, covered in his shirt.

"Walker, how dare you?" she hissed.

"What did you expect when I woke up and you were gone?"

"I expected you to still be sleeping after the long night you had with Layne."

Walker looked blank-faced. "I don't know what you mean."

Edie rolled her eyes at him. "Walker, I hate to break it to you, brother, but you are neither subtle nor silent, *if* you know what I mean. If you'd stop this overprotective BS and let Tris stay at my house, this wouldn't happen."

"Actually, I like the idea of them staying at your house and you and me staying here," Tristan said with a bright smile, knowing he was pushing Walker's buttons a little.

"Yeah, then I wouldn't have to go looking for you when I get calls about your coup!"

"Well, why didn't you say so?" Tristan rushed to throw on a T-shirt and slide his feet into his tennis shoes. "What happened?"

"Zain called. The finger has been delivered. They bugged the house and the delivery driver, who was an undercover agent. It was Tommaso Pastor. Zain is emailing a link to the live footage."

"What are we waiting for? Let's go!" Edie raced out of the room, the T-shirt moving just enough as she hurried by for Tristan to get a glimpse of the bottom of a butt cheek.

The punch to the stomach made him look away. "Stop staring. That's my sister."

"I really hope Layne's family put you through the wringer," Tristan called out as he hurried to follow Edie.

"You have no idea," Walker grumbled.

Tristan and Walker caught up with Edie halfway across the lawn. They didn't talk as they rushed into the house where Layne was on the phone and pulling something up on her laptop.

"Finally. Here they are," Layne said.

"What took you so long?" Tristan recognized Dylan's voice.

"Walker went all crazy big brother because Edie was next door having sex with Tristan last night," Layne said as if it were no big deal.

"Sisters don't have sex," Dylan said, sounding dead serious.

"They certainly do not," Zain said, sounding like a stuffy royal.

"Then just how did Piper manage to have a baby?" Layne asked as if they were all idiots.

"Audrey was born through immaculate conception," Dylan responded about his niece. "Aiden has never laid a hand on her. I hope you punched him, Walker."

"Just a little," Walker responded.

Edie whirled around with wide eyes but Tristan just smiled at her. Walker had pulled the punch. It was worth it to have the night with Edie. Hell, he'd take a beating every day if he had to, to be with her.

"What's going on with Tommaso?" Tristan asked, getting off the topic of his sex life.

"Here, I got it pulled up," Layne said as she turned the laptop and pressed Play. Tommaso came into view. He was looking down at a laptop and speaking rapidly.

"He's talking to Annette," Tristan said, as he quickly translated the French conversation. "He's in the middle of the conversation, but he's asking her what to do with the finger. She's telling him to have it delivered to the king. No writing, just the finger attached to official Millevian stationary. She thinks they'll run the print and see it's Abby's and put two and two together and attack Millevia. When they do that, they'll have the proof to the conspiracy lies they've been spreading about Rahmi wanting to take over Millevia for her port."

Tommaso continued to talk, but everyone looked to Tristan when Tommaso said his name. "He's asking about framing me for Gastaud's murder." Tristan waited, anger coursing through him as Annette laid out her plan. "They're going to kill Emily Gastaud so no one would be left to challenge Annette for power. Emily is young, but she's much loved in Millevia. People would overthrow Annette for her. Annette says they're going to use weapons stolen from Rahmi to kill her so it'll further back up the conspiracy that Rahmi wants to take over Millevia. Annette is now saying their plans are all coming together and by Friday it'll all be over and she'll be president for life."

Tristan watched as the video call ended. Tommaso pulled on a pair of gloves before taking out a piece of stationery. He folded it and the finger together, placed it in an envelope, and grabbed his bag. He then began a wipe-down of the house, making sure to leave no fingerprints of his behind. Thirty minutes later, he was out of the house with a hat pulled low over his head, and the finger in his hand.

"He'll probably toss it over the main gate at any moment," Tristan said and then heard Zain speaking quietly in the background.

A moment later, Zain was back on the call. "He was smart. Our men are following him. He handed the envelope to a man who looked addicted to drugs. He also gave him a wad of cash and then left. They are trailing Tommaso now. The man with the finger is just sitting there while Tommaso is hightailing it to the airport."

"Where's Emily Gastaud?" Greer asked over the phone.

"In Italy. We have to warn her," Tristan said. He was one of the few people who knew where she was.

"I'll get her," Greer said. "Give me her location."

"You're in Italy?" Edie asked.

"No," Greer said but didn't say where she was.

"She and Dylan are in Millevia. They're Plan B," Tristan said before giving Greer the address Emily had provided.

"I'll get her to a secure location and give her a phone with our numbers in it," Greer told them, not addressing what Tristan just said about them being in Millevia.

"It sounds as if they'll be moving in on you next week sometime," Dylan said. "Be careful."

Today was Saturday. In six days, this could all be over with. Only then could he really begin his future with Edie. But first, kill Jean, overthrow Annette, and establish a government for his country.

Tristan's phone rang and he almost jumped with surprise. It was the burner cell with a blocked number calling him. "It's Pastor!" he yelled and the room went quiet. Walker pulled out his own phone and pressed Record.

Tristan answered on speaker. "Yes?"

"It's me. Do you have Abby Mueez?" President Pastor asked.

"Madam President," Tristan said, more for evidence than out of respect. "I do."

"Good. We've gotten new evidence, Tristan. We have proof of her spying on Millevia for Rahmi. I want to talk to her."

Layne was already moving, frantically sending a text to Abby. "Of course. Give me one moment to get to her."

Tristan walked around the house as Layne got Abby on the phone. As he walked, he tried to figure out Pastor's angle. Why would she want Abby convicted of espionage?

When Walker waved at him, Tristan walked back into the living room, making sure to flip the lock on the front door several times before opening and closing it. "Abby, I have someone who wants to talk to you."

Layne put her phone close to his and Abby played it perfectly. She was on video so she could watch Tristan for clues on how to act. "What do you want from me? Let me go, please. My baby—"

"Abby, this is President Pastor of Millevia. We have evidence of you spying on our country for Rahmi during your recent visit. The court has looked at the evidence and has found you guilty of espionage. The penalty is death. It is so ruled. Tristan, you will carry out the penalty now."

"Yes, Madam President. Would you like her shot or her throat slit?"

"Shot. First in the stomach so she sees her baby die and then in the head."

Abby began to beg for her life as Tristan rushed to the closet, pulled his gun and gave Abby a nod. She screamed, and he fired the first shot into the floor of the closet. The echo of the closet made it seem more realistic of the holding cell Abby was supposedly in. She screamed. This time it was filled with pain, and then Tris fired the second shot. Abby instantly fell silent. The look on her face spoke enough that words weren't needed. Tristan had never seen a look like that. It was the look of living nightmares.

"Would you like me to come home now, ma'am?" Tristan asked.

"Not yet. I have another assignment for you, but it's not ready yet."

"What is it?" Tristan asked, knowing the assignment was for him to die.

"The Rahmi royal family in the United States holds a lot of sway. If they don't cave to our demands, I need you to make a statement for me."

"What kind of statement, ma'am?"

"A big one. But wait for my order. It'll be many days yet until I'll need you to move. Until then, consider yourself having some time off. Just be ready for my call when it comes. Good work, Durand."

The line went dead and no one said a word until Tristan hung up the phone.

"I'm going to kill her," Dylan said into the silence. "I'm going to kill her slowly. Ripping her limb from fucking limb."

Tristan looked down and saw two people standing behind Abby. One was Ahmed. The other was a beautiful woman who had Abby's eyes. Her mother. Jesus. Abby's parents shouldn't have had to hear that.

Ahmed pulled out his phone. "Mo, I need your jet. Guys' trip to Millevia."

Then he spun around and stalked from the video. No one spoke, but it wasn't the look on Ahmed's face that had scared him. It was his wife's face that had made Tristan's blood turn cold.

"I'm sorry to put you through that, Abby," Tristan said. "But thank you for your help." Abby nodded and hung up.

Tears ran down Layne's face. Edie's face was so pale that Tristan was worried she'd pass out. The cursing going on from Dylan and Zain said all Tristan felt. Pastor was out of control, but she'd be dealt with. One way or another.

"I'm sorry I brought her into your lives. I'm sorry I brought this trouble to your doorstep," Tristan said as humbly as he could. He was ruining innocent lives and he couldn't do it. No matter how much he loved Edie. He couldn't put her in danger. He couldn't put any of these people in danger. Sure, they busted his balls, but they were honest about it. Even while they did it, there was respect and kindness behind it. They weren't doing it just to be dicks—they were doing it to protect Edie and to make sure Tristan was worthy of her. Right now, he felt anything but worthy.

"I'm going to leave. I can't put you all in any more danger. Pastor is unhinged. I don't want her hurting any of you. If she finds out you've helped me, she'll have you killed." Tristan turned to leave the room, but Walker stopped him.

"You're not leaving, Assassin Boy. You didn't bring this on us. Well, okay, maybe on Edie, but you saved Abby and did the right thing by refusing a direct order. You saved Abby's life. Would Jean have killed her?"

Tristan nodded. "Without hesitation."

"But you didn't. You warned them. That was honorable, Tristan. And as an honorable man you wouldn't turn your back and leave the woman you love heartbroken."

Tristan looked at Walker and almost smiled. "Are you saying you'll kick my ass if I leave Edie?"

"For some reason, my sister loves you. And, well, you're not horrible."

"Does this mean you're done busting my balls?"

"Never," Walker said instantly. "That's my right as her brother. But I'll stand by you and defend you while I do it."

"I can live with that."

Edie's face regained some color as she ran into his arms and buried her face in his chest. The others began talking and it was decided that the Keeneston contingent would come down on Monday to help Tristan with whatever Pastor was sending his way. Layne's cousins would be arriving while Ahmed and Layne's father and uncles were flying to Millevia.

"Don't leave me, Tris," Edie whispered. "I don't know if I could survive it if something happened to you."

Tristan kissed the top of her head. He wouldn't leave her. He never wanted to be away from her again. He was a man in love, and a man in love had something to live for. Pastor had better send an army because nothing was going to keep him from a future with Edie.

## 25

There had been a shift that day. Edie lay in Tristan's bed after they'd made love. Walker and Tris had seemed almost brotherly today. Her brother still gave Tris crap, but they were laughing and ribbing each other now.

Layne had noticed it too. Then, rather awkwardly after dinner together, Walker had said he'd see them both tomorrow. It had been decided she'd have tonight and tomorrow to spend with Tris alone. But come Monday, everyone was going to be buckling down and preparing for battle. That gave her tonight and tomorrow to pretend everything was going to be fine. To pretend their future wasn't riding on a group of assassins.

"I can feel you thinking," Tristan whispered into the dark as he absently stroked her hair.

"I don't want Monday to come. I want to pretend we have this great future laid out in front of us."

"We do have a great future," Tristan said. "Why would you think we didn't?"

"A group of assassins are on their way to take you out, you have to overthrow Pastor, and then what? We haven't discussed the reality of our situation. Do we stay in Shadows Landing? Is your duty to Millevia's new leader? Are we a 'we' or does real life take over and we go in separate directions?" Edie finally admitted what she'd been worrying about. She wanted a future with him so badly, but she didn't know if they could have one. Deep down she knew the real reason. She couldn't survive Tris going out on a mission and not coming back, but she also couldn't ask him to give up his career.

Tristan continued gently running his hand over her hair and down her back. It was soothing as he began to talk. "Do you know how I see our future?"

"How?" Edie asked as she snuggled into him a little more, hoping the closer she was to him, he'd take her fear away.

"I kill Jean and dispense with the threat to take me out. We overthrow Pastor and help set up the new government. Then we live in Shadows Landing, but vacation in Millevia every year. We also vacation in Keeneston so I can see Carolina again and try out that military training facility Walker was telling me about because that sounds seriously cool. We get married, have as many children as you want, and live the rest of our lives together."

Edie felt like crying. Tristan had just laid out her dream. But that's what it was: a dream. Edie stopped herself. No. It might be a dream now, but when did she give up on dreams? Probably when Shane had died, but no longer. Her spirit, heart, and body had broken when Shane was killed, but she'd picked herself back up, slowly putting herself together piece by piece. She now had a dream and it was within her grasp, she just had to fight for it. If there was one thing a woman raised in Shadows Landing knew how to do, it was fight.

"Tomorrow evening you're on your own after dinner for a bit. I have a class at church I need to go to."

"Women's Bible study?" Tristan asked.

"Something like that," Edie said as her hand itched to get a weapon in it. She'd lost one husband, she wasn't going to lose another, that was for damned sure.

"Edie's been strange all day," Tristan whispered to Walker. "Have you noticed that?"

"You didn't piss her off, did you?" Walker whispered back as they watched their women trotting down the stairs in athletic clothes. Both were in those tight running pants that made their butts look great. Layne had on a Keeneston High School T-shirt and Edie wore a Coast Guard T-shirt. Layne also wore an excited smile, but the look on Edie's face could only be described as determined.

"We're off to the church. See you in a couple of hours," Edie said, finally looking up after grabbing a large duffle bag. "You guys okay here?"

Walker looked amused. Tristan felt slightly insulted that she didn't think he could be on his own for two hours. "Yeah, we're good," he answered as he gave her a look, letting her know he was worried about her.

"I've invited the guys over. We're going to play some poker. Have fun, babe," Walker said to Layne as he stood to give her a kiss goodbye.

Edie was already out the door or Tris would have done the same.

"See, strange. Right?" Tris asked as soon as the front door closed.

"Yeah, even I saw that."

Tristan didn't have time to ask anything further as the front door opened and Granger, Kord, Ryker, Trent, Dare, Paxton, and Wade walked in. Each carried either a plate of food or a case of beer. Let guys' night commence.

Chaos quickly ensued, but within minutes the dining room table was cleared, cards were out, and a buffet of food and beer were laid out.

"So, tomorrow is the start of lockdown, huh?" Granger asked as he shuffled the cards.

"Pastor said Friday was the day it would all be over, so we think they'll come after me Thursday night," Tristan told them as they waited for the cards to be dealt.

"What do you need us to do?" Wade asked. "I already have the ports and marinas on the lookout for any boats with either Millevian registration or passengers."

"Yeah, I'll have a friend tracking flights leaving Millevia as well," Ryker told them as he looked at his cards.

"The FBI will be on the lookout as well," Paxton said before frowning and looking up at Wade in disgust. "What kind of hammered horseshit deal was this?"

Wade chuckled and smiled. He obviously didn't think it was a bad deal.

"ATF too," Dare said, looking a little sheepish. "And the knitting club."

"Heck, the knitting club will probably have better info than the FBI," Kord teased.

Paxton shrugged. "It's true. I can't argue that."

"I think the better conversation would be about what the heck happened between Granger and Olivia the other night. The whole men vs. women thing was very . . . interesting," Trent smirked and Kord hid a smile behind his cards as Granger frowned.

"There's nothing going on. Never has been, never will be," Granger said. "Where's Gavin?"

"Tinsley said she'd watch baby Chase so he took Ellery out for date night," Paxton answered.

"And Ridge won't leave Savannah and Scarlett's side," Trent said before looking down at his phone. He held it up for everyone to see. "This is the thirty-second photo of Scarlett he sent me today."

"Did he send you the picture of the first poopy diaper?" Wade asked with a grimace. "I promise, y'all, I won't send you diaper pictures when little Wade is born."

"You'll be just as obsessed as Ridge," Dare said with a shake of his head. "You know it."

"I won't be nearly as bad as Ryker," Wade answered with a shrug. "I mean, he can't go ten minutes without mentioning 'my wife.' He'll be a blubbering mess when he has a child."

Ryker narrowed his eyes and glared at Wade, who only winked at him in return.

"Yes, because you never talk about your wife," Kord shot back to Wade.

"Guilty. I'm a man in love," Wade said, dramatically putting his hands over his heart. "Just like Granger. Only I was brave enough to go after the girl. He insulted his."

"It's not an insult if it's true," Granger muttered as he tossed another chip on the pile.

"When have you asked Olivia out?" Ryker asked, his tone neutral.

"What?" Granger didn't know where Ryker was going with his seemingly casual question.

"When have you asked her out?" Ryker repeated.

"I haven't. Why would I? I'm obviously not the type of

man she dates." Granger shrugged and tossed down his cards. "Pair of kings and a pair of sixes."

Everyone groaned as Granger scooped up the chips.

"Then everything you accused her of is false," Ryker calmly said, throwing the gauntlet down along with his chips for the next hand.

"What?" Granger snapped.

Tristan tried not to laugh when Ryker rolled his eyes. "You've never given Olivia the chance to date someone like you, so you can't say you're not her type. Therefore, your generalization of her and her dating habits is unfounded. Ergo, you're wrong." Ryker tossed chips on the table, then looked Granger in the eyes as if challenging him.

"She's not going to date a mere sheriff. A scarred one at that," Granger grumbled.

Tristan frowned. Scarred? He looked at the others but none of them seemed surprised by that.

"Darcy would beat your ass if she heard you talk like that," Wade said, putting two cards on the table.

Granger tossed him two more but didn't say anything else.

"She didn't grow up rich, you know. Damon never went to college because there wasn't money to send him. Stone didn't either. He went straight from high school to the minors, then turned pro a year later. Olivia only made it through college and then law school on scholarships. So, you know that whole average-Joe argument you made?" Ryker asked, but he didn't wait for Granger to answer. "Total bullshit."

"Damon reminds me of you," Wade said out of the blue.

Ryker frowned. "I don't know whether I should punch you or thank you."

"Yeah, I got nothing on the Townsend brothers. They are

a secretive bunch. I didn't even know Stone played hockey until I saw the trade in the paper," Kord admitted, taking the subject away from Granger and Olivia. "I can't even figure out how many there are. Damon, Stone, Kane—" Kord said, holding up three fingers.

"Isn't there a Hunter?" Dare asked.

"Yeah, and I heard them mention 'others' but never heard their names," Paxton added.

Tristan sat back as the conversation moved from the Townsend brothers to stupid things they did growing up with brothers or friends who were like brothers, to asking Tristan about growing up in Millevia with David.

Overall, it was just the kind of night he needed.

## 26

Edie grunted as she ran the saber through a straw dummy with enough force to rip it from its hanger. Lydia stopped fencing with a very amused Layne and stared.

"Miss E, is something wrong?" Lacy asked from where she was practicing with her own saber. Lacy had a gift. You started out with the smaller weapons like daggers and moved up to the larger ones as you mastered each weapon. At twelve, Lacy was already nearly as good as Edie.

"Just getting ready to protect what's mine." Edie wiped the sweat from her brow and looked around the packed room.

On their tenth birthday, the girls of Shadows Landing were allowed to begin taking weapons class. It had been that way for centuries. The practice began when the pirates who founded the town had to leave to do their plundering. They taught their wives and daughters to defend the town while they were away. The practice continued today.

Edie had begun when she was ten and only stopped when she left Shadows Landing at eighteen. When she returned three years ago, she immediately came back to class. And when Layne came to visit, she enthusiastically took the class as well.

All across the room, women aged twelve to eighty were throwing knives, fencing, battling with boarding pikes, and shooting crossbows. In the center of it all was Reverend Winston. His father had been the pastor there before him and his grandfather before that.

If you looked at Reverend Winston, you would see he was born for the job. He held himself in a quietly commanding way that told you he might be a man of the cloth but he'd protect his flock. He was in his mid-forties and was normally cool as a cucumber. But tonight, sweat glistened across his brow and his normally styled coils were natural and a couple were stuck to his forehead as he and Tinsley battled each other with their cutlasses. Skye Jessamine, the actress married to Trent Faulkner, was working with Miss Winnie on how to better handle her small dagger. On the far side, waitresses from The Pink Pig and the competing BBQ restaurant, Lowcountry Bistro, were going at it with hatchets. The church also had an armory of old guns, but their aim could be a bit tricky so only an elite group of the women practiced with them before church on Sundays.

"I tried to protect my video game once and threatened Landry with my dagger, but Mom told me I wasn't allowed to do that. What are you trying to protect, Miss E?" Lacy asked.

Edie hung the dummy back up and took a deep breath as she turned to Lacy. "You know Mr. Tristan? Someone wants to hurt him, and I'm not going to allow it."

Lacy nodded with understanding. "My siblings might get on my nerves, but I'd do the same if someone tried to hurt them. I like Mr. Tristan. He's funny. You should have seen how worried he got when Landry and I rode Bubba and Bertha. It's like he's never seen alligator-surfing before."

Edie smiled and felt a little of the tension melt from her shoulders. Sometimes you just needed to see the world through the eyes of a twelve-year-old. "Don't tell Mr. Tristan, but Walker and I used to do that too," Edie said with a wink.

Tristan tossed his cards on the table. "I fold." Granger was kicking their butts. Apparently teasing him about Olivia was not the way to throw him off his game. "Who wants another beer?"

Tristan stood up and counted the hands that were raised. He needed to get another six-pack and headed into the kitchen. He pulled a pack from the fridge and set it on the counter so he could grab another bag of chips. His hand was in the cabinet when a movement out the window caught his attention.

A person in head-to-toe black was crouched and racing across the back lawn with a military grade rifle in hand. Tristan didn't have time to yell for the guys as the man leaped up the stairs and into the screened-in porch.

Tristan dropped the chips and had his gun in hand as he ducked down behind the countertop. He had a straight shot to the back door as the door handle jiggled. Although it was locked, but it wasn't long until the person jimmied the door open and rolled inside.

Tristan moved quickly and had his gun pressed to the man's head before he could even stand up.

"I'm David!" the man said quickly as he raised his hands in surrender.

Tristan lowered his gun as soon as he heard his best friend's voice. "David? What the hell are you doing here?"

"You have three minutes tops. They took my phone so I couldn't contact you. They're here to kill you." David ripped his mask off and Tristan saw the worry in his eyes. "I broke ranks as they were coming through the woods to warn you."

"Come on," Tristan ordered, already running toward the dining room. "Pastor made her move!"

Tristan slid to a stop facing the roomful of men who looked up with surprise. Suddenly Walker, Granger, Kord, Dare, and Paxton had an alarming number of weapons in their hands and pointed at him.

Tristan saw then that David was behind him with his hands back up. "This is David," Tristan said quickly. "He came to warn us. Less than three minutes until Pastor's men attack."

Kord shoved away from the table. "I've got guns in the car."

"Go, I'll cover you." Granger and Kord ran from the room as Walker raced around drawing curtains and checking locks. He came back in the room wearing a windbreaker and Tristan wondered why he'd put on a jacket.

"Here! I saw at least ten men in the distance closing in from all directions out front. I kept it cool, though, and called out that I was getting more beer," Kord said as he tossed a large duffle bag on the table.

Granger unzipped it and he and Kord put on their bulletproof vests with SHERIFF emblazoned on the back before handing out a weapon to everyone and an extra vest to Trent.

"We need to barricade the doors," Walker said at the same time Tristan did.

Walker grimaced, but then backed down. "Tristan's in charge."

Tristan gave him a nod before turning to David. "Rundown?"

"Main team of eighteen ranging from our teams down to regular soldiers. A second team of ten soldiers who will hang outside of town and provide backup if needed. Pastor appointed Jean point. They are to surround and then storm."

"Night vision?" Tristan asked.

"Yes."

"Turn off the lights and the second they breach, turn them on. It'll buy you a second to take them out if they actually breach. Move the kitchen table so its side faces the door. Same with the couch. Use them for cover if they breach the house," Tristan ordered. These men weren't his team, but they seemed to move as a well-trained unit nonetheless.

"I've sent a text to the town, including Edie," Ryker said, putting on a windbreaker that matched Walker's.

"I don't think a jacket will help right now," Tristan said as he shoved a knife into his pocket and loaded up on ammo.

"It's bulletproof. My cousin invented it using nanotech." Ryker didn't seem as worried about assassins as Tristan thought he would, which made his job easier.

"Here," Dare said, tossing a bulletproof vest to him. ATF was on the back and front of it.

"Where did this come from?" Tristan asked as he saw Paxton fastening an FBI vest and handing a spare to Wade.

"We figured we'd need it sooner or later. It was under the chips in the bag I brought in." Dare grinned as he checked his gun. "Let's do this. And someone watch Wade. Coasties aren't used to shootouts."

Wade flipped him the bird before getting to work

moving a dining hutch with David to cover the window in the dining room.

"Tristan Durand!" Tris froze as Jean's voice boomed out. "I want to let you know I'm going to kill the woman you turned traitor for. You have two options. Come out and I'll kill you both quickly. Or stay in there and we'll torture her first. You make up your mind while I go say hi to your woman. Maybe she'll prefer a real man to a traitor."

David cursed and even though no one else spoke the language, they all guessed his meaning.

"He's going to kill Edie. If I surrender, he'll kill us both quickly. If not . . ." Tristan didn't need to finish. They all knew what the threat was.

Anger unlike anything Tristan had ever felt filled him. If they so much as looked at Edie, he would kill them. "I have to get to her before Jean does."

"And I have to get to Layne," Walker said immediately after.

Tristan and Walker shared a look. They didn't need words. They were completely in sync.

"I guess we know your answer," Jean shouted with a laugh. "One thing I didn't tell David—the backup team wasn't for backup. They were to capture your woman. They've surrounded the church already. No prayer will save her from me, Tristan."

"We got this. Go protect the women as soon as you see an opening. It's not just Edie and Layne there," Granger said with hard determination. "Lydia, her daughter, Miss Ruby, Miss Winnie—they're all there. I'm warning them. They'll be ready."

"Move the hutch," Tristan ordered. "They'll come in stronger from the front and back. Walker, go out the side as soon as you can."

Walker nodded and moved into position as David and Wade moved the hutch out of the way.

"What about you?" Kord asked.

"Granger is in charge after I leave. David, stay and help. I'm going right out the front." Tristan wasn't aware of time. He didn't feel anger anymore. Instead, his body was a machine as he climbed onto the side table by one of the front windows. He didn't bother trying to open it. The glass was going to break anyway. He rested the rifle's muzzle on the window casement. He hid out of sight to the side of the window as much as possible.

"Is everyone ready?" Tristan asked.

"Let's do this," Walker said and then it was on.

With cool efficiency Tristan fired until he ran out of bullets. He'd taken out six men and pushed others back enough for him to make his move.

He jumped off the table as the rest of his team began picking off those they could see. Tristan threw open the front door and stalked out as the back door crashed in. Windows broke upstairs and he heard soldiers racing toward the stairs. His team was shouting inside as Tristan let his rage loose on the unfortunate soldiers still out front.

## 27

Maggie Bell was helping Miss Mitzy with sighting the crossbow when Lacy's phone went off. Edie was sparring Lydia in hand-to-hand combat when Lydia rolled her eyes and stopped the fight.

"Lacy, how many times have I told you to turn off your phone while we're in class." Lydia placed her hands on her hips as her tween daughter rolled her eyes and raced to turn off her phone, which was now ringing. "Sorry," Lydia said to Edie. "Ready?"

Edie held up her hands, but Lacy gasped.

"What now?" Lydia asked her daughter. "I don't care who is 'shipped' with who or any of that other middle school dating crap. Get back to training."

"Mr. Tristan is under attack!" Lacy cried out. "And bad guys are coming here to kill Miss Edie!"

So many emotions ran through Edie that she didn't know what to do first. She wanted to run to Tristan to protect him, but then people were coming here to kill her.

Reverend Winston appeared in front of her. He took her hands in his and made her look him in the eyes. "We are ready to defend you and the town. You are well trained for this. Let your instincts and training take over."

Edie nodded and ripped the gloves from her hands as Lydia tossed her and Lacy their sabers.

"Ladies," Reverend Winston said, his voice demanding their full attention. "Let's show them what the women of Shadows Landing are made of—not only sugar and spice and everything nice, but of steel and iron, and no prisoners left alive."

Maggie Bell was an Olympic shooter and one of the few women trained on the muskets. She grabbed several from the armory as other women grabbed blunderbusses along with their cutlasses, sabers, daggers, boarding pikes, and hatchets.

"Ladies, to the pews and altar. Take your positions. We've practiced this," Reverend Winston called out.

"Should we bar the door?" Miss Winnie asked.

"No, they'll know something is up then," Reverend Winston answered calmly. "We'll lure them in and then ambush them. Edie, you and I are to sit halfway down the pews looking as if we're in prayer. Those able, under the pews both sides of the aisle behind and in front of Edie and me. Those who can't make it under, hide behind the altar or in the cloakroom by the entrance. When Maggie fires her first shot, everyone close-in for the ambush."

"Yes, Reverend!"

Edie watched as everyone went scattering into positions. "Lydia," Edie said, grabbing her friend. "You and Lacy need to get out of here."

Lydia looked at Edie as if she were crazy. "Are you kidding? I haven't had sex in seven months. I need this, badly. Plus, if I don't kill one of these guys, I might kill Lacy. Do you have any idea what kind of sass I put up with from a tween? This will be a very good bonding experience for us. Blood will be shed, but it won't be from a mother-daughter fight!"

"Come," Reverend Winston said calmly as he led Edie down the aisle, "let's talk about how you are doing while we wait. I imagine this must be very difficult for you after Shane."

Edie sat numbly down in the pew as Reverend Winston slid in next to her. "I can't lose another man I love."

Reverend Winston calmly slid a dagger up his sleeve before patting her hand. "And you won't."

Edie jumped when she felt a sudden breeze tickle the nape of her neck. Reverend Winston's hand squeezed hers, stopping her from turning. "Let us reflect on our teachings, my dear," Reverend Winston said in a calm voice that seemed to echo through the church.

Edie heard the boots filling the church and only turned to look up when Reverend Winston stood to face the army now filling his church. "Gentleman, please put your weapons down. A church is no place for violence."

"Excuse me, Father," the leader said in very French-accented English.

"Reverend."

"Reverend then. We will leave immediately as soon as Mrs. Wecker comes with us." The man was covered from head to toe in black. Black bulletproof vest, black cargo pants, black utility belt, and black helmet with black face paint.

"Me?" Edie asked, standing slowly to keep the saber concealed slightly behind her. "Why? Who are you?"

"Jean Moreau. You have been found guilty of espionage and treason. You are being detained on behalf of the country of Millevia. You are coming with us." Jean motioned for one of his men to grab her. Edie was about to make her move when the click of a musket hammer falling was the only warning they got before the near-deafening shot. The thick ball slammed into the man's face, sending blood spraying.

Edie was momentarily surprised, but then all chaos erupted. Battle cries that would've made their pirate ancestors proud rang through the church as women rolled out from under the pews, stepped from behind the altar, and closed in on them from the entrance of the church.

Jean reached for his gun, but Reverend Winston moved first. In a flash, he'd planted his dagger in Jean's arm, causing the man to drop his weapon, which Reverend Winston kicked under the pew. Jean leaped back as Edie bounded onto the pew with her saber raised, ready to attack.

Jean shouted in French and his men were no longer stunned.

"For Shadows Landing!" Reverend Winston shouted, and the fight was on.

Shadows Landing might not have believed Tristan was a deadly assassin before, but they would now. Tristan shot the first soldier in the head. The second grabbed him from behind, knocking his gun to the ground. Tristan felt the man's arm try for a chokehold, but he was well trained. He evaded the hold and grabbed his knife. Tristan cocked his head to the side, reached behind him, and stabbed the man through the neck. The third man raised a gun to Tristan's head but should have fired instantly. The slight hesitation allowed Tristan to knock the gun from his hand and after a few rapid punches and blocks, Tristan saw his opening and slashed the man's throat.

Tristan shot, slashed, and fought his way through the men out front of Edie's house. His mind was blank, his rage was loose, and nothing was going to stop him from getting to Edie before Jean could hurt her.

"Thanks for clearing a path," Granger said, running to catch up with him.

They turned the corner of the house to find Walker wiping blood from his knife. "If we cut through the woods and backyards, we can come out across the street from the church." Walker didn't wait for a discussion. He just took off with Granger and Tristan running to catch up.

They ran in silence through backyards, jumping fences and navigating through woods until they reached the back of Wade and Darcy's treasure museum. The three plastered themselves against the side of the building, keeping to the shadows as they edged closer to the sidewalk.

Tristan could finally see the church. Dread filled him as he saw the front door open. Then a resounding boom went off and he pressed back against the wall. "What the hell was that?"

"Musket fire. I bet Maggie is up in the choir loft, picking off men," Granger said as if it were no surprise.

Then confusion set in as the sound of women screaming echoed out the door. They weren't screams of fear, though. They were battle cries. Down the street the deep growl of an engine roared up the street as headlights came into view.

"That's Gator and his crew. They must have gotten the text. If you don't want them running in first, we'd better get going." Granger stepped out to take the lead and Tristan instantly fell into position by his side.

The trio raced across the street and peeled off to climb

the dual staircases to the church. Walker took the left and Granger and Tristan took the right.

"I'll go in first and take the right side," Granger whispered as the sound of fighting only grew louder. "Walker, take the left. Tristan, go up the middle."

Reverend Winston strode out to the middle of the aisle issuing commands like a pirate captain of old. Edie knew where she was going. Straight to Jean.

"Where's Tristan?" Edie yelled, with her saber at the ready.

"Dead!" Jean's lips lifted into a little smirk as if expecting the bad news to drop her to the ground in grief. From experience, Edie knew the grief would come, but first there was anger.

Edie roared and lunged forward. Jean was fast on his feet as he sidestepped and began walking backward slowly toward the altar. "Is Pastor worth it? You know she killed Gastaud, and she'll turn your country into a dictatorship. Is your freedom worth it?"

"That's the thing about dictatorships, not everyone loses their freedom. Only the lower classes do. If you're valuable enough, you become a lord over your own fiefdom. I'm too skilled a killer for Pastor to reduce me to mere citizenship, to be herded and cowed into submission. I'll lead her armies, put down the rebellions, and bask in the wealth of it." Jean held out his arms as if he were a god.

From the corner of Edie's eye, she saw Lacy walk up to a man who was holding several women hostage with his rifle. Edie was torn between racing to save her and killing Jean, but Lacy took the decision from Edie. Tears leaked down her face. Her lower lip trembled as she reached up to gently tapped him on the arm. "Have you seen my mommy?"

The man turned to Lacy, not knowing how to handle a crying twelve-year-old girl. Lacy smiled brightly. "Oh! There she is!"

Lydia rolled out from under a pew across the aisle and sprang to her feet. She lifted her cutlass and clobbered the man over the head with its pommel. The man staggered and turned around only for Lydia to ram the elaborate metal guard into his face, sending him to the ground where Miss Mitzy stepped on him and pointed a crossbow at his face.

Edie shouldn't have worried as Lydia high-fived her daughter. Instead, she turned all her attention back to Jean. "It won't matter, Jean. You've already lost and you don't even know it. Let me ask you something. Did you see Tristan die?"

Jean paused, but then puffed his chest back up. "Doesn't matter if I did or didn't. I sent eighteen men after him. Tristan is good, but he's not that good."

Hope sparked to life inside her and she smiled. There was something Jean didn't know—Tristan wasn't alone. "You know, Tristan wasn't alone."

Jean shrugged as he paused in the aisle. "I saw one man in jeans and a T-shirt. I'm not worried."

Fighting was all around them. Every minute or so, Maggie took down another man with her musket as Layne cursed about wanting a spoon. Groups of women teamed up on the men who had not expected to be asked to kill senior citizens, women, or children. A group of women had the captives in a huddle, guarding them with a combination of blunderbusses, boarding pikes, and the men's own guns they'd confiscated from the soldiers.

Of course, there were a couple who had to dive for cover

as the men tried to shoot, but they were usually Maggie's next target.

Edie was growing impatient. She would advance, Jean would retreat. She couldn't get close enough to him to make a move. He was quick, and worse, she knew she only had one chance to take him down. She was good in her own way, but she wasn't a trained assassin.

"We'll have to agree to disagree," Edie said with a smirk, mocking Jean's confidence in Tristan's death.

A sound by the front door drew Jean's attention away from her and that was all Edie needed. It was her opening and she went for him. She lunged ahead, thrusting her saber forward and sinking it into Jean's shoulder.

Tristan charged into the church and had to admit that he hesitated. He hadn't expected to see Miss Mitzy in a giant cat face T-shirt over athletic shorts with her foot on a soldier's chest and an ancient crossbow holding him hostage.

He also hadn't expected to see Lydia and her daughter wielding swords, Layne bringing a man down with a chokehold, Reverend Winston issuing orders like a field general, and women battling trained soldiers with hatchets, blunderbusses, and boarding pikes.

That split second of surprise was all Tristan needed to assess the situation. The women of Shadows Landing were beating the absolute crap out of Millevia's soldiers. And there, two-thirds of the way down the aisle were Jean and Edie. Her back was to Tristan and she held a saber confidently in her hand. Jean's eyes glanced behind her and saw Tristan. The moment of surprise at finding Tristan alive was all Edie needed. She lunged forward and the saber cut through his clothing, through muscle, and into his shoulder.

Jean howled as Edie twisted the sword hard before yanking it out, readying herself to stab him again. Only she didn't get the chance. Jean charged forward just as Edie pulled the sword out. Edie stepped back in surprise, trying to evade Jean.

Tristan plowed through the fighting, over the captives, and shoved past Reverend Winston as Jean's hands reached Edie's throat and the two of them crashed to the floor. Tristan's focus zeroed in on Edie as she fought with everything she had against Jean. Tristan didn't see Walker and Granger shooting a few remaining soldiers still battling with the women of Shadows Landing. He didn't see Gator picking up a soldier and tossing him over four rows of pews. He didn't see the hunting knife Turtle used to pin a man to the pew by the neck. And he didn't see Skeeter, in his oversized baggy clothes, throwing a knife across the aisle and into the arm of a man who was holding a gun to the diner waitress's head.

Instead, all Tristan saw was Edie throwing an elbow into Jean's nose, wriggling, twisting, and kicking beneath him as he fought to choke her. A breeze whipped through the church, a shiver ran down his spine, but not with fear. Be it God, a ghost, or karma coming for Jean, Tristan was filled with power and determination as he slammed into Jean's side, ripping him off Edie.

They rolled across the floor, Tristan's head collided with a pew, but it wasn't enough to distract him.

"Hello, Jean. Miss me?" Tristan asked as he clenched his fist and slammed it into Jean's face.

"I'm thrilled to see you so that I can kill you with my

bare hands." Jean scrambled to his feet as Tristan did the same.

The church was quiet, no one moved around them as Reverend Winston helped Edie up, and they scrambled out of the way of the fight. Tactical knives were pulled as they circled each other slowly looking for a weakness. Tristan didn't bother talking. Jean tried to taunt him with threats of what he was going to do to Tristan and Edie, but he didn't even hear them. It was a strange dance of slow circling, then rapid slashing, followed by retreating back to their circling of each other.

Tristan saw a movement behind Jean and fought not to show a reaction. Lacy was crawling out from a pew into the aisle behind Jean. Tristan stopped circling to protect Lacy from being seen because he knew Jean would use her as a shield for his escape. Tristan's breathing was harsh but controlled as he faced Jean head on.

"Why are you doing this, Jean?" Tristan asked, focusing Jean's attention on him. "What did Pastor promise you?"

"General of her new national army. I will be in charge of keeping the citizens in line. I'll get any house in Millevia I want, along with a fortune to keep people from challenging her rule. Plus, I get the pleasure of killing not only you, but the one woman you fell for. Does she know?" Jean asked mockingly.

"Know what?" Tristan asked as Lacy came to a stop on her hands and knees directly behind Jean.

"That you killed her friend, Abby."

Tristan smiled, knowing that victory was his as Lacy motioned with her hand for Tristan to come toward her. It was a childish prank, but it could work.

"Abby? She's not dead. She's alive and well. She was just up for a bit of fun. A little paint, a fake video call, and suddenly everyone thinks she's dead. Instead, I've earned Rahmi's eternal favor for protecting both Abby and Princess Ariana."

Tristan saw the moment Jean paused to process the truth of the deception. Tristan took advantage and leaped forward on attack. Jean stepped back to avoid the slice of Tristan's knife. Only, Jean's legs hit Lacy, his arms pinwheeled, and almost in slow motion, he fell backward over her.

Lydia grabbed her daughter's arms and yanked her free of Jean's legs as Walker and Granger sprang up from either side of the aisle, their guns aimed at Jean's head.

"Hello. We haven't been introduced. I'm Edie's brother." Walker's expression was menacing as Layne and Edie joined them and they all stared down at Jean.

Jean glanced around, seeing Kord, Dare, Paxton, Trent, and most of Shadows Landing filling the church. Even the sweet bartender, Georgie, stood with a paring knife in one hand and a zester in the other. Gage Bell and his parents were armed with shotguns, but most surprisingly was Kenzie, who stood off to the side of the crowd with a big freaking alligator next to her.

"I'm sorry, Jean. I don't think you're going to get that mansion you wanted. Tell me, how does it feel to be taken down by a twelve-year-old girl?" Tristan asked with a smile as he high-fived Lacy.

"I think we need to become better acquainted," Walker said with a smile now.

"I want asylum," Jean said desperately. "My life is in danger if I go back to Millevia. I can talk. I know all of Pastor's plans."

Tristan put his arm around Edie. There was no way he was letting Jean live. He was pretty sure it would be a nice brotherly bonding time with Walker if they killed him together.

"Excuse me," Layne said, coming up to Tristan with her phone. "Zain wants a word."

Tristan took the phone from Layne and held it to his ear. "Yes, Your Highness." he added the last part for Jean and was rewarded when Jean's eyes widened in surprise. "Of course. It would be my honor." Tristan paused as Zain continued to talk. "That's very kind of you and I will gladly take you and Rahmi up on that. I'll call you when it's done."

Tristan handed the phone back to Layne and looked at Walker and grinned slowly. "I've just been sworn in as a Rahmi diplomat. How would you like to escort our prisoners to Washington, D.C., where they will be interrogated by United States and Rahmi officials?"

"I would like that. I assume Jean doesn't have to arrive in D.C. unharmed?" Walker asked.

"That arm was already broken," Tristan said blandly as Granger hauled Jean to his feet and slapped cuffs on him. "We could use an assist from local law enforcement too."

"This is like our guys' trip to Atlanta," Paxton was positively gleeful as he, Dare, and Harper slid a long chain through the cuffs connecting all the prisoners together.

"A plane will be waiting for us at the airbase." Tristan turned to Edie and anger flared back to life at the red marks on her neck. "I'm sorry I have to leave. I will be back though. I promise."

There was so much more to say, but now wasn't the time. He had to see this through. Only then could he move forward with Edie. Their happily-ever-after was in sight. There was just one more thing to deal with: Pastor.

## 28

Edie reached up and cupped Tristan's cheek with her hand. She saw the determination in his eyes and recognized it. Shane always had the same look before a mission. It was the need to see a job through—to protect those who couldn't protect themselves.

"I'll be waiting right here for you." Edie rose onto her toes. Her lips brushed his and then his arms were around her.

"You were amazing tonight. I about died when I saw you armed with a saber. This is one very strange Bible study."

Edie chuckled and when she pulled back they were both smiling. "I'll let the guys tell you about our ladies' group on the plane." She reached out and took his hand in hers and gave it a little squeeze. "I love you, Tristan. Please be safe."

"Nothing can keep me from coming back to you. I love you, Edie." Tristan kissed her again and this time it wasn't soft or sweet. It was hard and hot, but over way too fast. "Let's go!"

Tristan worked with the town to round up the men from both Edie's house and the church and load them into a horse trailer the Bell family lent them. Tristan looked over his shoulder once more at her and smiled before he got into the truck with Kord behind the wheel. Granger and David stood guard over the men in the trailer.

"Edie," Walker said, coming to stand by her, "I couldn't protect Shane and because I failed, you lost the man you love. I swear on my life I will bring Tristan back to you. Unless you want me to ditch him in Millevia. I'd totally do that for you too."

The tears that had started to fall quickly turned to tears of laughter at her brother. "Bring him back to me, Walker. I love him."

Walker playfully grumbled, but then wrapped his arms around her. Edie sank into her brother's hug and took a deep breath. "I love you too, Walker. Thanks for always being there for me."

"Anytime, Sis. And for the record, he's not so bad." Walker gave her a wink before turning to jump in the truck.

Tinsley and Layne were by her side before Kord even got the truck in gear. "It'll be okay," Tinsley said reassuringly. "Tristan will be back before you know it."

"Walker will look out for him. But after what I heard Tristan did to get to you, it may be the other way around," Layne told her.

"What did he do?" Edie asked.

"Walker said he reminded him of Ahmed. He moved so fast, taking out men to get to you," Layne said. "That is a man deeply in love."

Edie nodded. The feeling was mutual. She turned to find the town milling around in the street as if no one knew what to do with themselves now that the action was over. Adrenaline was still high and Edie knew one way to thank them. "Harper, think we could do a street party? Have a couple of kegs I can buy?"

"Don't even worry about it. I can't think of a better cost for my Black Law fund to cover," Harper said before hugging her. "I'm so glad you're safe. I love you."

"I love all of you. And what's the Black Law fund?" Edie asked as the tension began to ease between her shoulders.

"The money I got after finding the jewel Black Law hid in my bar. Well, I have some set aside to fund things I thought he'd approve of. I think some drinks for the town fighting with the weapons he donated would be just the thing. You were a badass tonight. He'd be proud," Harper said of one of the pirates who had founded Shadows Landing.

"Nowhere near as badass as Kenzie coming in with Bubba all ready to fight. She has a freaking attack gator," Edie said, laughing as Kenzie joined them.

"Fickle male. He already left me for some booty. And not the pirate kind," Kenzie said, acting upset before laughing.

Harper put her fingers in her mouth and whistled. The crowd quieted and turned to her. "Listen up! Edie wants to thank you for helping her and Tristan. Shut down Main Street—Black Law and the pirates are giving us free beer tonight!" Harper saw Lacy and winked. "And free virgin daiquiris."

Lacy perked up and started begging her mother if they could stay when Lydia interrupted her, "Of course we can. It's our mother-daughter night!"

"And Lacy is our hero of the night!" Edie called out, wrapping the young lady in a big hug. "Thank you for being so brave. You helped Tristan beat Jean tonight."

Lacy blushed. "Aw, Miss E, it was fun."

A breeze rushed down the street, merrily dancing

merrily among the townsfolk, as the beer was brought out. Cheers burst out, toasts were made, and Skeeter swore that the pirate ghosts were happy and celebrating, too.

Tristan watched a group of men from the U.S. and Rahmi, all in black suits and carrying automatic weapons, load the last of the Millevia prisoners into an unmarked secure vehicle.

"Well, this wasn't what I expected to be doing when I joined the sheriff's department," Kord said, laughing.

Tristan turned and held out his hand. "You two are more than some small-town lawmen. I would go into any battle with you guys beside me any time."

"Thank you," Granger said, shaking Tristan's hand. "If you decide to stay in Shadows Landing, know you have a job with us."

"I might just take you up on that." Could he really have a future like that? Be a sheriff's deputy in Shadows Landing and Edie's husband? It sounded too good to be true.

"The job is yours if you want it. Now, I think our pilot is ready to take us back," Granger said as he, Kord, Paxton, Dare, and Walker began to walk back up to the cargo hold of the plane, leaving David and Tristan standing behind.

"David and I are not going back, yet," Tristan called out. "As a thank-you from Rahmi, I have a private plane waiting to sneak us into Millevia. I have to see this through."

Walker stopped walking and turned to him. "You're going to kill Pastor, aren't you?"

"You know I can't let what she did go. She has to pay for the murder of my president and the attack on Edie," Tristan told Walker. "And then I have to make sure the country is stable. I can't have someone worse filling the power void that will occur when she's killed."

"I'll go with you," Walker said, leaving no room for argument. "Edie is my sister and I want payback too. Plus, I promised to bring you back alive."

Tristan's first thought was to say no, but instead he gave one small dip of his chin in acquiescence. "I'd appreciate the help."

"Want us to go too?" Granger offered.

"No, thank you. I'll feel better with you back in Shadows Landing watching over Edie," Tristan told him.

"Be safe and get back home," Granger said, holding out his hand. Tristan shook it and Kord's before they shook David's and got back on the plane.

"What's your plan?" Walker asked. "Should we call Dylan and Greer?"

"Yes," Tristan told Walker as they boarded their own plane. "I don't want them moving in and killing her before I get the chance to talk to her."

"Who're Dylan and Greer?" David asked. Tristan told him a bit about the duo, in the vaguest terms possible, as Walker made the call.

By the time they were at cruising altitude, there was a plan fully in place. "Tommaso was arrested at the Rahmi airport right before his plane took off. The finger was tossed over the gate at the palace at the same time the plane was scheduled to depart. Rahmi guards used Tommaso's phone to text his wife, letting her know the plane was going to be late as it developed a maintenance issue, but he'd be back in no time. That should give us enough time to get to Pastor without her getting suspicious."

Tristan pulled up his phone displaying an aerial photo

of the palace for Walker to see. "This is what I was thinking."

They spent the next three hours working with Dylan and Greer to finalize their plan to sneak into the well-guarded palace and apprehend Pastor. When everything was finally set and everyone knew their roles, they closed their eyes and slept. They'd need all their energy for the next part of the plan.

Emily Gastaud had reassured Tristan she was safe and was being moved by CIA agents to a safe house closer to the border with Millevia. She would come out of hiding as soon as Pastor was neutralized. Her presence would calm the nation. Plus, she told Tristan of secret tunnels leading into the palace he hadn't known about, which would make their plan a lot easier and less risky to execute.

That was how Tristan's group waltzed into the palace without seeing a single guard. It was strange operating with David and the group from Keeneston. It was as if the two different parts of his life were joining together. David, Walker, Dylan, and Greer were prime examples of like recognizing like. They'd eyed each other, told a couple of jokes making fun of the other's respective military training, and then were like a group of old buddies.

"Here's the hidden entrance to Pastor's office," Tristan whispered. "If she's not in here, there's a door that connects to a private sitting room. We clear that before moving to the main residence."

His team nodded and Greer got into position to open the door, allowing David and Tristan to enter the room first. "One," Greer whispered. "Two. Three."

Greer pulled the door open and Tristan rushed in with his gun drawn and David at his side. "What the hell?" Tristan said with surprise.

Walker, Dylan, and Greer quickly flanked him and cursed at the sight before them, but before they could question it further, the outer door to the office slammed open and a group of five men dressed in head-to-toe black rushed in with guns drawn.

Tristan and his group raised their guns and the two groups of armed soldiers stared at each other before the leader of the team that had just entered lowered his gun.

"What the hell?" the leader of the team exclaimed as everyone hesitantly lowered their weapons.

Dylan shoved past Tristan and stared at his wife, the very picture of calm, cool, and collected as she relaxed in the chair behind the president's desk. "Abby, what the hell are you doing here?"

The leader of the group of men in black threw something, and suddenly a knife landed right next to where Dylan's hand was placed on the desk. David and Tristan had their guns raised and yelled at the leader to put his hands up, but Abby stood from behind the desk and everyone stopped talking.

"You let her put herself in danger?" the leader snarled to Dylan, but it was Abby who commanded the attention.

"Tristan, I'd like to introduce my father, Ahmed Mueez," Abby said with a fond smile. "I'm guessing the rest of the men are Miles Davies, Walker's father-in-law, Marshall Davies, Cade Davies, and Cy Davies, collectively known as the Davies Brothers, or *the uncles*. Gentlemen, meet Tristan Durand. He's in love with Edie."

Suddenly the five men had their guns pointed at him. "That's my daughter-in-law," one of the men growled. That must be Miles, Layne's father. "I think my brothers and I need to have a chat with you."

Tristan looked to Walker, who just shrugged. "Told you that you had no idea what I went through to marry Layne. I'm a downright pushover compared to them."

"There you are, dear. What took you so long?" Tristan turned to the voice of a woman coming from the sitting room. It was the woman who had been standing behind Abby and next to Ahmed on the video call after Abby had faked her death.

"Bridget?" Ahmed exclaimed in surprise. "What the hell is going on? What are you two doing here? Where is Pastor?"

"We thought we'd take a little mother-daughter trip to Millevia. Eliminate Pastor, overthrow the government, get some things for the baby." Bridget smiled sweetly and Tristan looked around.

"Where is Pastor?" Tristan asked. The family drama could wait. He had a mission.

"In there," Abby said, inclining her head toward the sitting room.

The men and Greer walked to the door and looked in. Pastor was slumped on the couch, dead.

"It was a suicide," Bridget said with a frown. "Tragic."

Tristan walked into the room and saw a piece of paper on the coffee table. He picked it up and read it. In the suicide note, Pastor took full responsibility for the murder of President Gastaud, the attempted framing of Tristan Durand, and the plan to draw Rahmi into war. It even spelled out Tommaso's involvement. It was all there. "That's her handwriting. How did you get her to confess to it all?" Tristan asked.

"I can be very persuasive," Abby said with a shrug,

before her expression turned icy hard. "No one threatens my child."

"Or my child and my grandchild," Bridget said fiercely.

Ahmed Mueez was pouting. "But she's my daughter and that's my grandchild too. I wanted to be the one to get vengeance. It's bad enough my daughter and wife got it, but then my son-in-law was trying to take it without me. Why didn't anyone call me?"

Tristan had to nearly swallow his lips to keep from laughing out loud. If Ahmed stomped his foot, Tristan was going to lose it.

"Would you like to help clear out the government officials loyal to Pastor?" Tristan offered politely.

"I guess we could help with that," Ahmed said, only slightly placated.

"Now that that is settled, let's get some gelato. Torture makes me hungry," Abby said, slipping her arm around Dylan and rising to kiss him.

"General Mueez," David said quietly as he stepped forward. "It would be such an honor to watch you work. You are my idol."

Ahmed perked up a little at that. "Well, then. Let's get to it. Durand, you and your friend come with us. We'll get this country straightened out by dinnertime."

"I'm having Emily brought in," Greer told them. "She wants to help. She'll also be the perfect person to deliver the news about Pastor and what she's done to the nation. Then I'll call Sebastian. He and Ryker can reassure her that Millevia's economy will be roaring back now that Pastor is out of power."

"I'm letting Zain know as well. Rahmi will be happy to work with Millevia moving forward," Abby said. "But now, gelato. I want three scoops. No, four."

Tristan laughed as Abby and Bridget headed out, talking about gelato flavors and baby clothes, leaving the two teams standing there.

Tristan took the lead since it was his country—even if only for a short while longer. "Let's start with the head of her military," Tristan said before shaking hands with everyone and introducing himself and David to *the uncles*, as they were called.

"Who do we put in power in their stead? You?" Miles asked Tristan.

Tristan shook his head. "Not me. I'm heading back to Shadows Landing as soon as I can. We need to put someone in power that both the people and the military forces respect. I propose General Bernard of the military academy." He looked at David, who nodded in agreement.

"Then let's get to work. Cade, can you bring him here to meet with Emily and fill him in?" Ahmed asked, and then things got really busy.

Tristan, David, and Emily spent the next two days with the uncles, weeding out those who were loyal to Pastor and working behind the scenes to fill key government positions. Rahmi approved the release of all the video footage regarding Tommaso and his part in the plan. Combined with Pastor's suicide letter and the evidence Tristan had collected along with Ryker and Sebastian, there were no doubts about her treasonous actions.

"Tristan," Emily said quietly as Greer was talking to President Stratton and Dylan was talking to Prince Zain about the role their countries would have in the announcement of Pastor's death.

Emily had always been a quiet woman with a calmness

about her that spoke of her innate confidence. She had dark brown hair that hung in curls around her rounded face, with big round brown eyes, which always made her seem younger than she was. At twenty-nine, she was young to be thrust into this situation, but she was handling it calmly and with intelligence that spoke to wisdom far beyond her years.

"I was hoping I could convince you to stay and run with me on a ticket. I'd be honored if you'd be my vice president."

Tristan smiled at her. Emily would win without question. While she didn't have previous experience, she'd grown up around politics and had been at her father's side since he became president when she was ten years old. Every eight years, her father had won re-election by a landslide. As Emily had grown up, she'd begun to help her father. She'd taken a job in the government to develop and aid small businesses and she helped build Millevia into the financial powerhouse it had been before Pastor ruined it. Tristan had no doubt she'd lead Millevia into a very bright future.

"If you'd asked me last month I wouldn't have hesitated," Tristan told her. It would have been a dream then, but right now it sounded more like a nightmare. He didn't know how, but in a very short time Shadows Landing had become home.

"What changed?" Emily asked.

"I fell in love," Tristan answered honestly. He also noticed Emily's gaze find David in the room before quickly going back to Tristan's. "You know, David is a good man. I bet he'd be an asset in your government."

"It's not mine yet. I need to win the election first."

"You will," Tristan said without any doubts.

"Will you be staying in Millevia?" Emily asked even as her eyes strayed back to David.

"No. I'm going back to Shadows Landing to ask the woman I love to marry me. But I hope that we'll come back to Millevia often."

Emily smiled and squeezed his hand. "I'm happy for you. My father would be too. Be sure to invite me to the wedding. You've been a good friend and trusted son of Millevia. Now, go get your bride."

## 29

Edie waved goodbye to Layne as she walked into the Charleston Airport. With Walker still in Millevia and her father's sudden trip with the guys, Layne decided to go home and rescue her mother from Carolina, who was finding great joy in sending food flying around the kitchen.

Tristan had been in Millevia for the past three days. He'd texted Edie often but had been too busy to talk longer than a couple of minutes on the phone the one time he'd called. He told her that they'd been quietly arresting anyone with connection to Pastor's crimes and that he was working nonstop with Emily, whom he began to call Em in their texts.

Edie didn't want to sound jealous, but she was. Em was intelligent, had a good head on her shoulders, knew how to navigate the choppy political waters, and was cute as a button. At least that was the impression Edie got when she'd looked Emily up. Tristan told her Em was relying on him to help her so they were working day and night together. And Edie knew Emily would ask Tristan to stay.

Edie pulled into her driveway as a text message came

through. She saw it was from Tristan and rushed to read it. The press conference was going to start in five minutes. Edie ran into her house and turned on BBN, hoping they'd cover the conference live.

The man and woman behind the desk looked serious as the graphic and ominous music played in the background. "We have breaking news," the woman said seriously. "We have reports coming out of Millevia that President Pastor is dead, leaving the small but wealthy country in turmoil. We're going live to the palace for a press conference."

The newsfeed changed to a podium with the Millevia flag on the wall. On one side of the stage the American flag stood on a pole. On the other side was the Rahmi flag. Then the stage began to fill with people. Edie's breath caught as she saw Tristan and David, looking powerful in black suits, come to stand in the middle of the stage. Tristan's shirt was red and David's blue—the colors of Millevia. Prince Jamal of Rahmi stood in front of the Rahmi flag, and then a woman she didn't recognize stopped in front of the American flag.

The room fell quiet, but that quiet didn't last when the side door opened and Emily Gastaud walked out. She wore tan high heels, a royal blue suit, and a red blouse to represent the colors of Millevia. The room was no longer quiet. It filled with gasps, cheers, and questions shouted in French, English, and Italian.

Emily held up her hand and the crowd quieted. She spoke quickly in her native language as she placed her hand over her heart before she switched to English. "Since this announcement has international ramifications, as well as domestic, I will be giving the rest of my remarks in English."

Emily took a deep breath and began to tell the world about President Pastor's rise to power. She showed and read the suicide note. She showed the video of Tommaso Pastor in Rahmi, and over the next twenty minutes all the evidence of the Pastors' treason was laid out, clearly and distinctly.

"The truth would not have come to light without the help of two Millevia's best soldiers who had been loyal to my father. Please help me thank Tristan Durand and David Parodi for their heroic actions in protecting Millevia."

Reporters erupted in cheers and pride swelled in her heart for Tristan. She knew what this moment meant to him.

"I also would like to thank the country of Rahmi, represented by Prince Jamal, and the United States, represented here today by Ambassador Rachel Singh, for their unwavering support of Millevia and the truth. Instead of falling for Pastor's lies, they worked hand in hand with Mr. Durand to find the truth. In our moment of need, our allies did not abandon us. I would also like to extend a special thanks to Sebastian Abel and Ryker Faulkner for also working with Mr. Durand. While it may have appeared that they turned their back on Millevia, in truth they did not. Their actions were at the request of Mr. Durand and I'm happy to announce that not only has all business with both men restarted, they've also invested heavily in new projects in our country. As we close the door on the darkest days in Millevia's history, we open a new door full of international cooperation, a prosperous economy, and a free people."

The reporters cheered again as Emily beamed. "A free election will be held in one month. Any candidate wanting to run will need to register by Friday."

"Miss Gastaud," a reporter yelled, "are you running for president?"

"I am. And in the meantime, so there is no worry about corruption, I will step away from the palace and relinquish any control I have taken to set the country to rights after Pastor's treason."

"Then who is running the country?" a reporter yelled.

"The mayor of La Roma will step in temporarily to help with the day–to-day running of the nation with the help of General Bernard, a long-time advocate of our country and head of the military academy. They will be the checks and balances in place until the election. Lastly, thank you for loving my father and thank you to all the people on this stage and all over the world who helped me discover the truth about his death. Today he can finally rest easily as Millevia heads toward a bright future."

Emily stopped in front of Prince Jamal, bowed her head, and then shook his hand. Next, she shook Tristan's hand, then David's, and lastly the American ambassador's before they filed off the stage.

BBN cut back to the studio where they had experts in international politics at the ready to go over every detail. Edie leaned forward and soaked up every word they shared. She also wondered if that meant Tristan was coming home now or next month after the new president was installed.

Tristan was beyond exhausted when he and Walker stepped off the plane in Washington, D.C. The second the press conference was done, he and David had accompanied Emily to file her paperwork as a candidate. She turned in her application for presidency to the clerk, who cried happy tears as she accepted it.

Tristan only left after promising to be back to vote in the election, making a quick stop at a very important store, taking Walker and David out for drinks to celebrate a mission completed, and packing up the rest of his things he'd left behind in Millevia City.

"We have three hours until our next flight," Tristan said, stretching. "I'm going to walk around a bit. I'll see you before you catch your plane to Lexington."

Walker nodded and didn't ask where Tristan was going. Instead, he took out his phone and called Layne. Tristan felt for the object in his pocket and hurried out the front doors of the airport. He held out his hand and a taxi pulled to a stop.

Tristan climbed in, gave the directions, and sat back. His heart was heavy. His palms were actually sweaty as he pulled up the information he needed on his phone.

"We're here."

Tristan looked up and nodded. He paid the driver and stepped out into the beautiful spring afternoon. The grass was freshly cut and the smell was somehow soothing as birds chirped.

Tristan followed the directions as he walked for what had to be over half a mile. But then he saw it. He'd arrived.

## SHANE JOHN WECKER
## SOC
## US NAVY SEAL

"Hello, Shane," Tristan said, standing at ease and looking down at Edie's husband's headstone. "Edie's told me a lot about you. She got a tattoo in your honor."

Tristan took a deep breath as his fingers ran over the object he was holding. "I would give anything for you to still be here. For Edie to never have experienced the pain of losing you, which makes why I'm here seem so selfish, but here it goes.

"I'm not what you would have wanted for her," Tristan admitted. "An assassin on the right side of the law is still an assassin. Not only that, but I brought danger into Edie's life when that's the last thing I wanted.

"I'd like to think we would have been friends so I feel as if I can say this on your behalf, but you would have been so proud of her. She was fearless in the face of danger, fighting for me and fighting for my country. I respect the hell out of her. Not only that, I love her, Shane. I love her with every fiber of my body." Tristan took a deep breath to calm himself. "I'm here to pay my respects to someone who clearly loved and cherished her and whom she still loves and cherishes, and ask your blessing."

Tristan took another deep breath and opened the palm of his hand. Inside was a bronze cross with the crest of Millevia in the middle. The ribbon was red with a royal blue stripe down the middle. "I was awarded this for bravery. I'm sure your country has given you one as well, but I knew this was meant for you. I don't fully understand it, but I feel a bond to you as a man who loved Edie."

Tristan knelt and pulled back a very small section of grass and buried the medal. "This is my pledge to you, Shane. I will stop at nothing to love, protect, and cherish Edie. Rest well, my brother in arms."

Tristan stood. He snapped his heels together and raised his hand to his forehead in a salute. He lowered his hand and spun on his heel to leave, only to pull up short.

Walker stood a short distance away with a frown on his face and his hands in his pockets. "I guess this means I can't call you Assassin Boy anymore."

"Why not?" Tristan asked as he closed the short distance between him and Walker.

"Because I'll be calling you my brother. Although Assassin Bro sounds pretty cool."

"Brother?" Tristan knew there was mutual respect between them, but he didn't know how Walker would handle Tristan's wish to marry Edie. They'd worked well together in Millevia, but Tristan had thought Walker was doing it out of duty rather than friendship.

"Shane might not be able to give his blessing, but as Shane's best friend, I feel confident in his answer. He would approve of you, Tristan. You're a good man who loves Edie. You didn't ask for it, but you have my blessing all the same. There's no one I trust more than you with my sister's life and heart."

Tristan had been emotional before, but shaking Walker's hand was next level. He nodded and stayed quiet as they both turned to Shane's grave. They talked silently to Shane and then Walker turned back to him. "We need to head back to the airport. You need to get to Shadows Landing and me to Keeneston. Let's go, Assassin Bro."

Tristan had never loved a nickname more.

## 30

Edie had heard from Layne that Walker had arrived home and her heart went into overdrive. Did that mean Tris would be back tonight? She'd asked Layne and even Walker, but they hadn't texted her back.

It had taken Edie all of a minute to decide that Tristan *was* coming home. He'd made a promise and so had Walker. If Walker had gone back to Keeneston, that would mean he brought Tristan safely home.

Edie gave herself a pep talk as she raced around the house. She dug out some old candles and placed them around for a romantic vibe. Of course, the clash of the scents of all the candles burning at once might be a tad overwhelming, but the candlelight screamed romance with a capital R.

Her refrigerator on the other hand—there was nothing romantic in it. She'd been so nervous the past days that she hadn't even gone shopping. Well, she'd do what she could with what she had.

She started a pot of water and raced upstairs. She fixed

her hair, spritzed some yummy-smelling body spray in just the right strategic locations, and grabbed a cute sundress. In the spur of the moment, she tossed the sundress back in the closet and pulled out the dress she'd worn for their first date in Millevia. Edie's heart pounded as she slipped her heels on, twisted her hair into a bun, and hurried back downstairs. She was racing against the clock and wanted everything to be set when Tristan arrived home.

Home. At least she hoped it would be his home.

"Buns, buns, buns . . ." she chanted as she opened cabinets looking for some buns to accompany dinner.

"You have very nice buns."

Edie gave a little yelp and jumped with surprise. Tristan was leaning against the kitchen wall, watching her frantic search for buns.

"You're home!" Any thought of acting calm and collected fled as relief coursed through her body. Edie ran to him and flung her arms around his neck.

Tristan was waiting for her and met her lips halfway with a kiss that started as a tingle in her lips and raced like lightning straight down to her toes.

"I missed you," Edie whispered against his lips as she moved back in for another kiss.

Tristan finally pulled back from the kiss but kept his hand on the nape of her neck. "I missed you too. It's good to be home." Tristan pulled her against him for one more quick kiss. "Did you make me dinner?"

"I did," Edie said with a laugh. "Um, mac and cheese with hot dogs." Edie tossed a loaf of bread on the table. "And no buns."

"Pulling out all the stops, huh?" Tristan laughed as he pulled her against him and kissed the top of her head.

Edie had never felt so content as she did in that moment. There was only one thing clouding her joy, but she couldn't ask him just yet. Instead, she served dinner and he told her about Millevia.

"Are you going back?" Edie asked as casually as she could with the pit in her stomach spinning with nerves.

"Millevia is still my country and I care about its future so I will be going back to vote and to visit. But right now, I want to visit with you. I see you dressed up for me."

"I did."

"That's the dress you wore on our date."

"You remember." Edie sounded surprised but instead felt incredibly special. If he could remember that, she needed to stop worrying about their future. He came home to her. He missed her. He loved her. That would be enough to build a future on. It might not be the future she had planned out, but it was hers and sometimes the best things happened when you stepped out of your comfort zone and took a calculated risk.

"How could I forget it? It's almost as stunning as you are." Tristan stood up and held out his hand.

Edie placed hers in his and knew she'd follow him anywhere. "I know we haven't talked about a future, but Tristan, I'm open to moving to Millevia. I'm sure if Emily wins, you'll have a very lucrative job offer."

Tristan took the first step upstairs before turning to look back at her. "I already have two very lucrative job offers."

"From Emily?" Edie asked, nervously. She could leave Shadows Landing again. She'd done it for Shane. She could do it for Tristan.

"Emily wanted me to run for vice president."

Tristan turned around and headed up another couple of

stairs. Edie went along in shock as their hands were still linked until she pulled him to a stop. "You're going to be vice president?"

"No. I just said it was an offer. I didn't take it. I think I might take the other offer, though. But first, there's one offer I really want to make."

"What's that?" Edie asked, her mind going a mile a minute. How long was her passport good for? Did she need to get a visa to stay so long in Millevia? What was the name of the relocation packers she'd used when she moved?

"How about I just show you?" Tristan reached for her, grabbed her waist, and picked her up. He flung her over his shoulder and took the stairs two at a time. Edie laughed as he set her on the edge of the bed and stepped back to look down at her. "I'm offering you me."

Edie reached for him then, hooking her fingers in the waistband of his jeans and pulling him on top of her. "That's an offer I will always accept."

"My little phoenix, it's time to rise," Edie heard Tristan whisper to her.

Edie cracked one eye open and pulled the covers back up over her naked body. "It's still dark out. It's probably only five o'clock."

"It is five, but I have a surprise for you."

"If it's not coffee, I don't want it," Edie grumbled.

"It *is* coffee. And breakfast. Come on, get dressed and meet me downstairs."

Edie swung her feet off the bed and then paused. "Wait, why do I need to get dressed?"

"Hurry up!" Tristan called from the base of the stairs.

Edie grumbled but got dressed quickly in shorts and an oversized sweatshirt. She pulled her hair back, and by the time she staggered downstairs, she was partially awake. If she and Tristan hadn't been up half the night making love, she'd be a little more conscious this morning.

"Here, put these on."

"Where are we going? I thought you made breakfast." Edie said, putting her feet into the shoes Tristan shoved forward.

"Right this way."

Edie followed him outside and then to his car. Ah, the diner. Tristan hadn't said he'd made breakfast, just that they were getting it. Only they drove past the diner. They drove into the marina instead. "What are we doing?"

"Wade said I could borrow his boat so we could have breakfast on the water."

Okay, that was romantic, not as cozy as her bed but still, romantic. As he helped her onto the boat, Edie silently apologized for all the mean things she'd thought about when Tris woke her up.

"I've missed being out on the water," Tristan told her as he set down a basket and pulled a blanket from it, revealing a thermos and some containers of food underneath.

He tucked the blanket around her legs and handed Edie a cup of hot coffee with a lid before navigating Wade's motorboat from the marina. Edie turned in the small sitting area in front of the console to look out over the still, dark water under the slightest glimmer of light on the horizon.

Edie sat back and closed her eyes as Tristan navigated the waters down to Charleston and out to the bay. She enjoyed the movement of the boat across the water, the wind in her hair, and the warmth of the blanket.

"We're here," Tristan said after he cut the engines.

Edie roused herself with a smile. It might have been early, but the ride had been so peaceful that she felt centered as she looked out over the water toward the impending sunrise. The sky was already filled with pinks, purples, and oranges as the sun stretched toward the horizon.

"You know," Tristan said, sitting beside her with his arm around her as the sun began to appear as if rising from the water. "In Greek mythology the phoenix rises time and time again, reborn from the ashes as an immortal symbol of renewal. Even through the darkest of nights, the sun, like your phoenix, rises again. You've been through the darkness, yet you rise, even brighter than the phoenix."

Edie snuggled against Tristan's chest as they watched the sun's rays reach for the sky over the water. It was almost as beautiful as Tristan's words to her.

"My wish for you is to soar among the clouds and shine as bright as the sun, Edie," Tristan said. Edie turned to kiss him because right now she couldn't form words to tell him how much what he said meant to her. Only she found Tristan holding up a ruby ring with a halo of small yellow diamonds around it that matched the colors of her phoenix tattoo. "My wish is you'll let my heart soar with you. Edie, will you marry me?"

Edie's heart beat so hard she trembled as she lifted her hand and nodded. A rush of warmth, love, and pure happiness seemed to surround her in that moment as she looked at the man she'd fallen so deeply in love with.

"Yes?" Tristan asked, holding the ring close to her finger.

Edie took a deep breath as tears rolled down her cheeks. "Yes!"

She didn't even look at the ring on her finger before she

flung her arms around his shoulders and kissed him. The man who had made her laugh again. The man who had made her love again. And the man who had given her a future of hopes and dreams again.

The sun's rays warmed her as they crested the horizon. Nothing could make this moment more perfect. "I guess I'd better start packing," Edie said with a laugh as she finally looked at her engagement ring.

"Where are we going? Tristan asked as he held her hand and brushed his thumb over the ring. "You know I'll follow you anywhere."

"To Millevia. To your new job."

Tristan smiled and she knew she'd made him happy. It would be an adjustment, but Tristan was worth it.

"I'm afraid I'm clipping my phoenix's wings already." Tristan reached into his back pocket and pulled out his wallet. "I hope you aren't too disappointed. I won't be the vice president of a country, but I did get the job I wanted."

He handed his wallet to her and Edie automatically took it. "I don't understand."

"Open it."

Edie pushed open the leather wallet and stared down at a five-pointed gold star. "Deputy Sheriff, Shadows Landing," Edie read the inscription out loud before looking up at Tristan. "Why do you have Kord's badge?"

"It's not Kord's badge. It's mine."

Edie looked back down at the badge and then back up at Tristan in confusion. "You're staying in Shadows Landing?"

"No, *we* are staying in Shadows Landing. The sheriff's office has graciously given me enough vacation days that we can visit Millevia for up to three weeks each year, and we will be dual citizens. I meant it when I said I want to share my life with you, Edie, and that includes your country and mine."

Words failed her so Edie just squealed with happiness and kissed Tristan soundly. The darkness had receded and now there was nothing but light, love, and a happily-ever-after.

# EPILOGUE

*Five weeks later . . .*

Edie looked around the weapons room of the Shadows Landing Church and smiled. It was filled with practically all the women in her life. The church must be half empty because they were all in here.

"No wonder Father Ben insisted on coming and blessing your wedding," Sophie Dagher, one of Walker's many cousins-in-law, said with a laugh about the priest from Keeneston. Sophie was a state-of-the-art weapons maker who came in to see the armory with a large group of her female relatives. "Look at this blunderbuss! It's in perfect condition."

"This is the dagger I've worked with," Layne said, showing her cousins the daggers and then the cutlasses and sabers.

Edie sat quietly as Tinsley put on the finishing touches to her wedding makeup as the women of Shadows Landing showed the women of Keeneston how to use the old pirate weapons.

Edie had wanted to marry quickly and had thought to just elope, but Walker freaked out. He promised her he'd take care of everything. He had told her she deserved the fairy tale and he wanted to give it to her. He'd sounded so sincere that she couldn't say no. So, she'd gone out and bought a simple white sundress and left everything else to her brother. She's seen the parties her brother had planned over the years and was cool with beer and BBQ for the reception. The sundress would fit Walker's casual theme.

Early that morning, Harper, Tinsley, Skye, and all the Faulkner women had shown up and dragged her to the church. They'd been locked in the armory for several hours as various people came and went. Karri, Skye's best friend, brought food and champagne as everyone talked, laughed, and hung out. Edie was starting to wonder why she was there so early when Skye insisted on doing Edie's hair. Then Tinsley insisted on doing the makeup.

As she sat through her beauty preparation, the Keeneston ladies started to join them. Now the armory was alive with the party-like atmosphere of women. Well, until Tinsley finished the makeup.

"Okay, everyone!" Tinsley called out. "It's dress time, so everyone out except the bridal party. We want this to be a surprise."

"It's not that much of a surprise," Edie said as everyone wished her luck, blew her kisses, and gave her thumbs-up as they headed out. "The dress has been hanging there the whole time."

"You're not wearing that dress to be married in. You're wearing this one," Skye said from behind her.

Edie turned to look at Skye and found her standing there with Sydney Davies McKnight. Syd was a former model-turned-fashion-house-owner and overall fashion mogul. She was also one of Layne's cousins.

"What's this?" Edie asked, eyeing the large black garment bag with Syd's logo on it.

"My wedding gift to you," Skye said with a smile. "I had Tristan steal one of your dresses and send it to Sydney who made you a wedding dress."

A custom Syd Inc. dress would cost tens of thousands of dollars. "That's too much!" Edie gasped.

Sydney smiled and shook her head. "It's my gift too. We went halfsies."

"It's still too much!"

Skye and Sydney just shrugged. Well, it probably wasn't too much for American's Sweetheart and a mogul, but it was for Edie.

"You're our friend, Edie, and we love you," Skye said before reaching for the zipper. "Now, do you want to see it?"

Edie could protest, but the truth was, she really wanted to see the dress. She'd bake them cakes for the next year to thank them.

Skye unzipped the garment bag and inside was the most beautiful dress she'd ever seen. The sheath of the dress was a sweetheart strapless gown that was not quite A-line, but also not overly form-fitting. However, it was the lace overlay that make Edie gasp. The delicate lace shimmered over the sheath like a whimsical dream.

It seemed to float along the floor and caressed her chest where it rose over the neckline and shoulders to meet in a button at the nape of her neck. Edie couldn't stop staring at herself in the mirror as Harper whistled, Layne and Tinsley cried, while Skye and Sydney's smile just beamed.

"Thank you so much. I have no words," Edie said in awe of the creation she got to wear to marry Tristan. "Oh no."

"What?" Sydney asked. "Do I need to make an alteration?"

"No, it's just that I'm so dressed up and I told Tristan it would all be casual."

"Oh, I don't think you need to worry about that. I'll see you out there. You're beautiful and we're all so happy for you, Edie." Sydney blew her a kiss and then she and Skye left the room.

"Now," Layne said, opening the last cabinet where the boarding pikes were stored to reveal three more black Syd Inc. bags. "Time for the bridesmaids to get dressed."

Edie couldn't protest when the prettiest dresses in the lightest blue were pulled out. They were simple, elegant, and something Edie could only dream of. "You all look so beautiful. I can't believe you all did this."

"Wasn't us," Harper said matter-of-factly, opening up her bag and pulling out a bottle of really good rum and four shot glasses. "Walker planned it all."

"Hey, my grandmother has a priest on speed dial. She helped too," Layne said with a laugh. "You wouldn't believe how fast we can throw together a wedding, so five weeks was a lifetime!"

"Ladies," Harper said, getting their attention. "We need to send Edie off in Shadows Landing fashion. Anne Bonny and Black Law wouldn't have it any other way."

Edie laughed as a dream she thought she'd never have became reality. She was surrounded by friends and family and marrying a man she was madly in love with.

"To Edie and Tristan!" Harper called out as they shot back the rum and then tapped the empty shot glasses twice on the table before they all broke out laughing.

The knock on the door had them turning to find Walker, looking handsome in a tuxedo. "You're a stunning bride,

Edie," Walker said, striding into the room. "Are you ready to get married?"

"I thought the guys were in slacks, not tuxedos."

"I told you I would plan the wedding. I wasn't going to let my sister get married in anything but the best and most beautiful gown. And I surely wouldn't let her groom look out of place. I've handled everything."

Edie hugged her brother tightly. "Thank you. You're the best brother in the whole world. I love you Walker."

"I love you too. Now, let's get you married to your assassin."

"Is he still here or did all the cousins and uncles scare him off?" Layne asked.

"He's still here. He actually told Ahmed he felt honored to have his life threatened by his idol. It was embarrassing," Walker said with a shake of his head.

Layne kissed Edie's cheek. "I'll see you up there. I'm so happy for you both."

Harper gave her a wink and followed after Layne to line up for their entrance.

"We're all very happy for you, Edie. I love you." Tinsley kissed her cheek and, as the music started, walked to join the others.

Edie slipped her hand into the crook of her brother's elbow and smiled up at him as the doors closed and they stepped up to them. The music changed and as the doors were opening, Walker whispered, "I'm happy for you, Edie. Tristan's a good man and loves you. I wouldn't accept anything else for you. I will, however, always be happy to kill him if you need me to."

Edie laughed as the doors opened to reveal her groom standing at the end of the aisle. He looked drop-dead sexy in a perfectly fitted tuxedo as he gazed at her as if no one else in the world existed. In fact, they didn't. Edie didn't see David or Granger standing next to Tristan or even the new president of Millevia sitting in the first row. All she saw was Tristan.

As soon as she reached him, Tristan held out his hand for her. Instantly, she reached for him as Walker gave her away and then went to stand between David and Granger. The ceremony was a blur, but Edie remembered Father Ben's hushed gasp of awe as Reverend Winston used a sword covered in jewels to bless them.

And then, finally, she heard the words *husband and wife* and Tristan was kissing her. The church cheered and Edie couldn't stop the enormous smile as they turned hand in hand to face their clapping friends and family.

Granger Fox looked out over the crowd of men lining up to catch the garter and took another shot of Ryker's very good bourbon. The town had really come together for the wedding. Walker had known his sister well enough to know she didn't do über fancy. She was all about friends and family. They'd set up a tent for the reception in the park overlooking the river. Ryker had provided the drinks. In a rare moment of community spirit, both Lowcountry Smokehouse and the competing Pink Pig both helped cater the dinner, and the women of the knitting club made desserts while Karri made the wedding cake.

It was elegant but casual. Lantern lights were hung in the trees and fairy lights in the tent. Country singer Holt Everett sang a selection of songs before the party band, also from Nashville, took over. No one seemed to think it strange that a country star was singing at a wedding in Shadows

Landing because he was part of this remarkable Keeneston family.

It was a family Granger had to admit he was beginning to feel a part of. When Walker brought the estranged Faulkner and Davies families together, he did more than reunite a family. He brought two small towns together as well. And when Edie moved back to Shadows Landing, it just solidified the bond as she was equally loved in both towns.

Granger scanned the crowd as the music stopped and the whole garter business was about to start. Ryker joined him at the bourbon bar and motioned for two more drinks. "What are you doing hiding back here?" Ryker asked.

Ryker handed Gavin a glass of bourbon as he joined them. "He's hiding," Gavin said.

Granger took a sip of the bourbon and didn't deny it. "Let someone who wants to get married do that nonsense."

"Yeah, and that's why when you mentioned marriage you looked right at Olivia," Ryker said smugly. Asshole.

Okay, so Granger hadn't been able to take his eyes off Olivia and that irritated him. She was breathtaking tonight in a royal blue and gold dress that was somehow incredibly classy, yet filled him with a lust that was so fierce he was back there trying to drink it away.

"Who's the new brother?" Granger asked instead of talking about Olivia.

"Hunter," Ryker answered for him. "Damon and Stone are on the right and Kane and Hunter are on the left of her."

"How many freaking brothers are there?" Gavin asked with a laugh.

"Olivia hasn't said. When I ask her, she just mutters 'lots' and shudders," Ryker said with a little smirk. "I have to admit I find it amusing. The more brothers appear, the more she takes it out on opposing counsel. You should see the deals she's making for Sebastian and me."

"Look, here's the garter throw," Gavin said, taking Granger's attention away from the Townsends. "Looks like Kord is ready."

Granger smiled at that. Kord looked as if he and Quad, who was currently a college basketball standout, were facing off for a tipoff.

Tristan glanced around the tent and turned his back to everyone. Then two things happened almost at once. First, Tristan spun and threw that garter like a major league fastball. Second, Gavin and Ryker shoved Granger forward hard.

Granger stumbled forward and the garter hit him right in the face before dropping into his bourbon. Well, crap.

Everyone cheered and Granger turned to glare at his two friends. "What the hell?"

The women lined up for the bouquet toss as Ryker and Gavin were practically bent over laughing hard at Granger's glare. Granger heard the cheers and turned to see Olivia standing between a wall of tall brothers with the bouquet in her hands.

"We thought you needed a little push. I guess fate did too," Ryker said, trying very hard to sound serious.

"Stop glaring. It's your dance," Gavin said, not bothering to try to mask his smirk.

Sure enough, the bandleader was calling him and Olivia to the dance floor, but the brothers wouldn't let her budge. Granger had seen his fair share of overprotective brothers, but the Townsend men were something else.

Granger approached, unfazed, even as they narrowed their eyes. "I believe this is our dance," he said, holding out his hand for Olivia.

"No marriage dance for our sister. You've already been staring enough," Damon, the clear leader and elder brother of the group, said, crossing his arms over his chest.

Granger saw Olivia's quick reaction to that news and wanted to punch Damon in his glaring face. "You're like the pied piper of Townsend brothers, aren't you? You play your flute and more just appear out of the woodwork. You may scare everyone else, but you don't scare me. I don't give a damn if you like me or not, but I am going to dance with Olivia."

Olivia reached out and took his hand. She shouldered her way between her glaring brothers and let him lead her onto the dance floor, which was a first for Olivia. Granger slid his arm around her waist as he swept her up into the dance.

"You're a good dancer," Olivia said. Granger didn't like the sad note in her voice. He was used to her fire.

"What's the matter?" Instantly every cell in his body was on alert.

Olivia just shook her head. "Nothing. I'm fine."

"Look, I may not be married, but I know there is nothing fine about being *fine*." Granger took a deep breath and her soft floral scent filled his mind with things that would definitely lead to her brothers killing him. "I'm sorry about our men vs. women fight at the bar. It's none of my business who you date."

Olivia frowned and he hated that he'd been the one to make her do so. "It's okay. You were probably right about the type of men I date, but they're the only ones who ask me out. But that's not what has me distracted. It's just a work thing."

"Do you want to talk about it?" Granger asked, giving in

to the desire to pull her closer. He did and felt her body fully brush up against his.

"You're already helping. Thank you for dancing with me tonight."

And damned if Granger didn't just feel like the biggest hero in the world. Too bad he was doomed to love a woman who would never be with a damaged man like him. But for right now he had her in his arms, and he was going to enjoy every moment.

Tristan had never been happier than he was that night. He had his wife in his arms as they danced with all their friends and family. The music came to an end and he saw Emily, the newly elected president of Millevia, walking toward them.

"Tristan, Edie, I'm so very happy for you." Emily had come in last night and had had dinner with him, Edie, and David. Interestingly, David had escorted Emily to the reception tonight. "I have a wedding gift for you."

Tristan handed the thick envelope for Edie to open. "You didn't have to get us anything," his wife said as she opened it. Her brows knit in confusion as she looked at the thick document. "I see my name and Tristan's, but I can't read it. I'm learning French as fast as I can, though."

Tristan took the document from her and read it in disbelief. "We've been bestowed the highest honor in Millevia," Tristan said, pulling the two medals from the bottom of the envelope out and handing one to Edie. "And as the country's gratitude for our service, they've honored us with the deed to a house."

"Now you always have a place in Millevia to come home to," Emily said with a smile. "You'll also find new Millevian citizenship papers for Edie. I can't thank you enough for all you did for our country."

Edie broke all kinds of protocol when she threw her arms around Emily and hugged her. "Getting Tristan as my husband was all the thanks I need."

"Madam President, would you care to dance?" David asked, joining them.

Emily blushed as she accepted his hand. "I thought I told you to call me Emily."

"Could tonight get any better?" Edie asked as she leaned her head against Tristan's shoulder.

"I can think of one way." Tristan pulled her to him and kissed her. "How about giving Lydia a run for her money. We can start tonight."

Edie tossed back her head and laughed. "I love you, Tristan, but I will not allow our kids to gator-surf."

"Not until they're sixteen. I agree. Twelve is just too young."

Tristan swept his laughing bride up into a dance, his heart soaring as together they found their happily-ever-after.

THE END

*Forever Concealed*

*Forever Devoted*

*Forever Hunted*

*Forever Guarded*

*Forever Notorious*

*Forever Ventured*

*Forever Freed*

*Forever Saved*

*Forever Bold*

*Forever Thrown*

*Forever Lies*

*Forever Protected (coming Aug/Sep 2022)*

*Shadows Landing Series*

*Saving Shadows*

*Sunken Shadows*

*Lasting Shadows*

*Fierce Shadows*

*Broken Shadows*

*Framed Shadows*

*Endless Shadows*

*Fading Shadows (coming April/May 2022)*

*Damaged Shadows (coming Oct 2022)*

Women of Power Series

*Chosen for Power*

*Built for Power*

*Fashioned for Power*

*Destined for Power*

# ABOUT THE AUTHOR

Kathleen Brooks is a New York Times, Wall Street Journal, and USA Today bestselling author. Kathleen's stories are romantic suspense featuring strong female heroines, humor, and happily-ever-afters. Her Bluegrass Series and follow-up Bluegrass Brothers Series feature small town charm with quirky characters that have captured the hearts of readers around the world.

Kathleen is an animal lover who supports rescue organizations and other non-profit organizations such as Friends and Vets Helping Pets whose goals are to protect and save our four-legged family members.

Email Notice of New Releases

**https://kathleen-brooks.com/new-release-notifications**

Kathleen's Website
**www.kathleen-brooks.com**
Facebook Page
**www.facebook.com/KathleenBrooksAuthor**
Twitter
**www.twitter.com/BluegrassBrooks**
Goodreads
**www.goodreads.com**

Made in United States
North Haven, CT
20 May 2022

19340157R00167